Jonathan Wild the Great

The Life of
Mr Jonathan Wild the Great

Henry Fielding

ET REMOTISSIMA PROPE

Hesperus Classics

Hesperus Classics
Published by Hesperus Press Limited
4 Rickett Street, London sw6 1ru
www.hesperuspress.com

First published in 1734
First published by Hesperus Press Limited, 2004
This edition is based on the revised 1754 edition of *Jonathan Wild the Great*

Foreword © Peter Ackroyd, 2004

Designed and typeset by Fraser Muggeridge
Printed in Italy by Graphic Studio Srl

isbn: 1-84391-089-6

CONTENTS

Henry Fielding, born in Somerset in 1707 and educated at Eton College, was a true son of London. The city became the landscape of his imagination and the centre of his multifarious activities. It is also the vibrant setting for the life and adventures of *Jonathan Wild*. Fielding was a dramatist long before he ever became a novelist. For eight years he wrote comedies, farces and burlesques, some of them considered to be notably lewd or 'loose', and was granted the title of 'the English Molière'. In less than three years, between 1730 and 1732, he wrote no less than thirteen plays. Even by the copious standards of the day it was an astonishing production. In true urban fashion he also earned his living as a journalist and a pamphleteer. He wrote pamphlets entitled *An Attempt Towards a Natural History of the Hanover Rat*, a satire on the use of Hanoverian mercenaries, and *A Dialogue between the Devil, the Pope and the Pretender* condemning the Stuart cause. He also edited newspapers and created a journalistic character, Hercules Vinegar, who commented on the topics of the day. His theatrical and journalistic gifts then came together in *Jonathan Wild* – or to give it its full title on its first appearance in 1743, *The Life of Mr Jonathan Wild the Great*.

It comprised the third volume of Fielding's scattered writings known as *Miscellanies*, largely devoted to the themes of grandiose ambition and false greatness. He seems to have composed *Jonathan Wild* in the spring and summer of 1742, just after completing *Joseph Andrews* and immediately following the resignation of Robert Walpole in February of that year – Walpole being the prime minister whose lavish use of bribes and patronage, and whose engineering of plots and cabals, rendered him the epitome of political corruption in the period. Walpole himself enters the plot of *Jonathan Wild* only obliquely, but the text is indebted to his example of villainy and chicanery in high places. Fielding does not make the point so deliberately as John Gay in *The Beggar's Opera*, staged some fifteen years before, but there is a clear resemblance between the sins of high life and of low life. Why should one deserve a peerage, and the other a gallows?

But *Jonathan Wild* is not a piece of contemporary political analysis, or even a social history. It is a work in which fact and fiction become strangely merged. As Fielding states in his preface to the *Miscellanies*, 'it is not a very faithful portrait of Jonathan Wild himself'. He goes on to confess that 'my narrative is rather of such actions which he might have performed, or would, or should have performed than what he really did'. But if it is not a biography, it can hardly be classified as a novel. Some of the events here related are indeed authentic, and the speeches as well as the maxims of Wild are not really appropriate in a fictional context. The book is essentially an exercise in irony, a philosophical satire that anticipates Johnson's *Rasselas* and Voltaire's *Candide*.

Wild was already a famous London figure before Fielding transmuted him in print. Daniel Defoe had written a book on his exploits, and there were other brief lives of dubious authenticity. Wild's urban career really began as a 'thief-taker', but this was cover for his more profitable activity as a fence of stolen goods. He would direct his criminal associates towards a target, take the proceeds of the theft from them, and then at a price return the same goods to the unfortunate victim. From his 'office' in Cripplegate he would miraculously 'find' important items. He would often betray his less successful or less complaisant confederates to the authorities, and thus gained a reputation as an honest member of the commonwealth. He posed as a useful citizen, when in fact he was one of the most ruthless and violent men of a ruthless and violent age.

Fielding was not in any case unacquainted with this world. He had himself been arrested and imprisoned for debt, and the scenes set in Newgate here are written with the full force of personal acquaintance. But he also knew the other face of the law, and seven years after writing *Jonathan Wild* he was appointed as a magistrate for Middlesex with his Court at Bow Street. It was he who set up a plan for two full-time police officers, who later became known as the 'Bow Street Runners'. He knew of what he wrote. He knew London to be a wilderness. It was, as he put it in another context, ' a vast wood or forest in which the thief may harbour with as great security as wild beasts do in the deserts of Arabia and Africa'. Wild, and such associates as Fierce, Fireblood and Molly Straddle, are the pitiless creatures of this forest which prey upon their victims.

But although *Jonathan Wild* derives in part from the rogue literature and criminal biographies of previous centuries, it is much more than that. It is an anti-epic and, as Fielding's prefatory material suggests, a parody of greatness in all its aspects. He detested the glamour and fame attached to 'greatness', whether in the form of Alexander the Great or Julius Caesar. The soubriquet of 'great man' disgusted him. That is why he implicitly compared Jonathan Wild to Robert Walpole, and why throughout this text there is a constant undermining of the idea and ideal of greatness in all its forms. As he remarks in the *Miscellanies* preface, 'Pride, Ostentation, Insolence, Cruelty, and every kind of Villany, are often construed into True Greatness of Mind'. This bombast, this 'false sublime', is unfavourably compared to 'goodness', of which the Heartfrees in this book are the symbolic representatives. In that sense *Jonathan Wild* is an allegory in which Wild himself is seen as a representative of evil, an example of selfishness and wanton appetite opposed to good nature and benevolence. These are the forces that war for the soul of the world. *The Life of Mr Jonathan Wild the Great* is a succinct study of a mighty theme, yet it is one that employs humour and satire as a way of conveying its moral. Note, as an example, the ending of the story when Wild is paraded on the gallows as the halter is placed around his neck – 'Wild, in the midst of the shower of stones, etc., which played upon him, applied his hands to the parson's pocket, and emptied it of his bottle-screw, which he carried out of the world in his hand'. It is the mark of literary genius to use the smallest detail to subvert the greatest moment. It is also the pervasive method of this book.

– Peter Ackroyd, 2004

Jonathan Wild the Great

BOOK I

CHAPTER I

*Showing the wholesome uses drawn from recording the achievements
of those wonderful productions of nature called great men*

As it is necessary that all great and surprising events, the designs of
which are laid, conducted, and brought to perfection by the utmost
force of human invention and art, should be produced by great and
eminent men, so the lives of such may be justly and properly styled the
quintessence of history. In these, when delivered to us by sensible
writers, we are not only most agreeably entertained, but most usefully
instructed; for besides the attaining hence a consummate knowledge
of human nature in general – of its secret springs, various windings,
and perplexed mazes – we have here before our eyes lively examples of
whatever is amiable or detestable, worthy of admiration or abhorrence,
and are consequently taught, in a manner infinitely more effectual than
by precept, what we are eagerly to imitate or carefully to avoid.

But besides the two obvious advantages of surveying as it were in
a picture the true beauty of virtue and deformity of vice, we may
moreover learn from Plutarch, Nepos, Suetonius[1] and other biographers this useful lesson: not too hastily, nor in the gross to bestow either
our praise or censure. Since we shall often find such a mixture of
good and evil in the same character that it may require a very accurate
judgement and a very elaborate inquiry to determine on which side the
balance turns. For though we sometimes meet with an Aristides or a
Brutus, a Lysander or a Nero[2], yet far the greater number are of the
mixed kind – neither totally good nor bad – their greatest virtues being
obscured and allayed by their vices, and those again softened and
coloured over by their virtues.

Of this kind was the illustrious person whose history we now
undertake; to whom, though nature had given the greatest and most
shining endowments, she had not given them absolutely pure and
without allay. Though he had much of the admirable in his character,

3

as much perhaps as is usually to be found in a hero, I will not yet venture to affirm that he was entirely free from all defects, or that the sharp eyes of censure could not spy out some little blemishes lurking amongst his many great perfections.

We would not therefore be understood to affect giving the reader a perfect or consummate pattern of human excellence, but rather by faithfully recording some little imperfections which shadowed over the lustre of those great qualities which we shall here record, to teach the lesson we have above mentioned, to induce our reader with us to lament the frailty of human nature, and to convince him that no mortal, after a thorough scrutiny, can be a proper object of our adoration.

But before we enter on this great work we must endeavour to remove some errors of opinion which mankind have, by the disingenuity of writers, contracted. For these, from their fear of contradicting the obsolete and absurd doctrines of a set of simple fellows – called, in derision, sages or philosophers – have endeavoured, as much as possible, to confound the ideas of greatness and goodness, whereas no two things can possibly be more distinct from each other. For greatness consists in bringing all manner of mischief on mankind, and goodness in removing it from them. It seems therefore very unlikely that the same person should possess them both, and yet nothing is more usual with writers, who find many instances of greatness in their favourite hero, than to make him a compliment of goodness into the bargain, and this, without considering that by such means they destroy the great perfection called uniformity of character. In the histories of Alexander and Caesar[3] we are frequently, and indeed impertinently, reminded of their benevolence and generosity, of their clemency and kindness. When the former had with fire and sword overrun a vast empire, had destroyed the lives of an immense number of innocent wretches, had scattered ruin and desolation like a whirlwind, we are told, as an example of his clemency, that he did not cut the throat of an old woman, and ravish her daughters, but was content with only undoing them. And when the mighty Caesar, with wonderful greatness of mind, had destroyed the liberties of his country, and with all the means of fraud and force had placed himself at the head of his equals, had corrupted and enslaved the greatest people whom the sun ever saw, we are reminded, as an evidence of his generosity, of his largesses to his followers and tools, by whose means he had accomplished his purpose, and by whose assistance he was to establish it.

Now, who does not see that such sneaking qualities as these are rather to be bewailed as imperfections than admired as ornaments in these great men, rather obscuring their glory, and holding them back in their race to greatness, indeed unworthy the end for which they seem to have come into the world, viz. of perpetrating vast and mighty mischief?

We hope our reader will have reason justly to acquit us of any such confounding ideas in the following pages, in which, as we are to record the actions of a great man, so we have nowhere mentioned any spark of goodness which had discovered itself either faintly in him, or more glaringly in any other person, but as a meanness and imperfection, disqualifying them for undertakings which lead to honour and esteem among men.

As our hero had as little as perhaps is to be found of that meanness – indeed only enough to make him partaker of the imperfection of humanity, instead of the perfection of diabolism – we have ventured to call him 'the Great'; nor do we doubt but our reader, when he has perused his story, will concur with us in allowing him that title.

CHAPTER II

Giving an account of as many of our hero's ancestors as can be gathered out of the rubbish of antiquity, which has been carefully sifted for that purpose

It is the custom of all biographers, at their entrance into their work, to step a little backwards (as far, indeed, generally as they are able) and to trace up their hero, as the ancients did the river Nile, until an incapacity of proceeding higher puts an end to their search.

What first gave rise to this method is somewhat difficult to determine. Sometimes I have thought that the hero's ancestors have been introduced as foils to himself. Again, I have imagined it might be to obviate a suspicion that such extraordinary personages were not produced in the ordinary course of nature, and may have proceeded from the author's fear that, if we were not told who their fathers were, they might be in danger, like Prince Prettyman, of being supposed to have had none. Lastly, and perhaps more truly, I have conjectured that the design of the biographer has been no more than to show his great learning and knowledge of antiquity. A design to which the world has probably owed many notable discoveries, and indeed most of the labours of our antiquarians.

But whatever original this custom had, it is now too well established to be disputed. I shall therefore conform to it in the strictest manner.

Mr Jonathan Wild, or Wyld, then (for he himself did not always agree in one method of spelling his name), was descended from the great Wolfstan Wild, who came over with Hengist, and distinguished himself very eminently at that famous festival where the Britons were so treacherously murdered by the Saxons; for when the word was given, i.e. '*Nemet eour saxes*', ('Take out your swords')[4], this gentleman, being a little hard of hearing, mistook the sound for '*Nemet her sacs*', ('Take out their purses'); instead therefore of applying to the throat, he immediately applied to the pocket of his guest, and contented himself with taking all that he had, without attempting his life.

The next ancestor of our hero who was remarkably eminent was Wild, surnamed Langfanger, or Longfinger. He flourished in the reign of Henry III, and was strictly attached to Hubert de Burgh, whose friendship he was recommended to by his great excellence in an art of which Hubert was himself the inventor. He could, without the knowledge of the proprietor, with great ease and dexterity, draw forth a man's purse from any part of his garment where it was deposited, and hence he derived his surname. This gentleman was the first of his family who had the honour to suffer for the good of his country: on whom a wit of that time made the following epitaph,

> *O shame o' justice! Wild is hanged,*
> *For thatten he a pocket fanged,*
> *While safe old Hubert and his gang*
> *Does pocket o' the nation fang.*

Langfanger left a son named Edward, whom he had carefully instructed in the art for which he himself was so famous. This Edward had a grandson, who served as a volunteer under the famous Sir John Falstaff, and by his gallant demeanour so recommended himself to his captain that he would have certainly been promoted by him, had Harry V kept his word with his old companion.

After the death of Edward the family remained in some obscurity down to the reign of Charles I, when James Wild distinguished himself on both sides the question in the civil wars, passing from one to the other, as Heaven seemed to declare itself in favour of either party. At the end of the war, James not being rewarded according to his merits, as is usually the case of such impartial persons, he associated himself with a brave man of those times, whose name was Hind, and declared open war with both parties. He was successful in several actions, and spoilt many of the enemy; until at length, being overpowered and taken, he was, contrary to the law of arms, put basely and cowardly to death by a combination between twelve men of the enemy's party, who after some consultation, unanimously agreed on the said murder.

This Edward took to wife Rebecca, the daughter of the above-mentioned John Hind, Esq., by whom he had issue John, Edward, Thomas, and Jonathan, and three daughters – namely, Grace, Charity, and Honour. John followed the fortunes of his father, and suffering with him, left no issue. Edward was so remarkable for his compassionate temper that he spent his life in soliciting the causes of the distressed captives in Newgate, and is reported to have held a strict friendship with an eminent divine who solicited the spiritual causes of the said captives. He married Editha, daughter and co-heiress of Geoffrey Snap, Gent., who long enjoyed an office under the high sheriff of London and Middlesex, by which, with great reputation, he acquired a handsome fortune. By her he had no issue. Thomas went very young abroad to one of our American colonies, and has not been since heard of. As for the daughters, Grace was married to a merchant of Yorkshire who dealt in horses. Charity took to husband an eminent gentleman, whose name I cannot learn, but who was famous for so friendly a disposition that he was bail for above a hundred persons in one year. He had likewise the remarkable humour of walking in Westminster Hall[5] with a straw in his shoe. Honour, the youngest, died unmarried. She lived many years in this town, was a great frequenter of plays, and used to be remarkable for distributing oranges to all who would accept of them.

Jonathan married Elizabeth, daughter of Scragg Hollow, of Hockley-in-the-Hole, Esq., and by her had Jonathan, who is the illustrious subject of these memoirs.

CHAPTER III

The birth, parentage, and education of Mr Jonathan Wild the Great

It is observable that Nature seldom produces anyone who is afterwards to act a notable part on the stage of life, but she gives some warning of her intention; and as the dramatic poet generally prepares the entry of every considerable character with a solemn narrative, or at least a great flourish of drums and trumpets, so does this our *Alma Mater*[6] by some shrewd hints pre-admonish us of her intention, giving us warning, as it were, and crying,

Venienti occurrite morbo[7]

Thus Astyages, who was the grandfather of Cyrus, dreamt that his daughter was brought to bed of a vine, whose branches overspread all Asia[8]; and Hecuba, while big with Paris, dreamt that she was delivered of a firebrand that set all Troy in flames[9]; so did the mother of our great man, while she was with child of him, dream that she was enjoyed in the night by the gods Mercury and Priapus. This dream puzzled all the learned astrologers of her time, seeming to imply in it a contradiction; Mercury being the god of ingenuity, and Priapus the terror of those who practised it. What made this dream the more wonderful, and perhaps the true cause of its being remembered, was a very extraordinary circumstance, sufficiently denoting something preternatural in it; for though she had never heard even the name of either of these gods, she repeated these very words in the morning, with only a small mistake of the quantity of the latter, which she chose to call Priăpus instead of

Priāpus; and her husband swore that, though he might possibly have named Mercury to her (for he had heard of such an heathen god), he never in his life could anywise have put her in mind of that other deity, with whom he had no acquaintance.

Another remarkable incident was that during her whole pregnancy she constantly longed for everything she saw; nor could be satisfied with her wish unless she enjoyed it clandestinely; and as nature, by true and accurate observers, is remarked to give us no appetites without furnishing us with the means of gratifying them; so had she at this time a most marvellous glutinous quality attending her fingers, to which, as to birdlime, everything closely adhered that she handled.

To omit other stories, some of which may be perhaps the growth of superstition, we proceed to the birth of our hero, who made his first appearance on this great theatre the very day when the plague first broke out in 1665[10]. Some say his mother was delivered of him in a house of an orbicular or round form in Covent Garden; but of this we are not certain. He was some years afterwards baptised by the famous Mr Titus Oates[11].

Nothing very remarkable passed in his years of infancy, save that as the letters '*th*' are the most difficult of pronunciation, and the last which a child attains to the utterance of, so they were the first that came with any readiness from young master Wild. Nor must we omit the early indications which he gave of the sweetness of his temper; for though he was by no means to be terrified into compliance, yet might he, by a sugarplum, be brought to your purpose. Indeed, to say the truth, he was to be bribed to anything, which made many say he was certainly born to be a great man.

He was scarce settled at school before he gave marks of his lofty and aspiring temper; and was regarded by all his schoolfellows with that deference which men generally pay to those superior geniuses who will exact it of them. If an orchard was to be robbed, Wild was consulted, and though he was himself seldom concerned in the execution of the design, yet was he always concerter of it, and treasurer of the booty, some little part of which he would now and then, with wonderful generosity, bestow on those who took it. He was generally very secret on these occasions; but if any offered to plunder of his own head without acquainting master Wild, and making a deposit of the booty, he was sure to have an information against him lodged with the schoolmaster, and to be severely punished for his pains.

He discovered so little attention to school learning that his master, who was a very wise and worthy man, soon gave over all care and trouble on that account, and acquainting his parents that their son proceeded extremely well in his studies, he permitted his pupil to follow his own inclinations, perceiving they led him to nobler pursuits than the sciences, which are generally acknowledged to be a very unprofitable study, and indeed greatly to hinder the advancement of men in the world. But though master Wild was not esteemed the readiest at making his exercise, he was universally allowed to be the most dexterous at stealing it of all his schoolfellows, being never detected in such furtive compositions – nor indeed in any other exercitations of his great talents, which all inclined the same way – but once when he had laid violent hands on a book called *Gradus ad Parnassum*[12], i.e. *A step towards Parnassus*, on which account his master, who was a man of most wonderful wit and sagacity, is said to have told him he wished it might not prove in the event *Gradus ad Patibulum*, i.e. *A Step towards the Gallows*.

But, though he would not give himself the pains requisite to acquire a competent sufficiency in the learned languages, yet did he readily listen with attention to others, especially when they translated the classical authors to him; nor was he in the least backward, at all such times, to express his approbation. He was wonderfully pleased with that passage in the eleventh Iliad where Achilles is said to have bound two sons of Priam upon a mountain, and afterwards to have released them for a sum of money[13]. This was, he said, alone sufficient to refute those who affected a contempt for the wisdom of the ancients, and an undeniable testimony of the great antiquity of priggism[a]. He was ravished with the account which Nestor gives in the same book of the rich booty which he bore off (i.e. stole) from the Eleans[14]. He was desirous of having this often repeated to him, and at the end of every repetition he constantly fetched a deep sigh, and said, 'It was a glorious booty.'

a. This word, in the cant language, signifies thievery.

When the story of Cacus was read to him out of the eighth *Aeneid* he generously pitied the unhappy fate of that great man, to whom he thought Hercules much too severe.[15] One of his schoolfellows commending the dexterity of drawing the oxen backward by their tails into his den, he smiled, and with some disdain said, 'He could have taught him a better way.'

He was a passionate admirer of heroes, particularly of Alexander the Great, between whom and the late king of Sweden he would frequently draw parallels.[16] He was much delighted with the accounts of the Czar's retreat from the latter, who carried off the inhabitants of great cities to people his own country.[17] 'This', he said, 'was not once thought of by Alexander'; but added, 'perhaps he did not want them.'

Happy had it been for him if he had confined himself to this sphere; but his chief, if not only blemish, was that he would sometimes, from a humility in his nature too pernicious to true greatness, condescend to an intimacy with inferior things and persons. Thus the *Spanish Rogue* was his favourite book, and the *Cheats of Scapin*[18] his favourite play.

The young gentleman being now at the age of seventeen, his father, from a foolish prejudice to our universities, and out of a false as well as excessive regard to his morals, brought his son to town, where he resided with him until he was of an age to travel. Whilst he was here, all imaginable care was taken of his instruction, his father endeavouring his utmost to inculcate principles of honour and gentility into his son.

CHAPTER IV

Mr Wild's first entrance into the world.
His acquaintance with Count La Ruse

An accident soon happened after his arrival in town which almost saved the father his whole labour on this head, and provided master Wild a better tutor than any aftercare or expense could have furnished him with. The old gentleman, it seems, was a follower of the fortunes of Mr Snap, son of Mr Geoffrey Snap, whom we have before mentioned to have enjoyed a reputable office under the Sheriff of London and

Middlesex, the daughter of which Geoffrey had intermarried with the Wilds. Mr Snap the younger, being thereto well warranted, had laid violent hands on – or – as the vulgar express it, arrested, one Count La Ruse, a man of considerable figure in those days, and had confined him to his own house until he could find two seconds who would in a formal manner give their words that the Count should, at a certain day and place appointed, answer all that one Thomas Thimble, a tailor, had to say to him. Which Thomas Thimble, it seems, alleged that the Count had, according to the law of the realm, made over his body to him as a security for some suits of clothes to him delivered by the said Thomas Thimble. Now as the Count, though perfectly a man of honour, could not immediately find these seconds, he was obliged for some time to reside at Mr Snap's house; for it seems the law of the land is that whoever owes another ten pounds, or indeed two pounds, may be, on the oath of that person, immediately taken up and carried away from his own house and family, and kept abroad until he is made to owe fifty pounds, whether he will or no. For which he is perhaps afterwards obliged to lie in gaol; and all these without any trial had, or any other evidence of the debt than the above said oath, which if untrue, as it often happens, you have no remedy against the perjurer: he was, forsooth, mistaken.

But though Mr Snap would not (as perhaps by the nice rules of honour he was obliged) discharge the Count on his parole, yet did he not (as by the strict rules of law he was enabled) confine him to his chamber. The Count had his liberty of the whole house, and Mr Snap, using only the precaution of keeping his doors well locked and barred, took his prisoner's word that he would not go forth.

Mr Snap had by his second lady two daughters, who were now in the bloom of their youth and beauty. These young ladies, like damsels in romance, compassionated the captive Count, and endeavoured by all means to make his confinement less irksome to him; which, though they were both very beautiful, they could not attain by any other way so effectually as by engaging with him at cards, in which contentions, as will appear hereafter, the Count was greatly skillful.

As Whisk and Swabbers[19] was the game then in the chief vogue, they were obliged to look for a fourth person in order to make up their parties. Mr Snap himself would sometimes relax his mind from the violent fatigues of his employment by these recreations; and sometimes a neighbouring young gentleman or lady came in to their assistance. But the most frequent guest was young master Wild, who had been educated from his infancy with the Miss Snaps, and was, by all the neighbours, allotted for the husband of Miss Tishy, or Laetitia, the younger of the two. For though, being his cousin-german, she was perhaps, in the eye of a strict conscience, somewhat too nearly related to him, yet the old people on both sides, though sufficiently scrupulous in nice matters, agreed to overlook this objection.

Men of great genius as easily discover one another as freemasons can. It was therefore no wonder that the Count soon conceived an inclination to an intimacy with our young hero, whose vast abilities could not be concealed from one of the Count's discernment. For though this latter was so expert at his cards that he was proverbially said to 'play the whole game', he was no match for master Wild, who inexperienced as he was, notwithstanding all the art, the dexterity, and often the fortune of his adversary, never failed to send him away from the table with less in his pocket than he brought to it, for indeed Langfanger himself could not have extracted a purse with more ingenuity than our young hero.

His hands made frequent visits to the Count's pocket before the latter had entertained any suspicion of him, imputing the several losses he sustained rather to the innocent and sprightly frolic of Miss Doshy, or Theodosia, with which, as she indulged him with little innocent freedoms about her person in return, he thought himself obliged to be contented. But one night, when Wild imagined the Count asleep, he made so unguarded an attack upon him, that the other caught him in the fact. However, he did not think proper to acquaint him with the discovery he had made, but preventing him from any booty at that time, he only took care for the future to button his pockets, and to pack the cards with double industry.

So far was this detection from causing any quarrel between these two prigs[a], that in reality it recommended them to each other; for a wise man – that is to say a rogue – considers a trick in life as a gamester does

a. Thieves.

a trick at play. It sets him on his guard, but he admires the dexterity of him who plays it. These, therefore, and many other such instances of ingenuity, operated so violently on the Count that, notwithstanding the disparity which age, title, and above all, dress, had set between them, he resolved to enter into an acquaintance with Wild. This soon produced a perfect intimacy, and that a friendship, which had a longer duration than is common to that passion between persons who only propose to themselves the common advantages of eating, drinking, whoring, or borrowing money; which ends, as they soon fail, so does the friendship founded upon them. Mutual interest, the greatest of all purposes, was the cement of this alliance, which nothing, of consequence, but superior interest, was capable of dissolving.

CHAPTER V

A dialogue between young master Wild and Count La Ruse,
which, having extended to the rejoinder, had a very quiet,
easy, and natural conclusion

One evening, after the Miss Snaps were retired to rest, the Count thus addressed himself to young Wild: 'You cannot, I apprehend, Mr Wild, be such a stranger to your own great capacity, as to be surprised when I tell you I have often viewed, with a mixture of astonishment and concern, your shining qualities confined to a sphere where they can never reach the eyes of those who would introduce them properly into the world, and raise you to an eminence where you may blaze out to the admiration of all men. I assure you I am pleased with my captivity, when I reflect I am likely to owe to it an acquaintance, and I hope friendship, with the greatest genius of my age; and, what is still more, when I indulge my vanity with a prospect of drawing from obscurity (pardon the expression) such talents as were, I believe, never before like to have been buried in it. For I make no question but, at my discharge from confinement, which will now soon happen, I shall be able to introduce you into company, where you may reap the advantage of your superior parts.

'I will bring you acquainted, sir, with those who, as they are capable of setting a true value on such qualifications, so they will have it both in their power and inclination to prefer you for them. Such an introduction is the only advantage you want, without which your merit might be your misfortune; for those abilities which would entitle you to honour and profit in a superior station may render you only obnoxious to danger and disgrace in a lower.'

Mr Wild answered, 'Sir, I am not insensible of my obligations to you, as well for the over-value you have set on my small abilities, as for the kindness you express in offering to introduce me among my superiors. I must own my father has often persuaded me to push myself into the company of my betters; but to say the truth, I have an awkward pride in my nature, which is better pleased with being at the head of the lowest class than at the bottom of the highest. Permit me to say, though the idea may be somewhat coarse, I had rather stand on the summit of a dunghill than at the bottom of a hill in Paradise. I have always thought it signifies little into what rank of life I am thrown, provided I make a great figure therein, and should be as well satisfied with exerting my talents well at the head of a small party or gang, as in the command of a mighty army. For I am far from agreeing with you that great parts are often lost in a low situation; on the contrary, I am convinced it is impossible they should be lost. I have often persuaded myself that there were not fewer than a thousand in Alexander's troops capable of performing what Alexander himself did.

'But, because such spirits were not elected or destined to an imperial command, are we therefore to imagine they came off without a booty? Or that they contented themselves with the share in common with their comrades? Surely, no. In civil life, doubtless, the same genius, the same endowments, have often composed the statesman and the prig, for so we call what the vulgar name a thief. The same parts, the same actions, often promote men to the head of superior societies, which raise them to the head of lower; and where is the essential difference if the one ends on Tower Hill and the other at Tyburn[20]? Has the block any preference to the gallows, or the axe to the halter, but was given them by the ill-guided judgement of men? You will pardon me, therefore, if I am not so hastily inflamed with the common outside of things, nor join the general opinion in preferring one state to another. A guinea is as valuable in a leathern as in an embroidered purse; and a cod's head is a cod's head still, whether in a pewter or a silver dish.'

The Count replied as follows: 'What you have now said does not lessen my idea of your capacity, but confirms my opinion of the ill effect of bad and low company. Can any man doubt whether it is better to be a great statesman or a common thief? I have often heard that the devil used to say, where or to whom I know not, that it was better to reign in Hell than to be a valet-de-chambre in Heaven, and perhaps he was in the right; but sure, if he had had the choice of reigning in either, he would have chosen better. The truth therefore is, that by low conversation we contract a greater awe for high things than they deserve. We decline great pursuits not from contempt but despair. The man who prefers the high road to a more reputable way of making his fortune does it because he imagines the one easier than the other; but you yourself have asserted, and with undoubted truth, that the same abilities qualify you for undertaking, and the same means will bring you to your end in both journeys – as in music it is the same tune, whether you play it in a higher or a lower key. To instance in some particulars, is it not the same qualification which enables this man to hire himself as a servant, and to get into the confidence and secrets of his master in order to rob him, and that to undertake trusts of the highest nature with a design to break and betray them? Is it less difficult by false tokens to deceive a shopkeeper into the delivery of his goods, which you afterwards run away with, than to impose upon him by outward splendour and the appearance of fortune into a credit by which you gain and he loses twenty times as much? Does it not require more dexterity in the fingers to draw out a man's purse from his pocket, or to take a lady's watch from her side, without being perceived of any (an excellence in which, without flattery, I am persuaded you have no superior), than to cog a die or to shuffle a pack of cards? Is not as much art, as many excellent qualities, required to make a pimping porter at a common bawdy-house as would enable a man to prostitute his own or his friend's wife or child? Does it not ask as good a memory, as nimble an invention, as steady a countenance, to forswear yourself in Westminster Hall as would furnish out a complete tool of state, or perhaps a statesman himself? It is needless to particularise every instance; in all we shall find that there is a nearer connection between high and low life than is generally imagined, and that a highwayman is entitled to more favour with the great than he usually meets with. If, therefore, as I think I have proved, the same parts which qualify a man for eminence in a low sphere qualify him likewise for eminence in a higher, sure it can be no doubt in which he would choose to exert them. Ambition, without which no one can be a great man, will immediately instruct him, in your own phrase, to prefer a hill in Paradise to a dung-hill; nay, even fear, a passion the most repugnant to greatness, will show him how much more safely he may indulge himself in the free and full exertion of his mighty abilities in the higher than in the lower rank; since experience teaches him that there is a crowd oftener in one year at Tyburn than on Tower Hill in a century.' Mr Wild with much solemnity rejoined, 'That the same capacity which qualifies a mill-ken[a], a bridle-cull[b] or a buttock-and-file[c], to arrive at any degree of eminence in his profession, would likewise raise a man in what the world esteem a more honourable calling, I do not deny; nay, in many of your instances it is evident that more ingenuity, more art, are necessary to the lower than the higher proficients. If, therefore, you had only contended that every prig might be a statesman if he pleased, I had readily agreed to it; but when you conclude that it is his interest to be so, that ambition would bid him take that alternative – in a word, that a statesman is greater or happier than a prig – I must deny my assent. But, in comparing these two together, we must carefully avoid being misled by the vulgar erroneous estimation of things, for mankind err in disquisitions of this nature as physicians do who in considering the operations of a disease have not a due regard to the age and complexion of the patient. The same degree of heat which is common in this constitution may be a fever in that; in the same manner that which may be riches or honour to me may be poverty or disgrace to another: for all these things are to be estimated by relation to the person who possesses them. A booty of £10 looks as great in the eye of a bridle-cull, and gives as much real

a. A housebreaker.
b. A highwayman.
c. A shoplifter. Terms used in the cant dictionary.

happiness to his fancy, as that of as many thousands to the statesman, and does not the former lay out his acquisitions in whores and fiddles with much greater joy and mirth than the latter in palaces and pictures? What are the flattery, the false compliments of his gang to the statesman, when he himself must condemn his own blunders, and is obliged against his will to give fortune the whole honour of success? What is the pride resulting from such sham applause, compared to the secret satisfaction which a prig enjoys in his mind in reflecting on a well-contrived and well-executed scheme? Perhaps, indeed, the greater danger is on the prig's side, but then you must remember that the greater honour is so too. When I mention honour, I mean that which is paid them by their gang; for that weak part of the world which is vulgarly called "the wise" see both in a disadvantageous and disgraceful light; and as the prig enjoys (and merits too) the greater degree of honour from his gang, so does he suffer the less disgrace from the world, who think his misdeeds, as they call them, sufficiently at last punished with a halter, which at once puts an end to his pain and infamy. Whereas the other is not only hated in power, but detested and contemned at the scaffold, and future ages vent their malice on his fame, while the other sleeps quiet and forgotten. Besides, let us a little consider the secret quiet of their consciences. How easy is the reflection of having taken a few shillings or pounds from a stranger, without any breach of confidence, or perhaps any great harm to the person who loses it, compared to that of having betrayed a public trust, and ruined the fortunes of thousands, perhaps of a great nation! How much braver is an attack on the highway than at a gaming table; and how much more innocent the character of a bawdy-house than a court pimp!' He was eagerly proceeding, when, casting his eyes on the Count, he perceived him to be fast asleep; wherefore having first picked his pocket of three shillings, then gently jogged him in order to take his leave, and promised to return to him the next morning to breakfast, they separated. The Count retired to rest, and master Wild to a night-cellar.

CHAPTER VI

Further conferences between the Count and master Wild,
with other matters of the great kind

The Count missed his money the next morning, and very well knew who had it; but as he knew likewise how fruitless would be any complaint, he chose to pass it by without mentioning it. Indeed it may appear strange to some readers that these gentlemen, who knew each other to be thieves, should never once give the least hint of this knowledge in all their discourse together, but on the contrary should have the words honesty, honour, and friendship as often in their mouths as any other men. This, I say, may appear strange to some; but those who have lived long in cities, courts, gaols, or such places, will perhaps be able to solve the seeming absurdity.

When our two friends met the next morning, the Count (who, though he did not agree with the whole of his friend's doctrine, was, however, highly pleased with his argument) began to bewail the misfortune of his captivity, and the backwardness of friends to assist each other in their necessities; but what vexed him – he said – most, was the cruelty of the fair. For he entrusted Wild with the secret of his having had an intrigue with Miss Theodosia, the elder of the Miss Snaps, ever since his confinement, though he could not prevail with her to set him at liberty. Wild answered, with a smile, 'It was no wonder a woman should wish to confine her lover where she might be sure of having him entirely to herself,' but added, he believed he could tell him a method of certainly procuring his escape. The Count eagerly besought him to acquaint him with it. Wild told him bribery was the surest means, and advised him to apply to the maid. The Count thanked him, but returned that he had not a farthing left besides one guinea, which he had then given her to change. To which Wild said he must make it up with promises, which he supposed he was courtier enough to know how to put off. The Count greatly applauded the advice, and said he hoped he should be able in time to persuade him to condescend to be a great man, for which he was so perfectly well qualified.

This method being concluded on, the two friends sat down to cards, a circumstance which I should not have mentioned but for the sake of observing the prodigious force of habit; for though the Count knew if he won ever so much of Mr Wild he should not receive a shilling, yet could he not refrain from packing the cards; nor could Wild keep his hands out of his friend's pockets, though he knew there was nothing in them.

When the maid came home the Count began to put it to her; offered her all he had, and promised mountains in futuro; but all in vain – the maid's honesty was impregnable. She said she would not break her trust for the whole world – no, not if she could gain a hundred pound by it. Upon which Wild stepping up and telling her she need not fear losing her place, for it would never be found out; that they could throw a pair of sheets into the street, by which it might appear he got out at a window; that he himself would swear he saw him descending; that the money would be so much gains in her pocket; that besides his promises, which she might depend on being performed, she would receive from him twenty shillings and nine pence in ready money (for she had only laid out three pence in plain Spanish); and lastly, that besides his honour, the Count should leave a pair of gold buttons (which afterwards turned out to be brass) of great value, in her hands, as a further pawn.

The maid still remained inflexible, until Wild offered to lend his friend a guinea more, and to deposit it immediately in her hands. This reinforcement bore down the poor girl's resolution, and she faithfully promised to open the door to the Count that evening.

Thus did our young hero not only lend his rhetoric, which few people care to do without a fee, but his money too (a sum which many a good man would have made fifty excuses before he would have parted with) to his friend, and procured him his liberty.

But it would be highly derogatory from the great character of Wild, should the reader imagine he lent such a sum to a friend without the least view of serving himself. As, therefore, the reader may easily account for it in a manner more advantageous to our hero's reputation, by concluding that he had some interested view in the Count's enlargement, we hope he will judge with charity, especially as the sequel makes it not only reasonable but necessary to suppose he had some such view.

A long intimacy and friendship subsisted between the Count and Mr Wild, who, being by the advice of the Count dressed in good clothes, was by him introduced into the best company. They constantly frequented the assemblies, auctions, gaming tables, and play houses; at which last they saw two acts every night, and then retired without paying – this being, it seems, an immemorial privilege which the beaus of the town prescribe for themselves. This, however, did not suit Wild's temper, who called it a cheat, and objected against it as requiring no dexterity, but what every blockhead might put in execution. He said it was a custom very much savouring of the sneaking-budge[a], but neither so honourable nor so ingenious.

Wild now made a considerable figure, and passed for a gentleman of great fortune in the funds. Women of quality treated him with great familiarity, young ladies began to spread their charms for him, when an accident happened that put a stop to his continuance in a way of life too insipid and inactive to afford employment for those great talents, which were designed to make a much more considerable figure in the world than attends the character of a beau or a pretty gentleman.

CHAPTER VII

Master Wild sets out on his travels, and returns home again.
A very short chapter, containing infinitely more time and less
matter than any other in the whole story

We are sorry we cannot indulge our reader's curiosity with a full and perfect account of this accident; but as there are such various accounts – one of which only can be true, and possibly and indeed probably none – instead of following the general method of historians, who in such cases set down the various reports, and leave to your own conjecture which you will choose, we shall pass them all over.

Certain it is that, whatever this accident was, it determined our hero's father to send his son immediately abroad for seven years; and which may seem somewhat remarkable, to his majesty's plantations in

a. Shoplifting.

America – that part of the world being, as he said, freer from vices than the courts and cities of Europe, and consequently less dangerous to corrupt a young man's morals. And as for the advantages, the old gentleman thought they were equal there with those attained in the politer climates; for travelling, he said, was travelling in one part of the world as well as another. It consisted in being such a time from home, and in traversing so many leagues; and appealed to experience whether most of our travellers in France and Italy did not prove at their return that they might have been sent as profitably to Norway and Greenland.

According to these resolutions of his father, the young gentleman went aboard a ship, and with a great deal of good company set out for the American hemisphere. The exact time of his stay is somewhat uncertain; most probably longer than was intended. But howsoever long his abode there was, it must be a blank in this history, as the whole story contains not one adventure worthy the reader's notice; being indeed a continued scene of whoring, drinking, and removing from one place to another.

To confess a truth, we are so ashamed of the shortness of this chapter, that we would have done a violence to our history, and have inserted an adventure or two of some other traveller; to which purpose we borrowed the journals of several young gentlemen who have lately made the tour of Europe; but to our great sorrow could not extract a single incident strong enough to justify the theft to our conscience.

When we consider the ridiculous figure this chapter must make, being the history of no less than eight years, our only comfort is that the histories of some men's lives, and perhaps of some men who have made a noise in the world, are in reality as absolute blanks as the travels of our hero. As, therefore, we shall make sufficient amends in the sequel for this inanity, we shall hasten on to matters of true importance and immense greatness. At present we content ourselves with setting down our hero where we took him up, after acquainting our reader that he went abroad, stayed seven years, and then came home again.

CHAPTER VIII

An adventure where Wild, in the division of the booty,
exhibits an astonishing instance of greatness

The Count was one night very successful at the hazard table[21], where
Wild, who was just returned from his travels, was then present; as
was likewise a young gentleman whose name was Bob Bagshot, an
acquaintance of Mr Wild's, and of whom he entertained a great
opinion. Taking therefore Mr Bagshot aside, he advised him to provide
himself (if he had them not about him) with a case of pistols, and to
attack the Count in his way home, promising to plant himself near with
the same arms, as a corps de reserve, and to come up on occasion. This
was accordingly executed, and the Count obliged to surrender to
savage force what he had in so genteel and civil a manner taken at play.

And as it is a wise and philosophical observation that one misfortune
never comes alone, the Count had hardly passed the examination of
Mr Bagshot when he fell into the hands of Mr Snap, who in company
with Mr Wild the elder and one or two more gentlemen – being, it
seems, thereto well warranted – laid hold of the unfortunate Count, and
conveyed him back to the same house from which, by the assistance
of his good friend, he had formerly escaped.

Mr Wild and Mr Bagshot went together to the tavern, where Mr
Bagshot (generously, as he thought) offered to share the booty, and
having divided the money into two unequal heaps, and added a golden
snuff-box to the lesser heap, he desired Mr Wild to take his choice.

Mr Wild immediately conveyed the larger share of the ready into his
pocket – according to an excellent maxim of his, 'First secure what
share you can before you wrangle for the rest' and then, turning to his
companion, he asked with a stern countenance whether he intended
to keep all that sum to himself. Mr Bagshot answered, with some
surprise, that he thought Mr Wild had no reason to complain; for it was
surely fair, at least on his part, to content himself with an equal share of
the booty, who had taken the whole. 'I grant you took it,' replied Wild,
'but pray, who proposed or counselled the taking it? Can you say that
you have done more than executed my scheme? And might not I,

if I had pleased, have employed another, since you well know there was not a gentleman in the room but would have taken the money if he had known how, conveniently and safely, to do it?' 'That is very true,' returned Bagshot, 'but did not I execute the scheme, did not I run the whole risk? Should not I have suffered the whole punishment if I had been taken, and is not the labourer worthy of his hire?' 'Doubtless,' says Jonathan, 'he is so, and your hire I shall not refuse you, which is all that the labourer is entitled to or ever enjoys. I remember when I was at school to have heard some verses, which for the excellence of their doctrine made an impression on me, purporting that the birds of the air and the beasts of the field work not for themselves. It is true, the farmer allows fodder to his oxen and pasture to his sheep; but it is for his own service, not theirs. In the same manner the ploughman, the shepherd, the weaver, the builder and the soldier work not for themselves but others; they are contented with a poor pittance (the labourer's hire), and permit us, the "Great", to enjoy the fruits of their labours. Aristotle, as my master told us, has plainly proved, in the first book of his *Politics*, that the low, mean, useful part of mankind, are born slaves to the wills of their superiors, and are indeed as much their property as the cattle. It is well said of us, the higher order of mortals, that we are born only to devour the fruits of the earth; and it may be as well said of the lower class, that they are born only to produce them for us. Is not the battle gained by the sweat and danger of the common soldier? Are not the honour and fruits of the victory the general's who laid the scheme? Is not the house built by the labour of the carpenter and the bricklayer? Is it not built for the profit only of the architect and for the use of the inhabitant, who could not easily have placed one brick upon another? Is not the cloth or the silk wrought into its form and variegated with all the beauty of colours by those who are forced to content themselves with the coarsest and vilest part of their work, while the profit and enjoyment of their labours fall to the share of others? Cast your eye abroad, and see who is it lives in the most magnificent buildings, feasts his palate with the most luxurious dainties, his eyes with the most beautiful sculptures and delicate paintings, and clothes himself in the finest and richest apparel; and tell me if all these do not fall to his lot who had not any the least share in producing all these conveniences, nor the least ability so to do? Why then should the state of a prig differ from all others? Or why should you, who are the labourer only, the executor of my scheme, expect a share in the profit? Be advised, therefore; deliver the whole booty to me, and trust to my bounty for your reward.' Mr Bagshot was some time silent, and looked like a man thunderstruck, but at last, recovering himself from his surprise, he thus began: 'If you think, Mr Wild, by the force of your arguments, to get the money out of my pocket, you are greatly mistaken. What is all this stuff to me? Damn me, I am a man of honour, and though I can't talk as well as you, by God you shall not make a fool of me; and if you take me for one, I must tell you you are a rascal.' At which words he laid his hand to his pistol. Wild, perceiving the little success the great strength of his arguments had met with, and the hasty temper of his friend, gave over his design for the present, and told Bagshot he was only in jest. But this coolness with which he treated the other's flame had rather the effect of oil than of water. Bagshot replied in a rage, 'Damn me, I don't like such jests; I see you are a pitiful rascal and a scoundrel.' Wild, with a philosophy worthy of great admiration, returned, 'As for your abuse, I have no regard to it; but to convince you I am not afraid of you, let us lay the whole booty on the table, and let the conqueror take it all.' And having so said, he drew out his shining hanger, whose glittering so dazzled the eyes of Bagshot, that in tone entirely altered, he said, 'No! he was contented with what he had already; that it was mighty ridiculous in them to quarrel among themselves; that they had common enemies enough abroad, against whom they should unite their common force; that if he had mistaken Wild he was sorry for it; and as for a jest, he could take a jest as well as another.' Wild, who had a wonderful knack of discovering and applying to the passions of men, beginning now to have a little insight into his friend, and to conceive what arguments would make the quickest impression on him, cried out in a loud voice, that he had bullied him into drawing his hanger, and, since it was out, he would not put it up without satisfaction. 'What satisfaction would you have?' answered the other. 'Your money or your blood,' said Wild. 'Why, look ye, Mr Wild,' said Bagshot, 'if you want to borrow a little of my part, since I know you to be a man of honour, I don't care if I lend you; for, though I am not afraid of any man living, yet rather than break with a friend, and as it may be necessary for your occasions–'. Wild, who often declared that he looked upon borrowing to be as good a way of taking as any, and – as he called it – the genteelest kind of sneaking-budge, putting up his hanger and shaking his friend by the hand, told him he had hit the nail on the head; it was really his present necessity only that prevailed with him against his will, for that his honour was concerned to pay a considerable sum the next morning. Upon which, contenting himself with one half of Bagshot's share, so that he had three parts in four of the whole, he took leave of his companion and retired to rest.

CHAPTER IX

Wild pays a visit to Miss Letitia Snap. A description of that lovely young creature, and the successless issue of Mr Wild's addresses

The next morning, when our hero waked, he began to think of paying a visit to Miss Tishy Snap, a woman of great merit and of as great generosity; yet Mr Wild found a present was ever most welcome to her, as being a token of respect in her lover. He therefore went directly to a toy shop, and there purchased a genteel snuff-box, with which he waited upon his mistress, whom he found in the most beautiful undress. Her lovely hair hung wantonly over her forehead, being neither white with, nor yet free from, powder. A neat double clout, which seemed to have been worn a few weeks only, was pinned under her chin; some remains of that art with which ladies improve nature shone on her cheeks; her body was loosely attired, without stays or jumps, so that her breasts had uncontrolled liberty to display their beauteous orbs, which they did as low as her girdle; a thin covering of a rumpled muslin handkerchief almost hid them from the eyes, save in a few parts, where a good-natured hole gave opportunity to the naked breast to appear. Her gown was a satin of a whitish colour, with about a dozen little silver spots upon it, so artificially interwoven at great distance that they looked as if they had fallen there by chance. This, flying open, discovered a fine yellow petticoat, beautifully edged round the bottom with a narrow piece of half gold lace which was now almost become fringe. Beneath this appeared another petticoat stiffened with whalebone, vulgarly called a hoop, which hung six inches at least below the other; and under this again appeared an undergarment of that colour which Ovid intends when he says,

...Qui color albus erat nunc est contrarius albo.[22]

She likewise displayed two pretty feet covered with silk and adorned with lace, and tied; the right with a handsome piece of blue ribbon, the left, as more unworthy, with a piece of yellow stuff, which seemed to have been a strip of her upper petticoat. Such was the lovely creature whom Mr Wild attended. She received him at first with some of that coldness which women of strict virtue, by a commendable though sometimes painful restraint, enjoin themselves to their lovers. The snuff-box, being produced, was at first civilly, and indeed gently, refused; but on a second application accepted. The tea-table was soon called for, at which a discourse passed between these young lovers, which, could we set it down with any accuracy, would be very edifying as well as entertaining to our reader; let it suffice then that the wit, together with the beauty, of this young creature, so inflamed the passion of Wild – which, though an honourable sort of a passion – was at the same time so extremely violent that it transported him to freedoms too offensive to the nice chastity of Laetitia, who was, to confess the truth, more indebted to her own strength for the preservation of her virtue than to the awful respect or backwardness of her lover. He was indeed so very urgent in his addresses that, had he not with many oaths promised her marriage, we could scarce have been strictly justified in calling his passion honourable; but he was so remarkably attached to decency that he never offered any violence to a young lady without the most earnest promises of that kind – these being, he said, a ceremonial due to female modesty, which cost so little, and were so easily pronounced, that the omission could arise from nothing but the mere wantonness of brutality. The lovely Laetitia, either out of prudence, or perhaps religion, of which she was a liberal professor, was deaf to all his promises, and luckily invincible by his force; for though she had not yet learnt the art of well clenching her fist, nature had not however left her defenceless, for at the ends of her fingers she wore arms which she used with such admirable dexterity that the hot blood of Mr Wild soon began to appear in several little spots on his face, and his full-blown cheeks to resemble that part which modesty forbids a boy to turn up anywhere but in a public school, after some pedagogue, strong of arm, has exercised his talents thereon. Wild now retreated from the conflict, and the victorious Laetitia, with becoming triumph and noble spirit, cried out, 'Damn your eyes, if this be your way of showing your love, I'll warrant I gives you enough on't.' She then proceeded to talk of her virtue, which Wild bid her carry to the devil with her, and thus our lovers parted.

CHAPTER X

A discovery of some matters concerning the chaste Laetitia which must wonderfully surprise, and perhaps affect, our reader

Mr Wild was no sooner departed than the fair conqueress, opening the door of a closet, called forth a young gentleman whom she had there enclosed at the approach of the other. The name of this gallant was Tom Smirk. He was clerk to an attorney, and was indeed the greatest beau and the greatest favourite of the ladies at the end of the town where he lived. As we take dress to be the characteristic or efficient quality of a beau, we shall, instead of giving any character of this young gentleman, content ourselves with describing his dress only to our readers. He wore, then, a pair of white stockings on his legs, and pumps on his feet. His buckles were a large piece of pinchbeck plate, which almost covered his whole foot. His breeches were of red plush, which hardly reached his knees; his waistcoat was a white dimity, richly embroidered with yellow silk, over which he wore a blue plush coat with metal buttons, a smart sleeve, and a cape reaching halfway down his back. His wig was of a brown colour, covering almost half his pate, on which was hung on one side a little laced hat, but cocked with great smartness. Such was the accomplished Smirk, who at his issuing forth from the closet, was received with open arms by the amiable Laetitia. She addressed him by the tender name of 'dear Tommy', and told him she had dismissed the odious creature whom her father intended for her husband, and had now nothing to interrupt her happiness with him.

Here, Reader, you must pardon us if we stop a while to lament the capriciousness of Nature in forming this charming part of the creation designed to complete the happiness of man; with their soft innocence to allay his ferocity, with their sprightliness to soothe his cares, and with their constant friendship to relieve all the troubles and disappointments which can happen to him. Seeing then that these are the blessings chiefly sought after and generally found in every wife, how must we lament that disposition in these lovely creatures which leads them to prefer in their favour those individuals of the other sex who do not seem intended by nature as so great a masterpiece! For surely, however useful they may be in the creation, as we are taught that nothing, not even a louse, is made in vain, yet these beaus – even that most splendid and honoured part which in this our island Nature loves to distinguish in red – are not, as some think, the noblest work of the Creator. For my own part, let any man choose to himself two beaus, let them be captains or colonels, as well-dressed men as ever lived, I would venture to oppose a single Sir Isaac Newton, a Shakespeare, a Milton, or perhaps some few others, to both these beaus; nay, and I very much doubt whether it had not been better for the world in general that neither of these beaus had ever been born than that it should have wanted the benefit arising to it from the labour of any one of those persons.

If this be true, how melancholy must be the consideration that any single beau, especially if he have but half a yard of ribbon in his hat, shall weigh heavier in the scale of female affection than twenty Sir Isaac Newtons! How must our reader, who perhaps had wisely accounted for the resistance which the chaste Laetitia had made to the violent addresses of the ravished (or rather ravishing) Wild from that lady's impregnable virtue – how must he blush, I say, to perceive her quit the strictness of her carriage, and abandon herself to those loose freedoms which she indulged to Smirk! But alas! When we discover all, as to preserve the fidelity of our history we must – when we relate that every familiarity had passed between them, and that the fair Laetitia (for we must, in this single instance, imitate Virgil when he drops the *pius* and the *pater*[23], and drop our favourite epithet of chaste), the fair Laetitia had I say, made Smirk as happy as Wild desired to be – what must then be our reader's confusion! We will, therefore, draw a curtain over this scene, from that philogyny which is in us, and proceed to matters which, instead of dishonouring the human species, will greatly raise and ennoble it.

CHAPTER XI

Containing as notable instances of human greatness as are to be met with in ancient or modern history. Concluding with some wholesome hints to the gay part of mankind

Wild no sooner parted from the chaste Laetitia than, recollecting that his friend the Count was returned to his lodgings in the same house, he resolved to visit him, for he was none of those half-bred fellows who are ashamed to see their friends when they have plundered and betrayed them; from which base and pitiful temper many monstrous cruelties have been transacted by men, who have sometimes carried their modesty so far as to the murder or utter ruin of those against whom their consciences have suggested to them that they have committed some small trespass, either by the debauching a friend's wife or daughter, belying or betraying the friend himself, or some other such trifling instance. In our hero there was nothing not truly great: he could, without the least abashment, drink a bottle with the man who knew he had the moment before picked his pocket; and, when he had stripped him of everything he had, never desired to do him any further mischief; for he carried good nature to that wonderful and uncommon height that he never did a single injury to man or woman by which he himself did not expect to reap some advantage. He would often indeed say that by the contrary party men often made a bad bargain with the devil, and did his work for nothing.

Our hero found the captive Count, not basely lamenting his fate nor abandoning himself to despair, but with due resignation, employing himself in preparing several packs of cards for future exploits. The Count, little suspecting that Wild had been the sole contriver of the misfortune which had befallen him, rose up and eagerly embraced him, and Wild returned his embrace with equal warmth. They were no sooner seated than Wild took an occasion, from seeing the cards lying on the table, to inveigh against gaming, and with an usual and highly commendable freedom, after first exaggerating the distressed circumstances in which the Count was then involved, imputed all his misfortunes to that cursed itch of play which, he said, he concluded had brought his present confinement upon him, and must unavoidably end in his destruction. The other, with great alacrity, defended his favourite amusement (or rather employment), and having told his friend the great success he had after his unluckily quitting the room, acquainted him with the accident which followed, and which the reader, as well as Mr Wild, has had some intimation of before; adding, however, one circumstance not hitherto mentioned, viz. that he had defended his money with the utmost bravery, and had dangerously wounded at least two of the three men that had attacked him. This behaviour Wild – who not only knew the extreme readiness with which the booty had been delivered, but also the constant frigidity of the Count's courage – highly applauded, and wished he had been present to assist him. The Count then proceeded to animadvert on the carelessness of the watch, and the scandal it was to the laws that honest people could not walk the streets in safety; and after expatiating some time on that subject, he asked Mr Wild if he ever saw so prodigious a run of luck (for so he chose to call his winning, though he knew Wild was well acquainted with his having loaded dice in his pocket). The other answered it was indeed prodigious, and almost sufficient to justify any person who did not know him better in suspecting his fair play. 'No man, I believe, dares call that in question,' replied he. 'No, surely,' says Wild, 'you are well known to be a man of more honour; but pray, sir,' continued he, 'did the rascals rob you of all?' 'Every shilling,' cries the other, with an oath, 'they did not leave me a single stake.'

While they were thus discoursing, Mr Snap, with a gentleman who followed him, introduced Mr Bagshot into the company. It seems Mr

Bagshot, immediately after his separation from Mr Wild, returned to the gaming table, where having trusted to Fortune that treasure which he had procured by his industry, the faithless goddess committed a breach of trust, and sent Mr Bagshot away with as empty pockets as are to be found in any laced coat in the kingdom. Now, as that gentleman was walking to a certain reputable house or shed in Covent Garden market, he fortuned to meet with Mr Snap, who had just returned from conveying the Count to his lodgings, and was then walking to and fro before the gaming house door; for you are to know, my good reader, if you have never been a man of wit and pleasure about town, that as the voracious pike lies snug under some weed before the mouth of any of those little streams which discharge themselves into a large river, waiting for the small fry which issue thereout, so hourly, before the door or mouth of these gaming-houses, does Mr Snap, or some other gentleman of his occupation, attend the issuing forth of the small fry of young gentlemen, to whom they deliver little slips of parchment, containing invitations of the said gentlemen to their houses, together with one Mr John Doe[a], a person whose company is in great request. Mr Snap, among many others of these billets, happened to have one directed to Mr Bagshot, being at the suit or solicitation of one Mrs Anne Sample, spinster, at whose house the said Bagshot had lodged several months, and whence he had inadvertently departed without taking a formal leave, on which account Mrs Anne had taken this method of speaking with him.

Mr Snap's house being now very full of good company, he was obliged to introduce Mr Bagshot into the Count's apartment, it being, as he said, the only chamber he had to lock up in. Mr Wild no sooner saw his friend than he ran eagerly to embrace him, and immediately presented him to the Count, who received him with great civility.

a. This is a fictitious name which is put into every writ; for what purpose the lawyers best know.

CHAPTER XII

*Other particulars relating to Miss Tishy, which perhaps may
not greatly surprise after the former. The description of a very
fine gentleman. And a dialogue between Wild and the Count,
in which public virtue is just hinted at, with etc.*

Mr Snap had turned the key a very few minutes before a servant of
the family called Mr Bagshot out of the room, telling him there was a
person below who desired to speak with him; and this was no other
than Miss Laetitia Snap, whose admirer Mr Bagshot had long been, and
in whose tender breast his passion had raised a more ardent flame than
that which any of his rivals had been able to raise. Indeed, she was so
extremely fond of this youth, that she often confessed to her female
confidantes, if she could ever have listened to the thought of living
with any one man, Mr Bagshot was he. Nor was she singular in this
inclination, many other young ladies being her rivals in this matter, who
had all the great and noble qualifications necessary to form a true
gallant, and which nature is seldom so extremely bountiful as to indulge
to any one person. We will endeavour, however, to describe them all
with as much exactness as possible. He was then six feet high, had large
calves, broad shoulders, a ruddy complexion, with brown curled hair,
a modest assurance, and clean linen. He had indeed, it must be
confessed, some small deficiencies to counterbalance these heroic
qualities; for he was the silliest fellow in the world, could neither write
nor read, nor had he a single grain or spark of honour, honesty, or good
nature, in his whole composition.

As soon as Mr Bagshot had quitted the room, the Count, taking Wild
by the hand, told him he had something to communicate to him of very
great importance. 'I am very well convinced,' said he, 'that Bagshot is
the person who robbed me.' Wild started with great amazement at this
discovery, and answered, with a most serious countenance, 'I advise
you to take care how you cast any such reflections on a man of Mr
Bagshot's nice honour, for I am certain he will not bear it.' 'Damn his
honour!' said the enraged Count; 'nor can I bear being robbed; I will
apply to a justice of peace.' Wild replied, with great indignation, 'Since

you dare entertain such a suspicion against my friend, I will henceforth disclaim all acquaintance with you. Mr Bagshot is a man of honour, and my friend, and consequently it is impossible he should be guilty of a bad action.' He added much more to the same purpose, which had not the expected weight with the Count; for the latter seemed still certain as to the person, and resolute in applying for justice – which, he said, he thought he owed to the public as well as to himself. Wild then changed his countenance into a kind of derision, and spoke as follows: 'Suppose it should be possible that Mr Bagshot had, in a frolic (for I will call it no other), taken this method of borrowing your money, what will you get by prosecuting him? Not your money again, for you hear he was stripped at the gaming table (of which Bagshot had during their short confabulation informed them); you will get then an opportunity of being still more out of pocket by the prosecution. Another advantage you may promise yourself is the being blown up at every gaming house in town, for that I will assure you of; and then much good may it do you to sit down with the satisfaction of having discharged what it seems you owe the public. I am ashamed of my own discernment when I mistook you for a great man. Would it not be better for you to receive part (perhaps all) of your money again by a wise concealment? For, however seedy[a] Mr Bagshot may be now, if he has really played this frolic with you, you may believe he will play it with others, and when he is in cash you may depend on a restoration; the law will be always in your power, and that is the last remedy which a brave or a wise man would resort to. Leave the affair therefore to me; I will examine Bagshot, and if I find he has played you this trick, I will engage my own honour you shall in the end be no loser.' The Count answered, 'If I was sure to be no loser, Mr Wild, I apprehend you have a better opinion of my understanding than to imagine I would prosecute a gentleman for the sake of the public. These are foolish words of course, which we learn a ridiculous habit of speaking, and will often break from us without any design or meaning. I assure you, all I desire is a reimbursement; and if I can by your means obtain that, the public may –' concluding with a phrase too coarse to be inserted in a history of this kind.

They were now informed that dinner was ready, and the company

a. Poor.

assembled below stairs, whither the reader may, if he please, attend these gentlemen.

There sat down at the table Mr Snap and the two Miss Snaps his daughters, Mr Wild the elder, Mr Wild the younger, the Count, Mr Bagshot, and a grave gentleman who had formerly had the honour of carrying arms in a regiment of foot, and who was now engaged in the office (perhaps a more profitable one) of assisting or following Mr Snap in the execution of the laws of his country.

Nothing very remarkable passed at dinner. The conversation (as is usual in polite company) rolled chiefly on what they were then eating and what they had lately eaten. In this the military gentleman, who had served in Ireland, gave them a very particular account of a new manner of roasting potatoes, and others gave an account of other dishes. In short, an indifferent bystander would have concluded from their discourse that they had all come into this world for no other purpose than to fill their bellies; and indeed, if this was not the chief, it is probable it was the most innocent design Nature had in their formation.

As soon as the dish was removed, and the ladies retired, the Count proposed a game at hazard, which was immediately assented to by the whole company, and, the dice being immediately brought in, the Count took up the box and demanded who would set him; to which no one made any answer, imagining perhaps the Count's pockets to be more empty than they were; for, in reality, that gentleman (notwithstanding what he had heartily swore to Mr Wild) had, since his arrival at Mr Snap's, conveyed a piece of plate to pawn, by which means he had furnished himself with ten guineas. The Count, therefore, perceiving this backwardness in his friends, and probably somewhat guessing at the cause of it, took the said guineas out of his pocket, and threw them on the table; when lo (such is the force of example), all the rest began to produce their funds – and immediately, a considerable sum glittering in their eyes – the game began.

CHAPTER XIII

A chapter of which we are extremely vain, and which indeed we look on as our chef-d'oeuvre; *containing a wonderful story concerning the devil, and as nice a scene of honour as ever happened*

My reader, I believe, even if he be a gamester, would not thank me for an exact relation of every man's success; let it suffice then that they played until the whole money vanished from the table. Whether the devil himself carried it away, as some suspected, I will not determine; but very surprising it was that every person protested he had lost, nor could anyone guess who, unless the devil, had won.

But though very probable it is that this arch fiend had some share in the booty, it is likely he had not all, Mr Bagshot being imagined to be a considerable winner – notwithstanding his assertions to the contrary. For he was seen by several to convey money often into his pocket; and what is still a little stronger presumption is that the grave gentleman whom we have mentioned to have served his country in two honourable capacities, not being willing to trust alone to the evidence of his eyes, had frequently dived into the said Bagshot's pocket, whence (as he tells us in the apology for his life afterwards published[a]), though he might extract a few pieces, he was very sensible he had left many behind. The gentleman had long indulged his curiosity in this way before Mr Bagshot, in the heat of gaming, had perceived him; but as Bagshot was now leaving off play, he discovered this ingenious feat of dexterity; upon which, leaping up from his chair in violent passion, he cried out, 'I thought I had been among gentlemen and men of honour, but, damn me, I find we have a pickpocket in company.' The scandalous sound of this word extremely alarmed the whole board, nor did they all show less surprise than the Convocation (whose not sitting of late is much lamented) would express at hearing there was an atheist in the room; but it more particularly affected the gentleman at whom it was levelled, though it was not addressed to him. He likewise started from

a. Not in a book by itself, in imitation of some other such persons, but in the ordinary's account, etc., where all the apologies for the lives of rogues and whores which have been published within these twenty years should have been inserted.

his chair, and with a fierce countenance and accent said, 'Do you mean me? Damn your eyes, you are a rascal and a scoundrel!' Those words would have been immediately succeeded by blows had not the company interposed, and with strong arm withheld the two antagonists from each other. It was, however, a long time before they could be prevailed on to sit down; which being at last happily brought about, Mr Wild the elder, who was a well-disposed old man, advised them to shake hands and be friends; but the gentleman who had received the first affront absolutely refused it, and swore he would 'have the villain's blood'. Mr Snap highly applauded the resolution, and affirmed that the affront was by no means to be put up by any who bore the name of a gentleman, and that unless his friend resented it properly he would never execute another warrant in his company; that he had always looked upon him as a man of honour, and doubted not but he would prove himself so; and that if it was his own case, nothing should persuade him to put up such an affront without proper satisfaction. The Count likewise spoke on the same side, and the parties themselves muttered several short sentences purporting their intentions. At last Mr Wild, our hero, rising slowly from his seat, and having fixed the attention of all present, began as follows: 'I have heard with infinite pleasure everything which the two gentlemen who spoke last have said with relation to honour, nor can any man possibly entertain a higher and nobler sense of that word, nor a greater esteem of its inestimable value, than myself. If we have no name to express it by in our cant dictionary, it were well to be wished we had. It is indeed the essential quality of a gentleman, and which no man who ever was great in the field or on the road (as others express it) can possibly be without. But alas! gentlemen, what pity is it that a word of such sovereign use and virtue should have so uncertain and various an application that scarce two people mean the same thing by it? Do not some by honour mean good nature and humanity, which weak minds call virtues? How then! Must we deny it to the great, the brave, the noble to the sackers of towns, the plunderers of provinces, and the conquerors of kingdoms? Were not these men of honour? And yet they scorn those pitiful qualities I have mentioned. Again, some few (or I am mistaken) include the idea of honesty in their honour. And shall we then say that no man who withholds from another what law – or justice perhaps, calls his own – or who greatly and boldly deprives him of such property, is a man of honour? Heaven forbid I should say so in this, or, indeed, in any other good company! Is honour truth? No, it is not in the lies going from us, but in its coming to us, our honour is injured. Does it then consist in what the vulgar call cardinal virtues? It would be an affront to your understandings to suppose it, since we see every day so many men of honour without any. In what then does the word honour consist? Why, in itself alone. A man of honour is he that is called a man of honour; and while he is so called he so remains, and no longer. Think not anything a man commits can forfeit his honour. Look abroad into the world; the prig, while he flourishes, is a man of honour; when in gaol, at the bar, or the tree, he is so no longer. And why is this distinction? Not from his actions; for those are often as well known in his flourishing estate as they are afterwards; but because men, I mean those of his own party or gang, call him a man of honour in the former, and cease to call him so in the latter condition. Let us see then – how has Mr Bagshot injured the gentleman's honour? Why, he has called him a pickpocket; and that, probably by a severe construction and a long roundabout way of reasoning, may seem a little to derogate from his honour, if considered in a very nice sense. Admitting it, therefore, for argument's sake, to be some small imputation on his honour, let Mr Bagshot give him satisfaction; let him doubly and triply repair this oblique injury by directly asserting that he believes he is a man of honour.' The gentleman answered he was content to refer it to Mr Wild, and whatever satisfaction he thought sufficient he would accept. 'Let him give me my money again first,' said Bagshot, 'and then I will call him a man of honour with all my heart.' The gentleman then protested he had not any, which Snap seconded, declaring he had his eyes on him all the while; but Bagshot remained still unsatisfied, until Wild, rapping out a hearty oath, swore he had not taken a single farthing, adding that whoever asserted the contrary gave him the lie, and he would resent it. And now, such was the ascendancy of this great man, that Bagshot immediately acquiesced, and performed the ceremonies required, and thus, by the exquisite address of our hero, this quarrel, which had so fatal an aspect, and which between two persons so extremely jealous of their honour would most certainly have produced very dreadful consequences, was happily concluded.

Mr Wild was indeed a little interested in this affair, as he himself had set the gentleman to work, and had received the greatest part of the booty; and as to Mr Snap's deposition in his favour, it was the usual height to which the ardour of that worthy person's friendship too frequently hurried him. It was his constant maxim that he was a pitiful fellow who would stick at a little rapping[a] for his friend.

CHAPTER XIV

In which the history of greatness is continued

Matters being thus reconciled, and the gaming over, from reasons before hinted, the company proceeded to drink about with the utmost cheerfulness and friendship, drinking healths, shaking hands, and professing the most perfect affection for each other. All which were not in the least interrupted by some designs which they then agitated in their minds, and which they intended to execute as soon as the liquor had prevailed over some of their understandings – Bagshot and the gentleman intending to rob each other; Mr Snap and Mr Wild the elder meditating what other creditors they could find out to charge the gentleman then in custody with; the Count hoping to renew the play, and Wild, our hero, laying a design to put Bagshot out of the way, or as the vulgar express it, to hang him with the first opportunity. But none of these great designs could at present be put in execution, for – Mr Snap being soon after summoned abroad on business of great moment which required likewise the assistance of Mr Wild the elder and his other friend, and as he did not care to trust to the nimbleness of the Count's heels, of which he had already had some experience – he declared he must lock up for that evening. Here, reader, if you please, as we are in no great haste, we will stop and make a simile. As when their lap is finished, the cautious huntsman to their kennel gathers the nimble-footed hounds, they with lank ears and tails slouch sullenly on, whilst

a. Rapping is a cant word for perjury.

he, with his whippers-in, follows close at their heels, regardless of their dogged humour, until having seen them safe within the door, he turns the key, and then retires to whatever business or pleasure calls him thence; so with lowering countenance and reluctant steps mounted the Count and Bagshot to their chamber, or rather kennel, whither they were attended by Snap and those who followed him, and where Snap, having seen them deposited, very contentedly locked the door and departed. And now, Reader, we will, in imitation of the truly laudable custom of the world, leave these our good friends to deliver themselves as they can, and pursue the thriving fortunes of Wild, our hero, who, with that great aversion to satisfaction and content which is inseparably incident to great minds, began to enlarge his views with his prosperity. For this restless, amiable disposition, this noble avidity which increases with feeding, is the first principle or constituent quality of these our great men; to whom, in their passage on to greatness, it happens as to a traveller over the Alps, or if this be a too far-fetched simile, to one who travels westward over the hills near Bath, where the simile was indeed made. He sees not the end of his journey at once; but passing on from scheme to scheme, and from hill to hill, with noble constancy, resolving still to attain the summit on which he has fixed his eye, however dirty the roads may be through which he struggles, he at length arrives – at some vile inn, where he finds no kind of entertainment nor conveniency for repose. I fancy, Reader, if you have ever travelled in these roads, one part of my simile is sufficiently apparent (and, indeed, in all these illustrations, one side is generally much more apparent than the other), but believe me, if the other does not so evidently appear to thy satisfaction, it is from no other reason than because you are unacquainted with these great men, and have not had sufficient instruction, leisure, or opportunity to consider what happens to those who pursue what is generally understood by *greatness*: for surely, if you have animadverted, not only on the many perils to which great men are daily liable while they are in their progress, but had discerned, as it were through a microscope (for it is invisible to the naked eye), that diminutive speck of happiness which they attain even in the consummation of their wishes, you would lament with me the unhappy fate of these great men, on whom nature has set so superior a mark that the rest of mankind are born for their use and emolument only, and be apt to cry out, 'It is pity that those for whose pleasure and profit mankind are to labour and sweat, to be hacked and hewed, to be pillaged, plundered, and every way destroyed, should reap so little advantage from all the miseries they occasion to others.' For my part, I own myself of that humble kind of mortals who consider themselves born for the behoof of some great man or other, and could I behold his happiness carved out of the labour and ruin of a thousand such reptiles as myself I might with satisfaction exclaim, '*Sic, sic juvat*'[24]. But when I behold one great man starving with hunger and freezing with cold, in the midst of fifty thousand who are suffering the same evils for his diversion – when I see another, whose own mind is a more abject slave to his own greatness, and is more tortured and racked by it than those of all his vassals – lastly, when I consider whole nations rooted out only to bring tears into the eyes of a great man, not indeed because he has extirpated so many, but because he had no more nations to extirpate – then truly I am almost inclined to wish that Nature had spared us this her masterpiece, and that no great man had ever been born into the world.

But to proceed with our history, which will, we hope, produce much better lessons, and more instructive, than any we can preach – Wild was no sooner retired to a night-cellar than he began to reflect on the sweets he had that day enjoyed from the labours of others, viz. first from Mr Bagshot, who had for his use robbed the Count; and secondly from the gentleman, who, for the same good purpose, had picked the pocket of Bagshot. He then proceeded to reason thus with himself: 'The art of policy is the art of multiplication, the degrees of greatness being constituted by those two little words *more* or *less*. Mankind are first properly to be considered under two grand divisions: those that use their own hands, and those who employ the hands of others. The former are the base and rabble; the latter, the genteel part of the creation. The mercantile part of the world, therefore, wisely use the term "employing hands", and justly prefer each other as they employ more or fewer; for thus one merchant says he is greater than another because he employs more hands. And now indeed the merchant should seem to challenge some character of greatness, did we not necessarily come to a second division, viz. of those who employ hands for the use

41

of the community in which they live, and of those who employ hands merely for their own use, without any regard to the benefit of society. Of the former sort are the yeoman, the manufacturer, the merchant, and perhaps the gentleman. The first of these being to manure and cultivate his native soil, and to employ hands to produce the fruits of the earth. The second being to improve them by employing hands likewise, and to produce from them those useful commodities which serve as well for the conveniences as necessaries of life. The third is to employ hands for the exportation of the redundance of our own commodities, and to exchange them with the redundancies of foreign nations, that thus every soil and every climate may enjoy the fruits of the whole earth. The gentleman is, by employing hands, likewise to embellish his country with the improvement of art and sciences, with the making and executing good and wholesome laws for the preservation of property and the distribution of justice, and in several other manners to be useful to society. Now we come to the second part of this division, viz. of those who employ hands for their own use only; and this is that noble and great part who are generally distinguished into conquerors, absolute princes, statesmen, and prigs. Now all these differ from each other in greatness only – they employ more or fewer hands. And Alexander the Great was only greater than a captain of one of the Tartarian or Arabian hordes, as he was at the head of a larger number. In what then is a single prig inferior to any other great man, but because he employs his own hands only; for he is not on that account to be levelled with the base and vulgar, because he employs his hands for his own use only. Now, suppose a prig had as many tools as any prime minister ever had, would he not be as great as any prime minister whatsoever? Undoubtedly he would. What then have I to do in the pursuit of greatness but to procure a gang, and to make the use of this gang centre in myself? This gang shall rob for me only, receiving very moderate rewards for their actions; out of this gang I will prefer to my favour the boldest and most iniquitous (as the vulgar express it); the rest I will, from time to time, as I see occasion, transport and hang at my pleasure; and thus (which I take to be the highest excellence of a prig) convert those laws which are made for the benefit and protection of society to my single use.'

Having thus preconceived his scheme, he saw nothing wanting to put it in immediate execution but that which is indeed the beginning as well as the end of all human devices: I mean money. Of which commodity he was possessed of no more than sixty-five guineas, being all that remained from the double benefits he had made of Bagshot, and which did not seem sufficient to furnish his house, and every other convenience necessary for so grand an undertaking. He resolved, therefore, to go immediately to the gaming house, which was then sitting, not so much with an intention of trusting to fortune as to play the surer card of attacking the winner in his way home. On his arrival, however, he thought he might as well try his success at the dice, and reserve the other resource as his last expedient. He accordingly sat down to play; and as Fortune, no more than others of her sex, is observed to distribute her favours with strict regard to great mental endowments, so our hero lost every farthing in his pocket. This loss however he bore with great constancy of mind, and with as great composure of aspect. To say truth, he considered the money as only lent for a short time, or rather indeed as deposited with a banker. He then resolved to have immediate recourse to his surer stratagem; and casting his eyes round the room, he soon perceived a gentleman sitting in a disconsolate posture, who seemed a proper instrument or tool for his purpose. In short (to be as concise as possible in these least shining parts of our history), Wild accosted this man, sounded him, found him fit to execute, proposed the matter, received a ready assent and, having fixed on the person who seemed that evening the greatest favourite of Fortune, they posted themselves in the most proper place to surprise the enemy as he was retiring to his quarters, where he was soon attacked, subdued, and plundered, but indeed of no considerable booty; for it seems this gentleman played on a common stock, and had deposited his winnings at the scene of action, nor had he any more than two shillings in his pocket when he was attacked.

This was so cruel a disappointment to Wild, and so sensibly affects us – as no doubt it will the reader – that, as it must disqualify us both from proceeding any further at present, we will now take a little breath, and therefore we shall here close this book.

BOOK II

CHAPTER I

*Characters of silly people, with the proper uses
for which such are designed*

One reason why we chose to end our first book as we did, with the last chapter, was that we are now obliged to produce two characters of a stamp entirely different from what we have hitherto dealt in. These persons are of that pitiful order of mortals who are in contempt called good natured; being indeed sent into the world by nature with the same design with which men put little fish into a pike pond, in order to be devoured by that voracious water-hero.

But to proceed with our history: Wild, having shared the booty in much the same manner as before, i.e. taken three quarters of it, amounting to eighteen pence, was now retiring to rest, in no very happy mood, when by accident he met with a young fellow who had formerly been his companion, and indeed intimate friend, at school. It has been thought that friendship is usually nursed by similitude of manners, but the contrary had been the case between these lads; for whereas Wild was rapacious and intrepid, the other had always more regard for his skin than his money; Wild therefore had very generously compassionated this defect in his school fellow, and had brought him off from many scrapes into most of which he had first drawn him, by taking the fault and whipping to himself. He had always indeed been well paid on such occasions; there are a sort of people who, together with the best of the bargain, will be sure to have the obligation too on their side; so it had happened here. For this poor lad had considered himself in the highest degree obliged to Mr Wild, and had contracted a very great esteem and friendship for him; the traces of which an absence of many years had not in the least effaced in his mind. He no sooner knew Wild, therefore, than he accosted him in the most friendly manner, and invited him home with him to breakfast (it being now near nine in the morning), which invitation our hero with no great difficulty consented to. This young man, who was about Wild's age, had some time before set up in the trade of a jeweller, in the materials or stock for which he had laid out the greatest part of a little fortune, and had married a very agreeable woman for love, by whom he then had two children. As our reader is to be more acquainted with this person, it may not be improper to open somewhat of his character, especially as it will serve as a kind of foil to the noble and great disposition of our hero, and as the one seems sent into this world as a proper object on which the talents of the other were to be displayed with a proper and just success.

Mr Thomas Heartfree then (for that was his name) was of an honest and open disposition. He was of that sort of men whom experience only, and not their own natures, must inform that there are such things as deceit and hypocrisy in the world, and who consequently are not at five-and-twenty so difficult to be imposed upon as the oldest and most subtle. He was possessed of several great weaknesses of mind, being good natured, friendly, and generous to a great excess. He had indeed too little regard to common justice, for he had forgiven some debts to his acquaintance only because they could not pay him, and had entrusted a bankrupt, on his setting up a second time, from having been convinced that he had dealt in his bankruptcy with a fair and honest heart, and that he had broke through misfortune only, and not from neglect or imposture. He was withal so silly a fellow that he never took the least advantage of the ignorance of his customers, and contented himself with very moderate gains on his goods; which he was the better enabled to do, notwithstanding his generosity, because his life was extremely temperate, his expenses being solely confined to the cheerful entertainment of his friends at home, and now and then a moderate glass of wine, in which he indulged himself in the company of his wife – who, with an agreeable person, was a mean-spirited, poor, domestic, low-bred animal, who confined herself mostly to the care of her family, placed her happiness in her husband and her children, followed no expensive fashions or diversions, and indeed rarely went abroad, unless to return the visits of a few plain neighbours, and twice a year afforded herself, in company with her husband, the diversion of a play, where she never sat in a higher place than the pit.

To this silly woman did this silly fellow introduce the great Wild, informing her at the same time of their school acquaintance and the many obligations he had received from him. This simple woman no sooner heard her husband had been obliged to her guest than her eyes sparkled on him with a benevolence which is an emanation from the heart, and of which great and noble minds, whose hearts never dwell but with an injury, can have no very adequate idea. It is therefore no wonder that our hero should misconstrue, as he did, the poor, innocent, and ample affection of Mrs Heartfree towards her husband's friend for that great and generous passion which fires the eyes of a modern heroine, when the colonel is so kind as to indulge his city creditor with partaking of his table today, and of his bed tomorrow. Wild, therefore, instantly returned the compliment as he understood it, with his eyes, and presently after bestowed many encomiums on her beauty, with which perhaps she, who was a woman though a good one, and misapprehended the design was not displeased any more than the husband.

When breakfast was ended, and the wife retired to her household affairs, Wild, who had a quick discernment into the weaknesses of men, and who, besides the knowledge of his good (or foolish) disposition when a boy, had now discovered several sparks of goodness, friendship, and generosity in his friend, began to discourse over the accidents which had happened in their childhood, and took frequent occasions of reminding him of those favours which we have before mentioned his having conferred on him. He then proceeded to the most vehement professions of friendship, and to the most ardent expressions of joy in this renewal of their acquaintance. He at last told him, with great seeming pleasure, that he believed he had an opportunity of serving him by the recommendation of a gentleman to his custom, who was then on the brink of marriage. 'And, if he be not already engaged, I will,' says he, 'endeavour to prevail on him to furnish his lady with jewels at your shop.'

Heartfree was not backward in thanks to our hero, and after many earnest solicitations to dinner, which were refused, they parted for the first time.

But here, as it occurs to our memory that our readers may be surprised (an accident which sometimes happens in histories of this kind) how Mr Wild the elder, in his present capacity, should have been able to maintain his son at a reputable school, as this appears to have been, it may be necessary to inform him that Mr Wild himself was then a tradesman in good business, but by misfortunes in the world – to wit, extravagance and gaming – he had reduced himself to that honourable occupation which we have formerly mentioned.

Having cleared up this doubt, we will now pursue our hero, who forthwith repaired to the Count, and having first settled preliminary articles concerning distributions, he acquainted him with the scheme which he had formed against Heartfree; and after consulting proper methods to put it in execution, they began to concert measures for the enlargement of the Count; on which the first, and indeed only point to be considered, was to raise money, not to pay his debts – for that would have required an immense sum, and was contrary to his inclination or intention – but to procure him bail. For as to his escape, Mr Snap had taken such precautions that it appeared absolutely impossible.

CHAPTER II

Great examples of greatness in Wild, shown as well by his behaviour to Bagshot as in a scheme laid, first, to impose on Heartfree by means of the Count, and then to cheat the Count of the booty

Wild undertook therefore to extract some money from Bagshot, who notwithstanding the depredations made on him, had carried off a pretty considerable booty from their engagement at dice the preceding day. He found Mr Bagshot in expectation of his bail, and with a countenance full of concern – which he could at any time, with wonderful art, put on – told him that all was discovered; that the Count knew him, and intended to prosecute him for the robbery, 'had not I exerted' (said he) 'my utmost interest, and with great difficulty prevailed on him in case you refund the money–' 'Refund the money!' cried Bagshot, 'that is in your power, for you know what an inconsiderable part of it fell to my share.' 'How!' replied Wild, 'is this your gratitude to me for saving your life? For your own conscience must convince you of your guilt, and with how much certainty the gentleman can give evidence against you.' 'Marry come up!' quoth Bagshot; 'I believe my life alone will not be in danger. I know those who are as guilty as myself. Do you tell me of conscience?' 'Yes, sirrah!' answered our hero, taking him by the collar; 'and since you dare threaten me I will show you the difference between committing a robbery and conniving at it, which is all I can charge myself with. I own indeed I suspected, when you showed me a sum of money, that you had not come honestly by it.' 'How!' says Bagshot, frightened out of one half of his wits, and amazed out of the other, 'can you deny?' 'Yes, you rascal,' answered Wild, 'I do deny everything; and do you find a witness to prove it. And, to show you how little apprehension I have of your power to hurt me, I will have you apprehended this moment.' At which words he offered to break from him; but Bagshot laid hold of his skirts, and with an altered tone and manner, begged him not to be so impatient. 'Refund then, sirrah,' cries Wild, 'and perhaps I may take pity on you.' 'What must I refund?' answered Bagshot. 'Every farthing in your pocket,' replied Wild; 'then I may have some compassion on you, and not only save your life, but, out of an excess of generosity, may return you something.' At which words Bagshot seeming to hesitate, Wild pretended to make to the door, and rapped out an oath of vengeance with so violent an emphasis that his friend no longer presumed to balance, but suffered Wild to search his pockets and draw forth all he found, to the amount of twenty-one guineas and a half, which last piece our generous hero returned him again, telling him he might now sleep secure but advised him for the future never to threaten his friends.

Thus did our hero execute the greatest exploits with the utmost ease imaginable, by means of those transcendent qualities which nature had indulged him with, viz. a bold heart, a thundering voice, and a steady countenance.

Wild now returned to the Count, and informed him that he had got ten guineas of Bagshot; for with great and commendable prudence, he sunk the other eleven into his own pocket, and told him with that money he would procure him bail – which he after prevailed on his father, and another gentleman of the same occupation, to become, for two guineas each – so that he made lawful prize of six more, making Bagshot debtor for the whole ten; for such were his great abilities, and so vast the compass of his understanding, that he never made any bargain without overreaching (or, in the vulgar phrase, cheating) the person with whom he dealt.

The Count being by these means enlarged, the first thing they did, in order to procure credit from tradesmen, was the taking a handsome house ready furnished in one of the new streets; in which as soon as the Count was settled, they proceeded to furnish him with servants and equipage, and all the insignia of a large estate proper to impose on poor Heartfree. These being all obtained, Wild made a second visit to his friend, and with much joy in his countenance acquainted him that he had succeeded in his endeavours, and that the gentleman had promised to deal with him for the jewels which he intended to present his bride, and which were designed to be very splendid and costly; he therefore appointed him to go to the Count the next morning, and carry with him a set of the richest and most beautiful jewels he had, giving him at the same time some hints of the Count's ignorance of that commodity, and that he might extort what price of him he pleased; but Heartfree told him, not without some disdain, that he scorned to take any such advantage; and, after expressing much gratitude to his friend for his recommendation, he promised to carry the jewels at the hour and to the place appointed.

I am sensible that the reader, if he has but the least notion of greatness, must have such a contempt for the extreme folly of this fellow that he will be very little concerned at any misfortunes which may befall him in the sequel; for to have no suspicion that an old schoolfellow, with whom he had, in his tenderest years, contracted a friendship, and who, on the accidental renewing of their acquaintance, had professed the most passionate regard for him, should be very ready to impose on him – in short, to conceive that a friend should, of his own accord, without any view to his own interest, endeavour to do him a service, must argue such weakness of mind, such ignorance of the world, and such an artless, simple, undesigning heart, as must render the person possessed of it the lowest creature and the properest object of contempt imaginable, in the eyes of every man of understanding and discernment.

Wild remembered that his friend Heartfree's faults were rather in his heart than in his head; that though he was so mean a fellow that he was never capable of laying a design to injure any human creature, yet was he by no means a fool, nor liable to any gross imposition, unless where his heart betrayed him. He therefore instructed the Count to take only one of his jewels at the first interview, and reject the rest as not fine enough, and order him to provide some richer. He said this management would prevent Heartfree from expecting ready money for the jewel he brought with him, which the Count was presently to dispose of, and by means of that money, and his great abilities at cards and dice, to get together as large a sum as possible, which he was to pay down to Heartfree at the delivery of the set of jewels, who would be thus void of all manner of suspicion and would not fail to give him credit for the residue.

By this contrivance, it will appear in the sequel that Wild did not only propose to make the imposition on Heartfree – who was (hitherto) void of all suspicion – more certain, but to rob the Count himself of this sum. This double method of cheating the very tools who are our instruments to cheat others is the superlative degree of greatness, and is probably, as far as any spirit crusted over with clay can carry it, falling very little short of diabolism itself.

This method was immediately put in execution, and the Count the first day took only a single brilliant, worth about three hundred pounds, and ordered a necklace, earrings, and solitaire, of the value of three thousand more, to be prepared by that day sevennight.

The interval was employed by Wild in prosecuting his scheme of raising a gang, in which he met with such success that within a few days he had levied several bold and resolute fellows, fit for any enterprise, howsoever dangerous or great, (i.e villainous).

We have before remarked that the truest mark of greatness is insatiability. Wild had covenanted with the Count to receive three quarters of the booty, and had, at the same time, covenanted with himself to secure the other fourth part likewise, for which he had formed a very great and noble design; but he now saw with concern that sum which was to be received in hand by Heartfree in danger of being absolutely lost. In order therefore to possess himself of that likewise, he contrived that the jewels should be brought in the afternoon, and that Heartfree should be detained before the Count could see him, so that the night should overtake him in his return, when two of his gang were ordered to attack and plunder him.

CHAPTER III

Containing scenes of softness, love, and honour all in the great style

The Count had disposed of his jewel for its full value, and this he had
by dexterity raised to a thousand pounds; this sum therefore he paid
down to Heartfree, promising him the rest within a month. His house,
his equipage, his appearance – but, above all, a certain plausibility in his
voice and behaviour – would have deceived any, but one whose great
and wise heart had dictated to him something within, which would
have secured him from any danger of imposition from without.
Heartfree therefore did not in the least scruple giving him credit; but as
he had in reality procured those jewels of another – his own little stock
not being able to furnish anything so valuable – he begged the Count
would be so kind to give his note for the money, payable at the time he
mentioned; which that gentleman did not in the least scruple; so he
paid him the thousand pound in specie, and gave his note for two
thousand eight hundred pounds more to Heartfree, who burnt with
gratitude to Wild for the noble customer he had recommended to him.

As soon as Heartfree was departed, Wild, who waited in another
room, came in and received the casket from the Count, it having been
agreed between them that this should be deposited in his hands, as he
was the original contriver of the scheme, and was to have the largest
share. Wild, having received the casket, offered to meet the Count late
that evening to come to a division, but such was the latter's confidence
in the honour of our hero, that he said, if it was any inconvenience to
him, the next morning would do altogether as well. This was more
agreeable to Wild, and accordingly, an appointment being made for that
purpose, he set out in haste to pursue Heartfree to the place where the
two gentlemen were ordered to meet and attack him. Those gentlemen
with noble resolution executed their purpose; they attacked and
spoiled the enemy of the whole sum he had received from the Count.

As soon as the engagement was over, and Heartfree left sprawling
on the ground, our hero, who wisely declined trusting the booty in
his friends' hands, though he had good experience of their honour,
made off after the conquerors. At length, they being all at a place of

safety, Wild, according to a previous agreement, received nine tenths of the booty, the subordinate heroes did indeed profess some little unwillingness (perhaps more than was strictly consistent with honour) to perform their contract; but Wild, partly by argument, but more by oaths and threatenings, prevailed with them to fulfil their promise.

Our hero having thus, with wonderful address, brought this great and glorious action to a happy conclusion, resolved to relax his mind after his fatigue in the conversation of the fair. He therefore set forward to his lovely Laetitia; but in his way accidentally met with a young lady of his acquaintance, Miss Molly Straddle, who was taking the air in Bridges Street. Miss Molly, seeing Mr Wild, stopped him, and with a familiarity peculiar to a genteel town education, tapped, or rather slapped him on the back, and asked him to treat her with a pint of wine at a neighbouring tavern. The hero, though he loved the chaste Laetitia with excessive tenderness, was not of that low snivelling breed of mortals who, as it is generally expressed, 'tie themselves to a woman's apron strings' – in a word, who are tainted with that mean, base, low vice – or virtue as it is called – of constancy; therefore he immediately consented, and attended her to a tavern famous for excellent wine, known by the name of *The Rummer and Horseshoe*, where they retired to a room by themselves. Wild was very vehement in his addresses, but to no purpose; the young lady declared she would grant no favour until he had made her a present; this was immediately complied with, and the lover made as happy as he could desire.

The immoderate fondness which Wild entertained for his dear Laetitia would not suffer him to waste any considerable time with Miss Straddle. Notwithstanding, therefore, all the endearments and caresses of that young lady, he soon made an excuse to go downstairs, and thence immediately set forward to Laetitia without taking any formal leave of Miss Straddle, or indeed of the drawer, with whom the lady was afterwards obliged to come to an account for the reckoning.

Mr Wild, on his arrival at Mr Snap's, found only Miss Doshy at home, that young lady being employed alone, in imitation of Penelope[25], with her thread or worsted, only with this difference, that whereas Penelope unravelled by night what she had knit or wove or spun by day, so what our young heroine unravelled by day she knit

53

again by night. In short, she was mending a pair of blue stockings with red clocks; a circumstance which perhaps we might have omitted, had it not served to show that there are still some ladies of this age who imitate the simplicity of the ancients.

Wild immediately asked for his beloved, and was informed that she was not at home. He then enquired where she was to be found, and declared he would not depart until he had seen her, nay, not until he had married her, for indeed, his passion for her was truly honourable in other words, he had so ungovernable a desire for her person that he would go any length to satisfy it. He then pulled out the casket, which he swore was full of the finest jewels, and that he would give them all to her, with other promises, which so prevailed on Miss Doshy – who had not the common failure of sisters in envying, and often endeavouring to disappoint each other's happiness – that she desired Mr Wild to sit down a few minutes, whilst she endeavoured to find her sister and to bring her to him. The lover thanked her, and promised to stay until her return; and Miss Doshy, leaving Mr Wild to his meditations, fastened him in the kitchen by barring the door (for most of the doors in this mansion were made to be bolted on the outside), and then, slapping to the door of the house with great violence, without going out at it, she stole softly upstairs where Miss Laetitia was engaged in close conference with Mr Bagshot. Miss Letty, being informed by her sister in a whisper of what Mr Wild had said, and what he had produced, told Mr Bagshot that a young lady was below to visit her whom she would despatch with all imaginable haste and return to him. She desired him therefore to stay with patience for her in the mean time, and that she would leave the door unlocked, though her papa would never forgive her if he should discover it. Bagshot promised on his honour not to step without his chamber; and the two young ladies went softly downstairs, when, pretending first to make their entry into the house, they repaired to the kitchen, where not even the presence of the chaste Laetitia could restore that harmony to the countenance of her lover which Miss Theodosia had left him possessed of – for during her absence he had discovered the absence of a purse containing banknotes for £900, which had been taken from Mr Heartfree, and which, indeed, Miss Straddle had, in the warmth of his amorous caresses, unperceived drawn from him. However, as he had that perfect mastery of his temper, or rather of his muscles, which is as necessary to the forming a great character as to the personating it on the stage, he soon conveyed a smile into his countenance, and sealing as well his misfortune as his chagrin at it, began to pay honourable addresses to Miss Letty. This young lady, among many other good ingredients, had three very predominant passions – to wit, vanity, wantonness, and avarice. To satisfy the first of these she employed Mr Smirk and company; to the second, Mr Bagshot and company; and our hero had the honour and happiness of solely engrossing the third. Now, these three sorts of lovers she had very different ways of entertaining. With the first she was all gay and coquette; with the second all fond and rampant; and with the last all cold and reserved. She therefore told Mr Wild, with a most composed aspect, that she was glad he had repented of his manner of treating her at their last interview, where his behaviour was so monstrous that she had resolved never to see him any more; that she was afraid her own sex would hardly pardon her the weakness she was guilty of in receding from that resolution, which she was persuaded she never should have brought herself to, had not her sister, who was there to confirm what she said (as she did with many oaths), betrayed her into his company, by pretending it was another person to visit her. But, however, as he now thought proper to give her more convincing proofs of his affections (for he had now the casket in his hand), and since she perceived his designs were no longer against her virtue, but were such as a woman of honour might listen to, she must own – and then she feigned a hesitation when Theodosia began, 'Nay, sister, I am resolved you shall counterfeit no longer. I assure you, Mr Wild, she has the most violent passion for you in the world; and indeed, dear Tishy, if you offer to go back, since I plainly see Mr Wild's designs are honourable, I will betray all you have ever said.' 'How, sister!' answered Laetitia; 'I protest you will drive me out of the room, I did not expect this usage from you.' Wild then fell on his knees, and taking hold of her hand, repeated a speech which, as the reader may easily suggest it to himself, I shall not here set down. He then offered her the casket, but she gently rejected it; and on a second offer, with a modest countenance and voice, desired to know what it contained. Wild then opened it, and took forth (with sorrow I write it, and with sorrow will it be read) one of those beautiful necklaces with which, at the fair of Bartholomew[26], they deck the well-bewhitened neck of Thalestris queen of Amazons, Anna Bullen, Queen Elizabeth, or some other high princess in Drollic story. It was indeed composed of that paste which Derdaeus Magnus[27], an ingenious toy-man, does at a very moderate price dispense of to the second-rate beaus of the metropolis. For, to open a truth – which we ask our reader's pardon for having concealed from him so long – the sagacious Count, wisely fearing lest some accident might prevent Mr Wild's return at the appointed time, had carefully conveyed the jewels which Mr Heartfree had brought with him into his own pocket, and in their stead had placed in the casket these artificial stones, which, though of equal value to a philosopher, and perhaps of a much greater to a true admirer of the compositions of art, had not however the same charms in the eyes of Miss Letty, who had indeed some knowledge of jewels. For Mr Snap, with great reason, considering how valuable a part of a lady's education it would be to be well instructed in these things, in an age when young ladies learn little more than how to dress themselves, had in her youth placed Miss Letty as the handmaid (or housemaid as the vulgar call it) of an eminent pawnbroker. The lightning, therefore, which should have flashed from the jewels, flashed from her eyes, and thunder immediately followed from her voice. She beknaved, be-rascalled, berogued the unhappy hero, who stood silent, confounded with astonishment, but more with shame and indignation at being thus outwitted and overreached. At length he recovered his spirits and, throwing down the casket in a rage, he snatched the key from the table, and without making any answer to the ladies – who both very plentifully opened upon him – and without taking any leave of them, he flew out at the door, and repaired with the utmost expedition to the Count's habitation.

CHAPTER IV

In which Wild, after many fruitless endeavours to discover his
friend, moralises on his misfortune in a speech which may be of use
(if rightly understood) to some other considerable speech-makers

Not the highest-fed footman of the highest-bred woman of quality
knocks with more impetuosity than Wild did at the Count's door,
which was immediately opened by a well-dressed liveryman, who
answered that his master was not at home. Wild, not satisfied with this,
searched the house, but to no purpose; he then ransacked all the
gaming houses in town, but found no Count. Indeed, that gentleman
had taken leave of his house the same instant Mr Wild had turned his
back, and equipping himself with boots and a post-horse, without
taking with him either servant, clothes, or any necessaries for the
journey of a great man, made such mighty expedition that he was now
upwards of twenty miles on his way to Dover.

Wild, finding his search ineffectual, resolved to give it over for that
night; he then retired to his seat of contemplation, a night-cellar, where
without a single farthing in his pocket he called for a sneaker of punch,
and placing himself on a bench by himself, he softly vented the
following soliloquy:

'How vain is human greatness! What avail superior abilities, and a
noble defiance of those narrow rules and bounds which confine the
vulgar, when his best-concerted schemes are liable to be defeated! How
unhappy is the state of priggism! How impossible for human prudence
to foresee and guard against every circumvention! It is even as a game of
chess, where while the rook, or knight, or bishop, is busied forecasting
some great enterprise, a worthless pawn exposes and disconcerts his
scheme. Better had it been for me to have observed the simple laws of
friendship and morality than thus to ruin my friend for the benefit
of others. I might have commanded his purse to any degree of moderation. I have now disabled him from the power of serving me. Well!
But that was not my design. If I cannot arraign my own conduct, why
should I, like a woman or a child, sit down and lament the disappointment of chance? But can I acquit myself of all neglect? Did I not

57

misbehave in putting it into the power of others to outwit me? But that is impossible to be avoided. In this a prig is more unhappy than any other. A cautious man may, in a crowd, preserve his own pockets by keeping his hands in them; but while the prig employs his hands in another's pocket, how shall he be able to defend his own? Indeed, in this light, what can be imagined more miserable than a prig? How dangerous are his acquisitions! How unsafe, how unquiet his possessions! Why then should any man wish to be a prig, or where is his greatness? I answer, in his mind, 'tis the inward glory, the secret consciousness of doing great and wonderful actions, which can alone support the truly great man, whether he be a conqueror, a tyrant, a statesman, or a prig. These must bear him up against the private curse and public imprecation, and while he is hated and detested by all mankind, must make him inwardly satisfied with himself. For what but some such inward satisfaction as this could inspire men possessed of power, wealth, of every human blessing which pride, avarice, or luxury could desire, to forsake their homes, abandon ease and repose, and at the expense of riches and pleasures, at the price of labour and hardship, and at the hazard of all that fortune has liberally given them, could send them at the head of a multitude of prigs, called an army, to molest their neighbours – to introduce rape, rapine, bloodshed, and every kind of misery among their own species? What but some such glorious appetite of mind could inflame princes, endowed with the greatest honours, and enriched with the most plentiful revenues, to desire maliciously to rob those subjects of their liberties who are content to sweat for the luxury, and to bow down their knees to the pride, of those very princes? What but this can inspire them to destroy one half of their subjects, in order to reduce the rest to an absolute dependence on their own wills, and on those of their brutal successors? What other motive could seduce a subject, possessed of great property in his community, to betray the interest of his fellow-subjects, of his brethren, and his posterity, to the wanton disposition of such princes? Lastly, what less inducement could persuade the prig to forsake the methods of acquiring a safe, an honest, and a plentiful livelihood, and at the hazard of even life itself, and what is mistaken called dishonour, to break openly and bravely through the laws of his country for uncertain, unsteady, and unsafe gain? Let me then hold myself contented with this reflection – that I have been wise though unsuccessful, and am a cheat though an unhappy man.'

His soliloquy and his punch concluded together – for he had at every pause comforted himself with a sip. And now it came first into his head that it would be more difficult to pay for it than it was to swallow it; when to his great pleasure he beheld at another corner of the room one of the gentlemen whom he had employed in the attack on Heartfree, and who, he doubted not, would readily lend him a guinea or two. But he had the mortification, on applying to him, to hear that the gaming table had stripped him of all the booty which his own generosity had left in his possession. He was therefore obliged to pursue his usual method on such occasions: so, cocking his hat fiercely, he marched out of the room without making any excuse, or anyone daring to make the least demand.

CHAPTER V

Containing many surprising adventures, which our hero,
with great greatness, achieved

We will now leave our hero to take a short repose, and return to Mr Snap's where, at Wild's departure, the fair Theodosia had again betaken herself to her stocking, and Miss Letty had retired upstairs to Mr Bagshot. But that gentleman had broken his parole, and having conveyed himself belowstairs behind a door, he took the opportunity of Wild's sally to make his escape. We shall only observe that Miss Letty's surprise was the greater as she had, notwithstanding her promise to the contrary, taken the precaution to turn the key; but in her hurry, she did it ineffectually. How wretched must have been the situation of this young creature, who had not only lost a lover on whom her tender heart perfectly doted, but was exposed to the rage of an injured father, tenderly jealous of his honour, which was deeply engaged to the sheriff of London and Middlesex for the safe custody of the said Bagshot, and for which two very good responsible friends had given not only their words but their bonds.

But let us remove our eyes from this melancholy object and survey our hero, who after a successless search for Miss Straddle, with wonderful greatness of mind and steadiness of countenance went early in the morning to visit his friend Heartfree, at a time when the common herd of friends would have forsaken and avoided him. He entered the room with a cheerful air, which he presently changed into surprise on seeing his friend in a nightgown, with his wounded head bound about with linen, and looking extremely pale from a great effusion of blood. When Wild was informed by Heartfree what had happened, he first expressed great sorrow, and afterwards suffered as violent agonies of rage against the robbers to burst from him. Heartfree, in compassion to the deep impression his misfortunes seemed to make on his friend, endeavoured to lessen it as much as possible, at the same time exaggerating the obligation he owed to Wild, in which his wife likewise seconded him, and they breakfasted with more comfort than was reasonably to be expected after such an accident; Heartfree expressing great satisfaction that he had put the Count's note in another pocket-book; adding, that such a loss would have been fatal to him, 'for to confess the truth to you, my dear friend,' said he, 'I have had some losses lately which have greatly perplexed my affairs; and though I have many debts due to me from people of great fashion, I assure you I know not where to be certain of getting a shilling.' Wild greatly felicitated him on the lucky accident of preserving his note, and then proceeded, with much acrimony, to inveigh against the barbarity of people of fashion, who kept tradesmen out of their money.

While they amused themselves with discourses of this kind, Wild meditating within himself whether he should borrow or steal from his friend – or indeed whether he could not effect both – the apprentice brought a banknote of £500 in to Heartfree, which he said a gentle-woman in the shop, who had been looking at some jewels, desired him to exchange. Heartfree, looking at the number, immediately recollected it to be one of those he had been robbed of. With this discovery he acquainted Wild, who with the notable presence of mind and un-changed complexion so essential to a great character, advised him to proceed cautiously; and offered (as Mr Heartfree himself was, he said, too much flustered to examine the woman with sufficient art) to take her into a room in his house alone. He would, he said, personate the master of the shop, would pretend to show her some jewels, and would undertake to get sufficient information out of her to secure the rogues, and most probably all their booty. This proposal was readily and thankfully accepted by Heartfree. Wild went immediately upstairs into the room appointed, whither the apprentice, according to appointment, conducted the lady.

The apprentice was ordered downstairs the moment the lady entered the room; and Wild, having shut the door, approached her with great ferocity in his looks, and began to expatiate on the complicated baseness of the crime she had been guilty of. But though he uttered many good lessons of morality – as we doubt whether from a particular reason they may work any very good effect on our reader – we shall omit his speech, and only mention his conclusion, which was by asking her what mercy she could now expect from him? Miss Straddle, for that was the young lady, who had had a good education, and had been more than once present at the Old Bailey, very confidently denied the whole charge, and said she had received the note from a friend. Wild then, raising his voice, told her she should be immediately committed, and she might depend on being convicted, 'but,' added he, changing his tone, 'as I have a violent affection for thee, my dear Straddle, if you will follow my advice, I promise you, on my honour, to forgive you, nor shall you be ever called in question on this account.' 'Why, what would you have me to do, Mr Wild?' replied the young lady, with a pleasanter aspect. 'You must know then,' said Wild, 'the money you picked out of my pocket (nay, by God you did, and if you offer to flinch you shall be convicted of it) I won at play of a fellow who it seems robbed my friend of it; you must, therefore, give an information on oath against one Thomas Fierce, and say that you received the note from him, and leave the rest to me. I am certain, Molly, you must be sensible of your obligations to me, who return good for evil to you in this manner.' The lady readily consented, and advanced to embrace Mr Wild, who stepped a little back and cried, 'Hold, Molly; there are two other notes of £200 each to be accounted for – where are they?' The lady protested with the most solemn asseverations that she knew of no more; with which, when Wild was not satisfied, she cried, 'I will stand search.'

'That you shall,' answered Wild, 'and stand strip too.' He then proceeded to tumble and search her, but to no purpose, until at last she burst into tears, and declared she would tell the truth (as indeed she did); she then confessed that she had disposed of the one to Jack Swagger, a great favourite of the ladies, being an Irish gentleman who had been bred clerk to an attorney, afterwards whipped out of a regiment of dragoons, and was then a Newgate solicitor, and a bawdy-house bully; and as for the other, she had laid it all out that very morning in brocaded silks and Flanders lace. With this account Wild, who indeed knew it to be a very probable one, was forced to be contented, and now, abandoning all further thoughts of what he saw was irretrievably lost, he gave the lady some further instructions, and then, desiring her to stay a few minutes behind him, he returned to his friend, and acquainted him that he had discovered the whole roguery. That the woman had confessed from whom she had received the note, and promised to give an information before a justice of peace; adding, he was concerned he could not attend him thither, being obliged to go to the other end of the town to receive thirty pounds, which he was to pay that evening. Heartfree said that should not prevent him of his company, for he could easily lend him such a trifle. This was accordingly done and accepted, and Wild, Heartfree, and the lady went to the justice together.

The warrant being granted, and the constable being acquainted by the lady, who received her information from Wild, of Mr Fierce's haunts, he was easily apprehended, and, being confronted by Miss Straddle – who swore positively to him, though she had never seen him before – he was committed to Newgate, where he immediately conveyed an information to Wild of what had happened, and in the evening received a visit from him.

Wild affected great concern for his friend's misfortune, and as great surprise at the means by which it was brought about. However, he told Fierce that he must certainly be mistaken in that point of his having had no acquaintance with Miss Straddle, but added that he would find her out, and endeavour to take off her evidence – which, he observed, did not come home enough to endanger him. Besides, he would secure him witnesses of an alibi, and five or six to his character; so that he need be under no apprehension, for his confinement until the sessions would be his only punishment.

Fierce, who was greatly comforted by these assurances of his friend, returned him many thanks, and both shaking each other very earnestly by the hand, with a very hearty embrace they separated.

The hero considered with himself that the single evidence of Miss Straddle would not be sufficient to convict Fierce, whom he resolved to hang, as he was the person who had principally refused to deliver him the stipulated share of the booty. He therefore went in quest of Mr James Sly, the gentleman who had assisted in the exploit, and found and acquainted him with the apprehending of Fierce. Wild then, intimating his fear least Fierce should impeach Sly, advised him to be beforehand, to surrender himself to a justice of peace and offer himself as an evidence. Sly approved Mr Wild's opinion, went directly to a magistrate, and was by him committed to the Gatehouse, with a promise of being admitted evidence against his companion.

Fierce was in a few days brought to his trial at the Old Bailey, where, to his great confusion, his old friend Sly appeared against him, as did Miss Straddle. His only hopes were now in the assistances which our hero had promised him. These unhappily failed him, so that, the evidence being plain against him, and he making no defence, the jury convicted him, the court condemned him, and Mr Ketch executed him.

With such infinite address did this truly great man know how to play with the passions of men, to set them at variance with each other, and to work his own purposes out of those jealousies and apprehensions which he was wonderfully ready at creating by means of those great arts which the vulgar call treachery, dissembling, promising, lying, falsehood, etc., but which are by great men summed up in the collective name of policy, or politics, or rather pollitrics – an art of which, as it is the highest excellence of human nature, perhaps our great man was the most eminent master.

CHAPTER VI

Of Hats

Wild had now got together a very considerable gang, composed of undone gamesters, ruined bailiffs, broken tradesmen, idle apprentices, attorneys' clerks, and loose and disorderly youth, who being born to no fortune, nor bred to any trade or profession, were willing to live luxuriously without labour. As these persons wore different principles, i.e. hats, frequent dissensions grew among them. There were particularly two parties, viz. those who wore hats fiercely cocked, and those who preferred the nab or trencher hat, with the brim flapping over their eyes. The former were called 'cavaliers' and 'tory rory ranter boys', etc.; the latter went by the several names of 'wags', 'roundheads', 'shakebags', 'old-nolls', and several others. Between these, continual jars arose, insomuch that they grew in time to think there was something essential in their differences, and that their interests were incompatible with each other, whereas in truth the difference lay only in the fashion of their hats. Wild, therefore, having assembled them all at an alehouse on the night after Fierce's execution, and perceiving evident marks of their misunderstanding from their behaviour to each other, addressed them in the following gentle, but forcible manner[a]:

a. There is something very mysterious in this speech, which probably that chapter written by Aristotle on this subject, which is mentioned by a French author, might have given some light into; but that is unhappily among the lost works of that philosopher. It is remarkable that *galerus*, which is Latin for a hat, signifies likewise a dog-fish, as the Greek word *kuneae* does the skin of that animal; of which I suppose the hats or helmets of the ancients were composed, as ours at present are of the beaver or rabbit. Sophocles, in the latter end of his *Ajax*, alludes to a method of cheating in hats, and the scholiast on the place tells us of one Crephontes, who was a master of the art. It is observable likewise that Achilles, in the first *Iliad* of Homer, tells Agamemnon, in anger, that he had dog's eyes. Now, as the eyes of a dog are handsomer than those of almost any other animal, this could be no term of reproach. He must therefore mean that he had a hat on, which perhaps, from the creature it was made of, or from some other reason, might have been a mark of infamy. This superstitious opinion may account for that custom, which has descended through all nations, of showing respect by pulling off this covering, and that no man is esteemed fit to converse with his superiors with it on. I shall conclude this learned note with remarking that the term 'old hat' is at present used by the vulgar in no very honourable sense.

'Gentlemen, I am ashamed to see men embarked in so great and glorious an undertaking as that of robbing the public so foolishly and weakly dissenting among themselves. Do you think the first inventors of hats, or at least of the distinctions between them, really conceived that one form of hats should inspire a man with divinity, another with law, another with learning, or another with bravery? No, they meant no more by these outward signs than to impose on the vulgar, and instead of putting great men to the trouble of acquiring or maintaining the substance, to make it sufficient that they condescend to wear the type or shadow of it. You do wisely, therefore, when in a crowd, to amuse the mob by quarrels on such accounts that while they are listening to your jargon you may with the greater ease and safety pick their pockets. But surely to be in earnest, and privately to keep up such a ridiculous contention among yourselves, must argue the highest folly and absurdity. When you know you are all prigs, what difference can a broad or a narrow brim create? Is a prig less a prig in one hat than in another? If the public should be weak enough to interest themselves in your quarrels, and to prefer one pack to the other, while both are aiming at their purses, it is your business to laugh at, not imitate their folly. What can be more ridiculous than for gentlemen to quarrel about hats, when there is not one among you whose hat is worth a farthing? What is the use of a hat further than to keep the head warm or to hide a bald crown from the public? It is the mark of a gentleman to move his hat on every occasion, and in courts and noble assemblies no man ever wears one. Let me hear no more therefore of this childish disagreement, but all toss up your hats together with one accord, and consider that hat as the best, which will contain the largest booty.'

He thus ended his speech, which was followed by a murmuring applause, and immediately all present tossed their hats together as he had commanded them.

CHAPTER VII

*Showing the consequence which attended Heartfree's adventures
with Wild; all natural and common enough to little wretches who
deal with great men; together with some precedents of letters,
being the different methods of answering a dun*

Let us now return to Heartfree, to whom the Count's note, which he had paid away, was returned with an account that the drawer was not to be found, and that on enquiring after him, they had heard he had run away, and consequently the money was now demanded of the endorser. The apprehension of such a loss would have affected any man of business, but much more one whose unavoidable ruin it must prove. He expressed so much concern and confusion on this occasion, that the proprietor of the note was frightened, and resolved to lose no time in securing what he could. So that in the afternoon of the same day Mr Snap was commissioned to pay Heartfree a visit, which he did with his usual formality, and conveyed him to his own house.

Mrs Heartfree was no sooner informed of what had happened to her husband than she raved like one distracted; but after she had vented the first agonies of her passion in tears and lamentations, she applied herself to all possible means to procure her husband's liberty. She hastened to beg her neighbours to secure bail for him. But, as the news had arrived at their houses before her, she found none of them at home, except an honest Quaker, whose servants durst not tell a lie. However, she succeeded no better with him, for unluckily he had made an affirmation the day before that he would never be bail for any man. After many fruitless efforts of this kind she repaired to her husband, to comfort him at least with her presence. She found him sealing the last of several letters, which he was despatching to his friends and creditors. The moment he saw her, a sudden joy sparkled in his eyes – which, however, had a very short duration, for despair soon closed them again; nor could he help bursting into some passionate expressions of concern for her and his little family, which she, on her part, did her utmost to lessen by endeavouring to mitigate the loss, and to raise in him hopes from the Count – who might, she said, be possibly only gone into the country. She comforted him likewise with the expectation of favour from his acquaintance, especially from those whom he had in a particular manner obliged and served. Lastly, she conjured him, by all the value and esteem he professed for her, not to endanger his health – on which alone depended her happiness – by too great an indulgence of grief; assuring him that no state of life could appear unhappy to her with him, unless his own sorrow or discontent made it so.

In this manner did this weak poor-spirited woman attempt to relieve her husband's pains, which it would have rather become her to aggravate by not only painting out his misery in the liveliest colours imaginable, but by upbraiding him with that folly and confidence which had occasioned it, and by lamenting her own hard fate in being obliged to share his sufferings.

Heartfree returned this goodness (as it is called) of his wife with the warmest gratitude, and they passed an hour in a scene of tenderness too low and contemptible to be recounted to our great readers. We shall therefore omit all such relations, as they tend only to make human nature low and ridiculous.

Those messengers who had obtained any answers to his letters now returned. We shall here copy a few of them, as they may serve for precedents to others who have an occasion – which happens commonly enough in genteel life – to answer the impertinence of a dun.

Letter 1

Mr Heartfree,
My lord commands me to tell you he is very much surprised at your assurance in asking for money which you know has been so little while due; however, as he intends to deal no longer at your shop, he has ordered me to pay you as soon as I shall have cash in hand, which, considering many disbursements for bills long due, etc., can't possibly promise any time, etc., at present. And am your humble servant,

Roger Morcraft

Letter 2

Dear Sir,

The money, as you truly say, has been three years due, but upon my soul I am at present incapable of paying a farthing; but, as I doubt not, very shortly, not only to content that small bill, but likewise to lay out very considerable further sums at your house, hope you will meet with no inconvenience by this short delay in, dear sir, your most sincere humble servant,

Cha. Courtly

Letter 3

Mr Heartfree,

I beg you would not acquaint my husband of the trifling debt between us; for as I know you to be a very good-natured man, I will trust you with a secret; he gave me the money long since to discharge it, which I had the ill luck to lose at play. You may be assured I will satisfy you the first opportunity, and am, sir, your very humble servant,

Cath. Rubbers

Please to present my compliments to Mrs Heartfree.

Letter 4

Mr Thomas Heartfree, Sir,

Yours received: but as to sum mentioned therein, does not suit at present. Your humble servant,

Peter Pounce

Letter 5

Sir,

I am sincerely sorry it is not at present possible for me to comply with your request, especially after so many obligations received on my side, of which I shall always entertain the most grateful memory. I am very greatly concerned at your misfortunes, and would have waited upon you in person, but am not at present very well, and besides, am obliged to go this evening to Vauxhall. I am, sir, your most obliged humble servant,

Cha. Easy

P.S.– I hope good Mrs Heartfree and the dear little ones are well.

There were more letters to much the same purpose; but we proposed giving our readers a taste only. Of all these, the last was infinitely the most grating to poor Heartfree, as it came from one to whom, when in distress, he had himself lent a considerable sum, and of whose present flourishing circumstances he was well assured.

CHAPTER VIII

In which our hero carries greatness to an immoderate height

Let us remove, therefore, as fast as we can, this detestable picture of ingratitude, and present the much more agreeable portrait of that assurance to which the French very properly annex the epithet of good. Heartfree had scarce done reading his letters when our hero appeared before his eyes – not with that aspect with which a pitiful parson meets his patron after having opposed him at an election, or which a doctor wears when sneaking away from a door when he is informed of his patient's death – not with that downcast countenance which betrays the man who, after a strong conflict between virtue and vice, has surrendered his mind to the latter, and is discovered in his first treachery – but with that noble, bold, great confidence with which a prime minister assures his dependant that the place he promised him was disposed of before. And such concern and uneasiness as he expresses in his looks on those occasions did Wild testify on the first meeting of his friend. And as the said prime minister chides you for neglect of your interest in not having asked in time, so did our hero attack Heartfree for his giving credit to the Count; and without suffering him to make any answer, proceeded in a torrent of words to overwhelm him with abuse – which, however friendly its intention might be – was scarce to be outdone by an enemy. By these means Heartfree, who might perhaps otherwise have vented some little concern for that recommendation which Wild had given him to the Count, was totally prevented from any such endeavour; and like an invading prince, when attacked in his own dominions, forced to recall his whole strength to defend himself at home. This indeed he did so well, by insisting on the figure and outward appearance of the Count and his equipage, that Wild at length grew a little more gentle, and with a sigh said, 'I confess I have the least reason of all mankind to censure another for an imprudence of this nature, as I am myself the most easy to be imposed upon, and indeed have been so by this Count, who, if he be insolvent, has cheated me of five hundred pounds. But, for my own part,' said he, 'I will not yet despair, nor would I have you. Many men have found it convenient to retire or abscond for a while, and afterwards have paid their debts, or at least handsomely compounded them. This I am certain of: should a composition take place, which is the worst I think that can be apprehended, I shall be the only loser; for I shall think myself obliged in honour to repair your loss, even though you must confess it was principally owing to your own folly. Zounds! had I imagined it necessary, I would have cautioned you, but I thought the part of the town where he lived sufficient caution not to trust him. And such a sum! The devil must have been in you certainly!'

This was a degree of impudence beyond poor Mrs Heartfree's imagination. Though she had before vented the most violent execrations on Wild, she was now thoroughly satisfied of his innocence, and begged him not to insist any longer on what he perceived so deeply affected her husband. She said trade could not be carried on without credit, and surely he was sufficiently justified in giving it to such a person as the Count appeared to be. Besides, she said, reflections on what was past and irretrievable would be of little service; that their present business was to consider how to prevent the evil consequences which threatened, and first to endeavour to procure her husband his liberty. 'Why does he not procure bail?' said Wild. 'Alas! sir,' said she, 'we have applied to many of our acquaintance in vain; we have met with excuses even where we could least expect them.' 'Not bail!' answered Wild, in a passion, 'he shall have bail, if there is any in the world. It is now very late, but trust me to procure him bail tomorrow morning.'

Mrs Heartfree received these professions with tears, and told Wild he was a friend indeed. She then proposed to stay that evening with her husband, but he would not permit her on account of his little family, whom he would not agree to trust to the care of servants in this time of confusion.

A hackney coach was then sent for, but without success; for these, like hackney friends, always offer themselves in the sunshine, but are never to be found when you want them. And as for a chair, Mr Snap lived in a part of the town which chairmen very little frequent. The good woman was therefore obliged to walk home, whither the gallant Wild offered to attend her as a protector. This favour was thankfully accepted, and the husband and wife having taken a tender leave of each other, the former was locked in and the latter locked out by the hands of Mr Snap himself.

As this visit of Mr Wild's to Heartfree may seem one of those passages in history which writers, Drawcansir-like[28], introduce only because they dare; indeed, as it may seem somewhat contradictory to the greatness of our hero, and may tend to blemish his character with an imputation of that kind of friendship which savours too much of weakness and imprudence, it may be necessary to account for this visit, especially to our more sagacious readers, whose satisfaction we shall always consult in the most especial manner. They are to know then that at the first interview with Mrs Heartfree, Mr Wild had conceived that passion, or affection, or friendship, or desire, for that handsome creature, which the gentlemen of this our age agreed to call love, and which is indeed no other than that kind of affection which, after the exercise of the dominical day is over, a lusty divine is apt to conceive for the well-dressed sirloin or handsome buttock which the well-edified squire in gratitude sets before him, and which, so violent is his love, he devours in imagination the moment he sees it. Not less ardent was the hungry passion of our hero, who from the moment he had cast his eyes on that charming dish, had cast about in his mind by what method he might come at it. This, as he perceived, might most easily be effected after the ruin of Heartfree – which, for other considerations, he had intended. So he postponed all endeavours for this purpose until he had first effected what, by order of time, was regularly to precede this latter design; with such regularity did this our hero conduct all his schemes, and so truly superior was he to all the efforts of passion, which so often disconcert and disappoint the noblest views of others.

CHAPTER IX

More greatness in Wild. A low scene between Mrs Heartfree and
her children, and a scheme of our hero worthy of the highest admiration,
and even astonishment

When first Wild conducted his flame (or rather his dish, to continue our metaphor) from the proprietor, he had projected a design of conveying her to one of those eating-houses in Covent Garden, where female flesh is deliciously dressed and served up to the greedy appetites of young gentlemen; but fearing lest she should not come readily enough into his wishes, and that, by too eager and hasty a pursuit, he should frustrate his future expectations – and luckily at the same time a noble hint suggesting itself to him, by which he might almost inevitably secure his pleasure, together with his profit – he contented himself with waiting on Mrs Heartfree at home, and after many protestations of friendship and service to her husband, took his leave, and promised to visit her early in the morning, and to conduct her back to Mr Snap's.

Wild now retired to a night-cellar, where he found several of his acquaintance, with whom he spent the remaining part of the night in revelling; nor did the least compassion for Heartfree's misfortunes disturb the pleasure of his cups. So truly great was his soul that it was absolutely composed, save that an apprehension of Miss Tishy's making some discovery (as she was then in no good temper towards him) a little ruffled and disquieted the perfect serenity he would otherwise have enjoyed. As he had, therefore, no opportunity of seeing her that evening, he wrote her a letter full of ten thousand protestations of honourable love, and (which he more depended on) containing as many promises, in order to bring the young lady into good humour, without acquainting her in the least with his suspicion, or giving her any caution; for it was his constant maxim never to put it into anyone's head to do you a mischief by acquainting him that it is in his power.

We must now return to Mrs Heartfree, who passed a sleepless night in as great agonies and horror for the absence of her husband as a fine well-bred woman would feel at the return of hers from a long voyage or journey. In the morning, the children being brought to her, the eldest asked where dear papa was. At which she could not refrain from bursting into tears. The child, perceiving it, said,

'Don't cry, mamma; I am sure papa would not stay abroad if he could help it.' At these words she caught the child in her arms, and, throwing herself into the chair in an agony of passion, cried out,

'No, my child; nor shall all the malice of hell keep us long asunder.'

These are circumstances which we should not, for the amusement of six or seven readers only, have inserted, had they not served to show that there are weaknesses in vulgar life to which great minds are so entirely strangers that they have not even an idea of them; and, secondly, by exposing the folly of this low creature, to set off and elevate that greatness of which we endeavour to draw a true portrait in this history.

Wild, entering the room, found the mother with one child in her arms, and the other at her knee. After paying her his compliments, he desired her to dismiss the children and servant, for that he had something of the greatest moment to impart to her.

She immediately complied with his request, and the door being shut, asked him with great eagerness if he had succeeded in his intentions of procuring the bail. He answered he had not endeavoured at it yet, for a scheme had entered into his head by which she might certainly preserve her husband, herself, and her family. In order to which he advised her instantly to remove with the most valuable jewels she had to Holland, before any statute of bankruptcy issued to prevent her; that he would himself attend her thither and place her in safety, and then return to deliver her husband, who would be thus easily able to satisfy his creditors. He added that he was that instant come from Snap's, where he had communicated the scheme to Heartfree, who had greatly approved of it, and desired her to put it in execution without delay, concluding that a moment was not to be lost.

The mention of her husband's approbation left no doubt in this poor woman's breast; she only desired a moment's time to pay him a visit in order to take her leave. But Wild peremptorily refused; he said by every moment's delay she risked the ruin of her family; that she would be absent only a few days from him, for that the moment he had lodged her safe in Holland, he would return, procure her husband his liberty, and bring him to her. 'I have been the unfortunate, the innocent cause of all my dear Tom's calamity, madam,' said he, 'and I will perish with him or see him out of it.' Mrs Heartfree overflowed with acknowledgments of his goodness, but still begged for the shortest interview with her husband. Wild declared that a minute's delay might be fatal; and added, though with the voice of sorrow rather than of anger, that if she had not resolution enough to execute the commands he brought her from her husband, his ruin would lie at her door – and for his own part, he must give up any further meddling in his affairs.

She then proposed to take her children with her; but Wild would not permit it, saying they would only retard their flight, and that it would be properer for her husband to bring them. He at length absolutely prevailed on this poor woman, who immediately packed up the most valuable effects she could find, and after taking a tender leave of her infants, earnestly recommended them to the care of a very faithful servant. Then they called a hackney coach, which conveyed them to an inn, where they were furnished with a chariot and six, in which they set forward for Harwich.

Wild rode with an exulting heart, secure, as he now thought himself, of the possession of that lovely woman, together with a rich cargo. In short, he enjoyed in his mind all the happiness which unbridled lust and rapacious avarice could promise him. As to the poor creature who was to satisfy these passions, her whole soul was employed in reflecting on the condition of her husband and children. A single word scarce escaped her lips, though many a tear gushed from her brilliant eyes, which, if I may use a coarse expression, served only as delicious sauce to heighten the appetite of Wild.

CHAPTER X

Sea adventures very new and surprising

When they arrived at Harwich, they found a vessel which had put in there just ready to depart for Rotterdam. So they went immediately on board, and sailed with a fair wind; but they had hardly proceeded out of sight of land when a sudden and violent storm arose and drove them to the southwest; insomuch that the captain apprehended it impossible to avoid the Goodwin Sands, and he and all his crew gave themselves up for lost. Mrs Heartfree, who had no other apprehensions from death but those of leaving her dear husband and children, fell on her knees to beseech the Almighty's favour, when Wild, with a contempt of danger truly great, took a resolution as worthy to be admired perhaps as any recorded of the bravest hero, ancient or modern – a resolution which plainly proved him to have these two qualifications so necessary to a hero, to be superior to all the energies of fear or pity. He saw the tyrant Death ready to rescue from him his intended prey, which he had yet devoured only in imagination. He therefore swore he would prevent him, and immediately attacked the poor wretch, who was in the utmost agonies of despair, first with solicitation, and afterwards with force.

Mrs Heartfree, the moment she understood his meaning – which, in her present temper of mind, and in the opinion she held of him, she did not immediately – rejected him with all the repulses which indignation and horror could animate. But when he attempted violence she filled the cabin with her shrieks, which were so vehement that they reached the ears of the captain, the storm at this time luckily abating. This man, who was a brute rather from his education and the element he inhabited than from nature, ran hastily down to her assistance, and finding her struggling on the ground with our hero, he presently rescued her from her intended ravisher, who was soon obliged to quit the woman in order to engage with her lusty champion, who spared neither pains nor blows in the assistance of his fair passenger.

When the short battle was over – in which our hero, had he not been overpowered with numbers, who came down on their captain's side, would have been victorious – the captain rapped out a hearty oath, and asked Wild if he had no more Christianity in him than to ravish a woman in a storm? To which the other greatly and sullenly answered it was very well, but damn him if he had not satisfaction the moment they came on shore. The captain with great scorn replied, 'Kiss ...' etc., and then, forcing Wild out of the cabin, he, at Mrs Heartfree's request, locked her into it, and returned to the care of his ship.

The storm was now entirely ceased, and nothing remained but the usual ruffling of the sea after it, when one of the sailors spied a sail at a distance, which the captain wisely apprehended might be a privateer (for we were then engaged in a war with France), and immediately ordered all the sail possible to be crowded. But his caution was in vain, for the little wind which then blew was directly adverse, so that the ship bore down upon them, and soon appeared to be what the captain had feared, a French privateer. He was in no condition of resistance, and immediately struck on her firing the first gun. The captain of the Frenchman, with several of his hands, came on board the English vessel, which they rifled of everything valuable, and amongst the rest, of poor Mrs Heartfree's whole cargo; and then, taking the crew, together with the two passengers, aboard his own ship, he determined, as the other would be only a burden to him, to sink her, she being very old and leaky, and not worth going back with to Dunkirk. He preserved, therefore, nothing but the boat, as his own was none of the best, and then, pouring a broadside into her, he sent her to the bottom.

The French captain, who was a very young fellow, and a man of gallantry, was presently enamoured to no small degree with his beautiful captive; and imagining Wild, from some words he dropped, to be her husband, notwithstanding the ill affection towards him which appeared in her looks, he asked her if she understood French. She answered in the affirmative, for indeed she did perfectly well. He then asked her how long she and that gentleman (pointing to Wild) had been married. She answered, with a deep sigh and many tears, that she was married indeed, but not to that villain, who was the sole cause of all her misfortunes. That appellation raised a curiosity in the captain, and he importuned her in so pressing but gentle a manner to acquaint him with the injuries she complained of that she was at last prevailed on to recount to him the whole history of her afflictions. This so moved the captain, who had too little notions of greatness, and so incensed him against our hero, that he resolved to punish him; and without regard to the laws of war, he immediately ordered out his shattered boat, and making Wild a present of half a dozen biscuits to prolong his misery, he put him therein; and then, committing him to the mercy of the sea, proceeded on his cruise.

CHAPTER XI

The great and wonderful behaviour of our hero in the boat

It is probable that a desire of ingratiating himself with his charming captive, or rather conqueror, had no little share in promoting this extraordinary act of illegal justice; for the Frenchman had conceived the same sort of passion or hunger which Wild himself had felt, and was almost as much resolved, by some means or other, to satisfy it. We will leave him however at present in the pursuit of his wishes, and attend our hero in his boat, since it is in circumstances of distress that true greatness appears most wonderful. For that a prince in the midst of his courtiers, all ready to compliment him with his favourite character or title, and indeed with everything else – or that a conqueror, at the head of a hundred thousand men, all prepared to execute his will, howsoever ambitious, wanton, or cruel, should, in the giddiness of their pride, elevate themselves many degrees above those their tools – seems not difficult to be imagined, or indeed accounted for. But that a man in chains, in prison – nay, in the vilest dungeon – should, with persevering pride and obstinate dignity, discover that vast superiority in his own nature over the rest of mankind, who to a vulgar eye seem much happier than himself – nay, that he should discover heaven and providence (whose peculiar care, it seems, he is) at that very time at work for him – this is among the arcana of greatness, to be perfectly understood only by an adept in that science.

What could be imagined more miserable than the situation of our hero at this season, floating in a little boat on the open seas, without oar, without sail, and at the mercy of the first wave to overwhelm him? Nay, this was indeed the fair side of his fortune, as it was a much more eligible fate than that alternative which threatened him with almost unavoidable certainty, viz. starving with hunger, the sure consequence of a continuance of the calm.

Our hero, finding himself in this condition, began to ejaculate a round of blasphemies, which the reader, without being over-pious, might be offended at seeing repeated. He then accused the whole female sex, and the passion of love (as he called it), particularly that which he bore to Mrs Heartfree, as the unhappy occasion of his present sufferings. At length, finding himself descending too much into the language of meanness and complaint, he stopped short, and after broke forth as follows: 'Damn it, a man can die but once! What signifies it? Every man must die, and when it is over it is over. I never was afraid of anything yet, nor I won't begin now; no, damn me, won't I. What signifies fear? I shall die whether I am afraid or no. Who's afraid then, damn me?' At which words he looked extremely fierce, but recollecting that no one was present to see him, he relaxed a little the terror of his countenance, and pausing a while, repeated the word, damn! 'Suppose I should be damned at last,' cries he, 'when I never thought a syllable of the matter? I have often laughed and made a jest about it, and yet it may be so, for anything which I know to the contrary. If there should be another world it will go hard with me, that is certain. I shall never escape for what I have done to Heartfree. The devil must have me for that undoubtedly. The devil! Pshaw! I am not such a fool to be frightened at him neither. No, no – when a man's dead there's an end of him. I wish I was certainly satisfied of it though: for there are some men of learning, as I have heard, of a different opinion. It is but a bad chance, methinks, I stand. If there be no other world, why I shall be in no worse condition than a block or a stone. But if there should… damn me I will think no longer about it. Let a pack of cowardly rascals be afraid of Death, I dare look him in the face. But shall I stay and be starved? No, I will eat up the biscuits the French son of a whore bestowed on me, and then leap into the sea for drink, since the unconscionable dog has not allowed me a single dram.' Having thus said, he proceeded immediately to put his purpose in execution, and, as his resolution never failed him, he had no sooner despatched the small quantity of provision which his enemy had with no vast liberality presented him than he cast himself headlong into the sea.

CHAPTER XII

The strange and yet natural escape of our hero

Our hero, having with wonderful resolution thrown himself into the sea, as we mentioned at the end of the last chapter, was miraculously within two minutes after replaced in his boat – and this without the assistance of a dolphin or a seahorse, or any other fish or animal, who are always as ready at hand when a poet or historian pleases to call for them to carry a hero through the sea, as any chairman at a coffee-house door near St. James's to convey a beau over a street, and preserve his white stockings. The truth is, we do not choose to have any recourse to miracles, from the strict observance we pay to that rule of Horace,

Nec Deus intersit, nisi dignus vindice nodus. [29]

The meaning of which is, 'Do not bring in a supernatural agent when you can do without him'; and indeed we are much deeper read in natural than supernatural causes. We will therefore endeavour to account for this extraordinary event from the former of these; and in doing this it will be necessary to disclose some profound secrets to our reader, extremely well worth his knowing, and which may serve him to account for many occurrences of the phenomenous kind which have formerly appeared in this our hemisphere.

Be it known then that the great Alma Mater, Nature, is of all other females the most obstinate and tenacious of her purpose. So true is that observation,

Naturam expellas furca licet, usque recurret.

Which I need not render in English, it being to be found in a book which most fine gentlemen are forced to read.[30] Whatever Nature, therefore, purposes to herself, she never suffers any reason, design, or accident to frustrate. Now, though it may seem to a shallow observer that some persons were designed by Nature for no use or purpose whatever, yet certain it is that no man is born into the world without his particular allotment; viz. some to be kings, some statesmen, some ambassadors, some bishops, some generals, and so on. Of these there be two kinds: those to whom Nature is so generous to give some endowment qualifying them for the parts she intends them afterwards to act on this stage, and those whom she uses as instances of her unlimited power, and for whose preferment to such and such stations Solomon himself could have invented no other reason than that Nature designed them so. These latter some great philosophers have, to show them to be the favourites of Nature, distinguished by the honourable appellation of naturals. Indeed, the true reason of the general ignorance of mankind on this head seems to be this: that, as Nature chooses to execute these her purposes by certain second causes, and as many of these second causes seem so totally foreign to her design, the wit of man – which, like his eye, sees best directly forward and very little and imperfectly what is oblique – is not able to discern the end by the means. Thus, how a handsome wife or daughter should contribute to execute her original designation of a general, or how flattery or half a dozen houses in a borough-town should denote a judge, or a bishop, he is not capable of comprehending. And, indeed, we ourselves, wise as we are, are forced to reason *ab effectu*; and if we had been asked what Nature had intended such men for, before she herself had by the event demonstrated her purpose, it is possible we might sometimes have been puzzled to declare; for it must be confessed that at first sight, and to a mind uninspired, a man of vast natural capacity and much acquired knowledge may seem by Nature designed for power and honour, rather than one remarkable only for the want of these, and indeed all other qualifications; whereas daily experience convinces us of the contrary, and drives us as it were into the opinion I have here disclosed.

Now, Nature having originally intended our great man for that final exaltation which, as it is the most proper and becoming end of all great men, it were heartily to be wished they might all arrive at, would by no means be diverted from her purpose. She therefore no sooner spied him in the water than she softly whispered in his ear to attempt the recovery of his boat, which call he immediately obeyed, and being a good swimmer, and it being a perfect calm, with great facility accomplished it.

Thus we think this passage in our history, at first so greatly surprising, is very naturally accounted for, and our relation rescued from the prodigious, which, though it often occurs in biography, is not to be encouraged nor much commended on any occasion, unless when absolutely necessary to prevent the history's being at an end. Secondly, we hope our hero is justified from that imputation of want of resolution which must have been fatal to the greatness of his character.

CHAPTER XIII

The conclusion of the boat adventure, and the end of the second book

Our hero passed the remainder of the evening, the night, and the next day in a condition not much to be envied by any passion of the human mind, unless by ambition; which provided it can only entertain itself with the most distant music of fame's trumpet, can disdain all the pleasures of the sensualist, and those more solemn, though quieter comforts, which a good conscience suggests to a Christian philosopher.

He spent his time in contemplation – that is to say, in blaspheming, cursing, and sometimes singing and whistling. At last, when cold and hunger had almost subdued his native fierceness, it being a good deal past midnight and extremely dark, he thought he beheld a light at a distance, which the cloudiness of the sky prevented his mistaking for a star. This light, however, did not seem to approach him, at least it approached by such imperceptible degrees that it gave him very little comfort, and at length totally forsook him. He then renewed his contemplation as before, in which he continued until the day began to break, when to his inexpressible delight, he beheld a sail at a very little distance, and which luckily seemed to be making towards him. He was likewise soon espied by those in the vessel, who wanted no signals to inform them of his distress, and as it was almost a calm, and their course lay within five hundred yards of him, they hoisted out their boat and fetched him aboard.

The captain of this ship was a Frenchman; she was laden with deal from Norway, and had been extremely shattered in the late storm. This captain was of that kind of men who are actuated by general humanity, and whose compassion can be raised by the distress of a fellow-creature, though of a nation whose king has quarrelled with the monarch of their own. He therefore, commiserating the circumstances of Wild, who had dressed up a story proper to impose upon such a silly fellow, told him that, as himself well knew, he must be a prisoner on his arrival in France, but that he would endeavour to procure his redemption; for which our hero greatly thanked him. But, as they were making very slow sail (for they had lost their main mast in the storm), Wild saw a little vessel at a distance – they being within a few leagues of the English shore – which, on enquiry, he was informed was probably an English fishing boat. And, it being then perfectly calm, he proposed that, if they would accommodate him with a pair of scullers, he could get within reach of the boat, at least near enough to make signals to her; and he preferred any risk to the certain fate of being a prisoner. As his courage was somewhat restored by the provisions (especially brandy) with which the Frenchmen had supplied him, he was so earnest in his entreaties that the captain, after many persuasions, at length complied, and he was furnished with scullers, and with some bread, pork, and a bottle of brandy. Then, taking leave of his preservers, he again betook himself to his boat, and rowed so heartily that he soon came within the sight of the fisherman, who immediately made towards him and took him aboard.

No sooner was Wild got safe on board the fisherman than he begged him to make the utmost speed into Deal, for that the vessel which was still in sight was a distressed Frenchman, bound for Havre de Grace, and might easily be made a prize if there was any ship ready to go in pursuit of her. So nobly and greatly did our hero neglect all obligations conferred on him by the enemies of his country that he would have contributed all he could to the taking his benefactor, to whom he owed both his life and his liberty.

The fisherman took his advice, and soon arrived at Deal, where the reader will, I doubt not, be as much concerned as Wild was that there was not a single ship prepared to go on the expedition.

Our hero now saw himself once more safe on terra firma, but unluckily at some distance from that city where men of ingenuity can most easily supply their wants without the assistance of money, or rather can most easily procure money for the supply of their wants. However, as his talents were superior to every difficulty, he framed so dextrous an account of his being a merchant, having been taken and plundered by the enemy, and of his great effects in London, that he was not only heartily regaled by the fisherman at his house, but made so handsome a booty by way of borrowing – a method of taking which we have before mentioned to have his approbation – that he was enabled to provide himself with a place in the stagecoach; which (as God permitted it to perform the journey) brought him at the appointed time to an inn in the metropolis.

And now, Reader, as you can be in no suspense for the fate of our great man, since we have returned him safe to the principal scene of his glory, we will a little look back on the fortunes of Mr Heartfree, whom we left in no very pleasant situation; but of this we shall treat in the next book.

BOOK III

CHAPTER I

The low and pitiful behaviour of Heartfree;
and the foolish conduct of his apprentice

His misfortunes did not entirely prevent Heartfree from closing his eyes. On the contrary, he slept several hours the first night of his confinement. However, he perhaps paid too severely dear both for his repose and for a sweet dream which accompanied it, and represented his little family in one of those tender scenes which had frequently passed in the days of his happiness and prosperity, when the provision they were making for the future fortunes of their children used to be one of the most agreeable topics of discourse with which he and his wife entertained themselves. The pleasantness of this vision, therefore, served only, on his awaking, to set forth his present misery with additional horror, and to heighten the dreadful ideas which now crowded on his mind.

He had spent a considerable time after his first rising from the bed on which he had, without undressing, thrown himself, and now began to wonder at Mrs Heartfree's long absence; but as the mind is desirous (and perhaps wisely too) to comfort itself with drawing the most flattering conclusions from all events, so he hoped the longer her stay was the more certain was his deliverance. At length his impatience prevailed, and he was just going to despatch a messenger to his own house when his apprentice came to pay him a visit, and on his enquiry informed him that his wife had departed in company with Mr Wild many hours before, and had carried all his most valuable effects with her; adding at the same time that she had herself positively acquainted him she had her husband's express orders for so doing, and that she was gone to Holland.

It is the observation of many wise men – who have studied the anatomy of the human soul with more attention than our young physicians generally bestow on that of the body – that great and violent surprise has a different effect from that which is wrought in a good housewife by perceiving any disorders in her kitchen – who on such occasions commonly spreads the disorder, not only over her whole family, but over the whole neighbourhood. Now, these great calamities, especially when sudden, tend to stifle and deaden all the faculties, instead of rousing them; and accordingly Herodotus tells us a story[31] of Croesus king of Lydia, who on beholding his servants and courtiers led captive, wept bitterly, but when he saw his wife and children in that condition, stood stupid and motionless; so stood poor Heartfree on this relation of his apprentice, nothing moving but his colour, which entirely forsook his countenance.

The apprentice, who had not in the least doubted the veracity of his mistress, perceiving the surprise which too visibly appeared in his master, became speechless likewise, and both remained silent some minutes, gazing with astonishment and horror at each other. At last Heartfree cried out in an agony, 'My wife deserted me in my misfortunes!' 'Heaven forbid, sir!' answered the other. 'And what is become of my poor children?' replied Heartfree. 'They are at home, sir,' said the apprentice. 'Heaven be praised! She has forsaken them too!' cries Heartfree, 'fetch them hither this instant. Go, my dear Jack, bring hither my little all which remains now; fly, child, if you do not intend likewise to forsake me in my afflictions.' The youth answered he would die sooner than entertain such a thought, and begging his master to be comforted, instantly obeyed his orders.

Heartfree, the moment the young man was departed, threw himself on his bed in an agony of despair; but recollecting himself after he had vented the first sallies of his passion, he began to question the infidelity of his wife as a matter impossible. He ran over in his thoughts the uninterrupted tenderness which she had always shown him and, for a minute, blamed the rashness of his belief against her; until the many circumstances of her having left him so long, and neither writ nor sent to him since her departure with all his effects and with Wild, of whom he was not before without suspicion, and lastly and chiefly, her false pretence to his commands, entirely turned the scale and convinced him of her disloyalty.

While he was in these agitations of mind the good apprentice, who had used the utmost expedition, brought his children to him. He embraced them with the most passionate fondness, and imprinted numberless kisses on their little lips. The little girl flew to him with almost as much eagerness as he himself expressed at her sight, and cried out, 'O papa, why did you not come home to poor mamma all this while? I thought you would not have left your little Nancy so long.' After which he asked her for her mother, and was told she had kissed them both in the morning, and cried very much for his absence. All which brought a flood of tears into the eyes of this weak, silly man, who had not greatness sufficient to conquer these low efforts of tenderness and humanity.

He then proceeded to enquire of the maid-servant, who acquainted him that she knew no more than that her mistress had taken leave of her children in the morning with many tears and kisses, and had recommended them in the most earnest manner to her care. She said she had promised faithfully to take care of them, and would, while they were entrusted to her, fulfil her promise. For which profession Heartfree expressed much gratitude to her, and, after indulging himself with some little fondnesses which we shall not relate, he delivered his children into the good woman's hands, and dismissed her.

CHAPTER II

A soliloquy of Heartfree's, full of low and base ideas,
without a syllable of greatness

Being now alone, he sat some short time silent, and then burst forth into the following soliloquy,

'What shall I do? Shall I abandon myself to a dispirited despair, or fly in the face of the Almighty? Surely both are unworthy of a wise man; for what can be more vain than weakly to lament my fortune if irretrievable, or, if hope remains, to offend that Being who can most strongly support it? But are my passions then voluntary? Am I so absolutely their master that I can resolve with myself – so far only will I grieve? Certainly no. Reason, however we flatter ourselves, has not such despotic empire in our minds that it can, with imperial voice, hush all our sorrow in a moment. Where then is its use? For either it is an empty sound, and we are deceived in thinking we have reason, or it is given us to some end, and has a part assigned it by the all-wise Creator. Why, what can its office be other than justly to weigh the worth of all things, and to direct us to that perfection of human wisdom which proportions our esteem of every object by its real merit, and prevents us from over- or undervaluing whatever we hope for, we enjoy, or we lose. It does not foolishly say to us, 'Be not glad', or, 'Be not sorry', which would be as vain and idle as to bid the purling river cease to run, or the raging wind to blow. It prevents us only from exulting, like children, when we receive a toy, or from lamenting when we are deprived of it. Suppose then I have lost the enjoyments of this world, and my expectation of future pleasure and profit is for ever disappointed – what relief can my reason afford? What, unless it can show me I had fixed my affections on a toy – that what I desired was not, by a wise man, eagerly to be affected, nor its loss violently deplored? For there are toys adapted to all ages, from the rattle to the throne; and perhaps the value of all is equal to their several possessors, for if the rattle pleases the ear of the infant, what can the flattery of sycophants give more to the prince? The latter is as far from examining into the reality and source of his pleasure as the former; for if both did, they must both equally despise it. And surely, if we consider them seriously, and compare them together, we shall be forced to conclude all those pomps and pleasures of which men are so fond, and which, through so much danger and difficulty, with such violence and villainy, they pursue, to be as worthless trifles as any exposed to sale in a toyshop. I have often noted my little girl viewing, with eager eyes, a jointed baby; I have marked the pains and solici- tations she has used until I have been prevailed on to indulge her with it. At her first obtaining it, what joy has sparkled in her countenance! With what raptures has she taken possession! But how little satisfaction has she found in it! What pains to work out her amusement from it! Its dress must be varied; the tinsel ornaments which first caught her eyes produce no longer pleasure; she endeavours to make it stand and walk in vain, and is constrained herself to supply it with conversation. In a day's time it is thrown by and neglected, and some less costly toy preferred to it. How like the situation of this child is that of every man!

What difficulties in the pursuit of his desires! What inanity in the possession of most, and satiety in those which seem more real and substantial! The delights of most men are as childish and as superficial as that of my little girl; a feather or a fiddle are their pursuits and their pleasures through life, even to their ripest years, if such men may be said to attain any ripeness at all. But let us survey those whose understandings are of a more elevated and refined temper; how empty do they soon find the world of enjoyments worth their desire or attaining! How soon do they retreat to solitude and contemplation, to gardening and planting, and such rural amusements, where their trees and they enjoy the air and the sun in common, and both vegetate with very little difference between them. But suppose (which neither truth nor wisdom will allow) we could admit something more valuable and substantial in these blessings – would not the uncertainty of their possession be alone sufficient to lower their price? How mean a tenure is that at the will of fortune, which chance, fraud, and rapine are every day so likely to deprive us of, and often the more likely by how much the greater worth our possessions are of! Is it not to place our affections on a bubble in the water, or on a picture in the clouds? What madman would build a fine house or frame a beautiful garden on land in which he held so uncertain an interest? But again, was all this less undeniable, did Fortune, the lady of our manor, lease to us for our lives, of how little consideration must even this term appear! For, admitting that these pleasures were not liable to be torn from us, how certainly must we be torn from them! Perhaps tomorrow – nay, or even sooner, for as the excellent poet says,

> *Where is tomorrow? In the other world.*
> *To thousands this is true, and the reverse*
> *Is sure to none.*[32]

But if I have no further hope in this world, can I have none beyond it? Surely those laborious writers, who have taken such infinite pains to destroy or weaken all the proofs of futurity, have not so far succeeded as to exclude us from hope. That active principle in man which with such boldness pushes us on through every labour and difficulty, to attain the most distant and most improbable event in this world, will not surely deny us a little flattering prospect of those beautiful mansions which, if they could be thought chimerical, must be allowed the loveliest which can entertain the eye of man; and to which the road, if we understand it rightly, appears to have so few thorns and briars in it, and to require so little labour and fatigue from those who shall pass through it, that its ways are truly said to be ways of pleasantness, and all its paths to be those of peace. If the proofs of Christianity be as strong as I imagine them, surely enough may be deduced from that ground only, to comfort and support the most miserable man in his afflictions. And this I think my reason tells me – that, if the professors and propagators of infidelity are in the right, the losses which death brings to the virtuous are not worth their lamenting; but if these are, as certainly they seem, in the wrong, the blessings it procures them are not sufficiently to be coveted and rejoiced at.

'On my own account, then, I have no cause for sorrow, but on my children's! – why, the same Being to whose goodness and power I entrust my own happiness is likewise as able and as willing to procure theirs. Nor matters it what state of life is allotted for them, whether it be their fate to procure bread with their labour, or to eat it at the sweat of others. Perhaps, if we consider the case with proper attention, or resolve it with due sincerity, the former is much the sweeter. The hind may be more happy than the lord, for his desires are fewer, and those such as are attended with more hope and less fear. I will do my utmost to lay the foundations of my children's happiness, I will carefully avoid educating them in a station superior to their fortune, and for the event trust to that being in whom whoever rightly confides, must be superior to all worldly sorrows.'

In this low manner did this poor wretch proceed to argue, until he had worked himself up into an enthusiasm which by degrees soon became invulnerable to every human attack; so that when Mr Snap acquainted him with the return of the writ, and that he must carry him to Newgate, he received the message as Socrates did the news of the ship's arrival, and that he was to prepare for death.[33]

CHAPTER III

Wherein our hero proceeds in the road to greatness

But we must not detain our reader too long with these low characters. He is doubtless as impatient as the audience at the theatre until the principal figure returns on the stage; we will therefore indulge his inclination, and pursue the actions of the Great Wild.

There happened to be in the stagecoach in which Mr Wild travelled from Dover a certain young gentleman who had sold an estate in Kent, and was going to London to receive the money. There was likewise a handsome young woman who had left her parents at Canterbury, and was proceeding to the same city, in order (as she informed her fellow-travellers) to make her fortune. With this girl the young spark was so much enamoured that he publicly acquainted her with the purpose of his journey, and offered her a considerable sum in hand and a settlement if she would consent to return with him into the country, where she would be at a safe distance from her relations. Whether she accepted this proposal or no we are not able with any tolerable certainty to deliver; but Wild, the moment he heard of his money, began to cast about in his mind by what means he might become master of it. He entered into a long harangue about the methods of carrying money safely on the road, and said he had at that time two bankbills of a hundred pounds each sewed in his coat; which, added he, 'is so safe a way, that it is almost impossible I should be in any danger of being robbed by the most cunning highwayman.'

The young gentleman, who was no descendant of Solomon or, if he was, did not, any more than some other descendants of wise men, inherit the wisdom of his ancestor, greatly approved Wild's ingenuity, and thanking him for his information, declared he would follow his example when he returned into the country; by which means he proposed to save the premium commonly taken for the remittance. Wild had then no more to do but to inform himself rightly of the time of the gentleman's journey, which he did with great certainty before they separated.

At his arrival in town he fixed on two whom he regarded as the most resolute of his gang for this enterprise; and accordingly, having summoned the principal – or most desperate, as he imagined him, of these two (for he never chose to communicate in the presence of more than one) – he proposed to him the robbing and murdering this gentleman.

Mr Marybone (for that was the gentleman's name, to whom he applied) readily agreed to the robbery, but he hesitated at the murder. He said, as to robbery, he had, on much weighing and considering the matter, very well reconciled his conscience to it; for though that noble kind of robbery which was executed on the highway was, from the cowardice of mankind, less frequent, yet the baser and meaner species, sometimes called cheating, but more commonly known by the name of robbery within the law, was in a manner universal. He did not therefore pretend to the reputation of being so much honester than other people; but could by no means satisfy himself in the commission of murder, which was a sin of the most heinous nature, and so immediately prosecuted by God's judgement that it never passed undiscovered or unpunished.

Wild, with the utmost disdain in his countenance, answered as follows: 'Are you he whom I have selected out of my whole gang for this glorious undertaking, and do you cant of God's revenge against murder? You have, it seems, reconciled your conscience (a pretty word) to robbery, from its being so common. Is it then the novelty of murder which deters you? Do you imagine that guns, and pistols, and swords, and knives, are the only instruments of death? Look into the world and see the numbers whom broken fortunes and broken hearts bring untimely to the grave. To omit those glorious heroes who, to their immortal honour, have massacred nations – what think you of private persecution, treachery, and slander, by which the very souls of men are in a manner torn from their bodies? Is it not more generous, nay, more good natured, to send a man to his rest, than, after having plundered him of all he has, or from malice or malevolence deprived him of his character, to punish him with a languishing death, or, what is worse, a languishing life? Murder, therefore, is not so uncommon as you weakly conceive it, though, as you said of robbery, that more noble kind which lies within the paw of the law may be so. But this is the most innocent in him who does it, and the most eligible to him who is to suffer it. Believe me, lad, the tongue of a viper is less hurtful than that of a slanderer, and the gilded scales of a rattle-snake less dreadful than the purse of the oppressor. Let me therefore hear no more of your scruples; but consent to my proposal without further hesitation, unless, like a woman, you are afraid of blooding your clothes, or, like a fool, are terrified with the apprehensions of being hanged in chains. Take my word for it, you had better be an honest man than half a rogue. Do not think of continuing in my gang without abandoning yourself absolutely to my pleasure; for no man shall ever receive a favour at my hands who sticks at anything, or is guided by any other law than that of my will.'

Wild then ended his speech, which had not the desired effect on Marybone. He agreed to the robbery, but would not undertake the murder, as Wild (who feared that, by Marybone's demanding to search the gentleman's coat, he might hazard suspicion himself) insisted. Marybone was immediately entered by Wild in his black book, and was presently after impeached and executed as a fellow on whom his leader could not place sufficient dependence; thus falling, as many rogues do, a sacrifice, not to his roguery, but to his conscience.

CHAPTER IV

In which a young hero, of wonderful good promise,
makes his first appearance, with many other great matters

Our hero next applied himself to another of his gang, who instantly received his orders, and instead of hesitating at a single murder, asked if he should blow out the brains of all the passengers, coachman and all. But Wild, whose moderation we have before noted, would not permit him; and therefore, having given him an exact description of the devoted person, with his other necessary instructions, he dismissed him, with the strictest orders to avoid, if possible, doing hurt to any other person.

The name of this youth, who will hereafter make some figure in this history – being the Achates of our Aeneas, or rather the Hephaestion of our Alexander[34] – was Fireblood. He had every qualification to make a second-rate great man; or, in other words, he was completely equipped for the tool of a real or first-rate great man. We shall therefore (which is the properest way of dealing with this kind of greatness) describe him negatively, and content ourselves with telling our reader what qualities he had not; in which number were humanity, modesty, and fear – not one grain of any of which was mingled in his whole composition.

We will now leave this youth, who was esteemed the most promising of the whole gang, and whom Wild often declared to be one of the prettiest lads he had ever seen – of which opinion, indeed, were most other people of his acquaintance. We will however leave him at his entrance on this enterprise, and keep our attention fixed on our hero, whom we shall observe taking large strides towards the summit of human glory.

Wild, immediately at his return to town, went to pay a visit to Miss Laetitia Snap, for he had that weakness of suffering himself to be enslaved by women, so naturally incident to men of heroic disposition. To say the truth, it might more properly be called a slavery to his own appetite; for could he have satisfied that, he had not cared three farthings what had become of the little tyrant for whom he professed so violent a regard. Here he was informed that Mr Heartfree had been conveyed to Newgate the day before, the writ being then returnable. He was somewhat concerned at this news; not from any compassion for the misfortunes of Heartfree, whom he hated with such inveteracy that one would have imagined he had suffered the same injuries from him which he had done towards him. His concern therefore had another motive; in fact, he was uneasy at the place of Mr Heartfree's confinement, as it was to be the scene of his future glory, and where consequently he should be frequently obliged to see a face which hatred, and not shame, made him detest the sight of.

To prevent this, therefore, several methods suggested themselves to him. At first he thought of removing him out of the way by the ordinary method of murder, which he doubted not but Fireblood would be very ready to execute; for that youth had, at their last interview, sworn, damn his eyes, he thought there was no better pastime than blowing a man's brains out. But, besides the danger of this method, it did not look horrible nor barbarous enough for the last mischief which he should do to Heartfree. Considering, therefore, a little further with himself, he at length came to a resolution to hang him, if possible, the very next session.

Now, though the observation – how apt men are to hate those they injure, or how unforgiving they are of the injuries they do themselves – be common enough, yet I do not remember to have ever seen the reason of this strange phenomenon as at first it appears. Know therefore, reader, that with much and severe scrutiny we have discovered this hatred to be founded on the passion of fear, and to arise from an apprehension that the person whom we have ourselves greatly injured will use all possible endeavours to revenge and retaliate the injuries we have done him. An opinion so firmly established in bad and great minds (and those who confer injuries on others have seldom very good or mean ones) that no benevolence, nor even beneficence, on the injured side, can eradicate it. On the contrary, they refer all these acts of kindness to imposture and design of lulling their suspicion, until an opportunity offers of striking a surer and severer blow; and thus, while the good man who has received it has truly forgotten the injury, the evil mind which did it has it in lively and fresh remembrance.

As we scorn to keep any discoveries secret from our readers – whose instruction, as well as diversion, we have greatly considered in this history – we have here digressed somewhat to communicate the following short lesson to those who are simple and well inclined. Though as a Christian you are obliged, and we advise thee, to forgive thy enemy, never trust the man who has reason to suspect that you know he has injured you.

CHAPTER V

More and more greatness, unparalleled in history or romance

In order to accomplish this great and noble scheme, which the vast genius of Wild had contrived, the first necessary step was to regain the confidence of Heartfree. But however necessary this was, it seemed to be attended with such insurmountable difficulties, that even our hero for some time despaired of success. He was greatly superior to all mankind in the steadiness of his countenance, but this undertaking seemed to require more of that noble quality than had ever been the portion of a mortal. However, at last he resolved to attempt it, and from his success I think we may fairly assert that what was said by the Latin poet of labour – that it conquers all things – is much more true when applied to impudence.

When he had formed his plan he went to Newgate, and burst resolutely into the presence of Heartfree, whom he eagerly embraced and kissed; and then, first arraigning his own rashness, and afterwards lamenting his unfortunate want of success, he acquainted him with the particulars of what had happened; concealing only that single incident of his attack on the other's wife, and his motive to the undertaking, which, he assured Heartfree, was a desire to preserve his effects from a statute of bankruptcy.

The frank openness of this declaration, with the composure of countenance with which it was delivered – his seeming only ruffled by the concern for his friend's misfortune; the probability of truth attending it, joined to the boldness and disinterested appearance of this visit, together with his many professions of immediate service at a time when he could not have the least visible motive from self-love – and above all, his offering him money, the last and surest token of friendship – rushed with such united force on the well-disposed heart, as it is vulgarly called, of this simple man, that they instantly staggered and soon subverted all the determination he had before made in prejudice of Wild; who, perceiving the balance to be turning in his favour, presently threw in a hundred imprecations on his own folly and ill-advised forwardness to serve his friend, which had thus unhappily produced his ruin; he added as many curses on the Count, whom he vowed to pursue with revenge all over Europe; lastly he cast in some grains of comfort, assuring Heartfree that his wife was fallen into the gentlest hands, that she would be carried no further than Dunkirk, whence she might very easily be redeemed.

Heartfree, to whom the lightest presumption of his wife's fidelity would have been more delicious than the absolute restoration of all his jewels, and who indeed, had with the utmost difficulty been brought to entertain the slightest suspicion of her inconstancy, immediately abandoned all distrust of both her and his friend, whose sincerity (luckily for Wild's purpose) seemed to him to depend on the same evidence. He then embraced our hero, who had in his countenance all the symptoms of the deepest concern, and begged him to be comforted; saying that the intentions, rather than the actions of men, conferred obligations – that as to the event of human affairs, it was governed either by chance or some superior agent – that friendship was concerned only in the direction of our designs; and suppose these failed of success, or produced an event never so contrary to their aim, the merit of a good intention was not in the least lessened, but was rather entitled to compassion.

Heartfree however was soon curious enough to enquire how Wild had escaped the captivity which his wife then suffered. Here likewise he recounted the whole truth, omitting only the motive to the French captain's cruelty, for which he assigned a very different reason – namely, his attempt to secure Heartfree's jewels (Wild indeed always kept as much truth as was possible in everything) – and this, he said, was turning the cannon of the enemy upon themselves.

Wild, having thus with admirable and truly laudable conduct achieved the first step, began to discourse on the badness of the world, and particularly to blame the severity of creditors, who seldom or never attended to any unfortunate circumstances, but without mercy inflicted confinement on the debtor, whose body the law, with very unjustifiable rigour, delivered into their power. He added that, for his part, he looked on this restraint to be as heavy a punishment as any appointed by law for the greatest offenders; that the loss of liberty was, in his opinion, equal to, if not worse than, the loss of life; that he had always determined, if by any accident or misfortune he had been subjected to the former, he would run the greatest risk of the latter to rescue himself from it; which he said, if men did not want resolution, was always enough – for that it was ridiculous to conceive that two or three men could confine two or three hundred, unless the prisoners were either fools or cowards, especially when they were neither chained nor fettered. He went on in this manner until, perceiving the utmost attention in Heartfree, he ventured to propose to him an endeavour to make his escape, which he said might easily be executed; that he would himself raise a party in the prison, and that, if a murder or two should happen in the attempt, he (Heartfree) might keep free from any share either in the guilt or in the danger.

There is one misfortune which attends all great men and their schemes, viz. that, in order to carry them into execution, they are obliged, in proposing their purpose to their tools, to discover themselves to be of that disposition in which certain little writers have advised mankind to place no confidence – an advice which has been sometimes taken. Indeed, many inconveniences arise to the said great men from these scribblers publishing without restraint their hints or alarms to society – and many great and glorious schemes have been thus frustrated – wherefore it were to be wished that in all well-regulated governments such liberties should be by some wholesome laws restrained, and all writers inhibited from venting any other instructions to the people than what should be first approved and licensed by the said great men, or their proper instruments or tools; by which means nothing would ever be published but what made for the advancing their most noble projects.

Heartfree, whose suspicions were again raised by this advice, viewing Wild with inconceivable disdain, spoke as follows: 'There is one thing the loss of which I should deplore infinitely beyond that of liberty and of life also – I mean that of a good conscience – a blessing which he who possesses can never be thoroughly unhappy; for the bitterest potion of life is by this so sweetened that it soon becomes palatable whereas, without it, the most delicate enjoyments quickly lose all their relish, and life itself grows insipid, or rather nauseous, to us. Would you then lessen my misfortunes by robbing me of what has been my only comfort under them, and on which I place my dependence of being relieved from them? I have read that Socrates refused to save his life by breaking the laws of his country, and departing from his prison when it was open. Perhaps my virtue would not go so far; but heaven forbid liberty should have such charms to tempt me to the perpetration of so horrid a crime as murder! As to the poor evasion of committing it by other hands, it might be useful indeed to those who seek only the escape from temporal punishment, but can be of no service to excuse me to that Being whom I chiefly fear offending – nay, it would greatly aggravate my guilt by so impudent an endeavour to impose upon Him, and by so wickedly involving others in my crime. Give me, therefore, no more advice of this kind; for this is my great comfort in all my afflictions – that it is in the power of no enemy to rob me of my conscience, nor will I ever be so much my own enemy as to injure it.'

Though our hero heard all this with proper contempt, he made no direct answer, but endeavoured to evade his proposal as much as possible, which he did with admirable dexterity. This method of getting tolerably well off, when you are repulsed in your attack on a man's conscience, may be styled the art of retreating, in which the politician, as well as the general, has sometimes a wonderful opportunity of displaying his great abilities in his profession.

Wild, having made this admirable retreat, and argued away all design of involving his friend in the guilt of murder, concluded however that he thought him rather too scrupulous in not attempting his escape and then, promising to use all such means as the other would permit in his service, took his leave for the present. Heartfree, having indulged himself an hour with his children, repaired to rest, which he enjoyed quiet and undisturbed; whilst Wild, disdaining repose, sat up all night, consulting how he might bring about the final destruction of his friend, without being beholden to any assistance from himself, which he now despaired of procuring. With the result of these consultations we shall acquaint our reader in good time, but at present we have matters of much more consequence to relate to him.

CHAPTER VI

The event of Fireblood's adventure; and a threat of marriage,
which might have been concluded either at Smithfield or St James's

Fireblood returned from his enterprise unsuccessful. The gentleman happened to go home another way than he had intended, so that the whole design miscarried. Fireblood had indeed robbed the coach, and had wantonly discharged a pistol into it, which lightly wounded one of the passengers in the arm. The booty he met with was not very considerable, though much greater than that with which he acquainted Wild; for of eleven pounds in money, two silver watches, and a wedding ring, he produced no more than two guineas and the ring, which he protested with numberless oaths was his whole booty. However, when an advertisement of the robbery was published, with a reward promised for the ring and the watches, Fireblood was obliged to confess the whole, and to acquaint our hero where he pawned the watches – which Wild, taking the full value of them for his pains, restored to the right owner.

He did not fail catechising his young friend on this occasion. He said he was sorry to see any of his gang guilty of a breach of honour; that without honour priggery was at an end; that if a prig had but honour he would overlook every vice in the world. 'But, nevertheless,' said he, 'I will forgive you this time, as you are a hopeful lad, and I hope never afterwards to find you delinquent in this great point.'

Wild had now brought his gang to great regularity – he was obeyed and feared by them all. He had likewise established an office, where all men who were robbed, paying the value only (or a little more) of their goods, might have them again. This was of notable use to several persons who had lost pieces of plate they had received from their grandmothers; to others who had a particular value for certain rings, watches, heads of canes, snuff-boxes, etc., for which they would not have taken twenty times as much as they were worth, either because they had them a little while or a long time, or that somebody else had had them before, or from some other such excellent reason, which often stamps a greater value on a toy than the great Bubble-boy[35] himself would have the impudence to set upon it.

By these means he seemed in so promising a way of procuring a fortune, and was regarded in so thriving a light by all the gentlemen of his acquaintance – as by the keeper and turnkeys of Newgate, by Mr Snap, and others of his occupation – that Mr Snap one day, taking Mr Wild the elder aside, very seriously proposed what they had often lightly talked over, a strict union between their families, by marrying his daughter Tishy to our hero. This proposal was very readily accepted by the old gentleman, who promised to acquaint his son with it.

On the morrow on which this message was delivered, our hero, little dreaming of the happiness which, of its own accord, was advancing so near towards him, had called Fireblood to him; and after informing that youth of the violence of his passion for the young lady, and assuring him what confidence he reposed in him and his honour, he despatched him to Miss Tishy with the following letter; which we here insert, not only as we take it to be extremely curious, but to be a much better pattern for that epistolary kind of writing which is generally called love-letters than any to be found in the academy of compliments, and which we challenge all the beaus of our time to excel either in matter or spelling.

Most divine and adwhorable creeture, – I doubt not but those IIs, briter than the son, which have kindled such a flam in my hart, have likewise the faculty of seeing it. It would be the hiest preassumption to imagin you eggnorant of my loav. No, madam, I sollemly purtest, that of all the butys in the unaversal glob, there is none kapable of hateracting my IIs like you. Corts and pallaces would be to me deserts without your kumpany, and with it a wilderness would have more charms than haven itself. For I hop you will beleve me when I sware every place in the univarse is a haven with you. I am konvinced you must be sinsibel of my violent passion for you, which, if I endevored to hid it, would be as impossible as for you, or the son, to hid your buty's. I assure you I have not slept a wink since I had the hapness of seeing you last; therefore hop you will, out of Kumpassion, let me have the honour of seeing you this afternune; for I am, with the greatest adwhoration,

Most deivine creeture, Iour most pessionate amirer, adwhorer, and slave,

Jonathan Wyld

If the spelling of this letter be not so strictly orthographical, the reader will be pleased to remember that such a defect might be worthy of censure in a low and scholastic character, but can be no blemish in that sublime greatness of which we endeavour to raise a complete idea in this history. In which kind of composition spelling, or indeed any kind of human literature, has never been thought a necessary ingredient. For if these sort of great personages can but complot and contrive their noble schemes, and hack and hew mankind sufficiently, there will never be wanting fit and able persons who can spell to record their praises. Again, if it should be observed that the style of this letter does not exactly correspond with that of our hero's speeches, which we have here recorded, we answer it is sufficient if in these the historian adheres faithfully to the matter, though he embellishes the diction with some flourishes of his own eloquence, without which the excellent speeches recorded in ancient historians (particularly in Sallust) would have scarce been found in their writings. Nay, even amongst the moderns, famous as they are for elocution, it may be doubted whether those inimitable harangues published in the monthly magazines came literally from the mouths of the Hurgos, etc., as they are there inserted, or whether we may not rather suppose one historian of great eloquence has borrowed the matter only, and adorned it with those rhetorical showers for which many of the said Hurgos are not so extremely eminent.[36]

CHAPTER VII

Matters preliminary to the marriage between Mr Jonathan Wild and the chaste Laetitia

But to proceed with our history: Fireblood, having received this letter, and promised on his honour with many voluntary asseverations to discharge his embassy faithfully, went to visit the fair Laetitia. The lady, having opened the letter and read it, put on an air of disdain, and told Mr Fireblood she could not conceive what Mr Wild meant by troubling her with his impertinence. She begged him to carry the letter back again, saying had she known from whom it came, she would have been damned before she had opened it. 'But with you, young gentleman,' says she, 'I am not in the least angry. I am rather sorry that so pretty a young man should be employed in such an errand.' She accompanied these words with so tender an accent and so wanton a leer that Fireblood, who was no backward youth, began to take her by the hand, and proceeded so warmly that, to imitate his actions with the rapidity of our narration, he in a few minutes ravished this fair creature, or at least would have ravished her, if she had not, by a timely compliance, prevented him.

Fireblood, after he had ravished as much as he could, returned to Wild, and acquainted him as far as any wise man would with what had passed, concluding with many praises of the young lady's beauty, with whom, he said, if his honour would have permitted him, he should himself have fallen in love; but, damn him if he would not sooner be torn to pieces by wild horses than even think of injuring his friend. He asserted indeed, and swore so heartily, that had not Wild been so thoroughly convinced of the impregnable chastity of the lady, he might have suspected his success; however, he was by these means entirely satisfied of his friend's inclination towards his mistress.

Thus constituted were the love affairs of our hero, when his father brought him Mr Snap's proposal. The reader must know very little of love, or indeed of anything else, if he requires any information concerning the reception which this proposal met with. 'Not guilty' never sounded sweeter in the ears of a prisoner at the bar, nor the sound of a reprieve to one at the gallows, than did every word of the old gentleman in the ears of our hero. He gave his father full power to treat in his name, and desired nothing more than expedition.

The old people now met, and Snap, who had information from his daughter of the violent passion of her lover, endeavoured to improve it to the best advantage, and would have not only declined giving her any fortune himself, but have attempted to cheat her of what she owed to the liberality of her relations, particularly of a pint silver caudle-cup, the gift of her grandmother. However, in this the young lady herself afterwards took care to prevent him. As to the old Mr Wild, he did not sufficiently attend to all the designs of Snap, as his faculties were busily employed in designs of his own, to overreach (or, as others express it, to cheat) the said Mr Snap by pretending to give his son a whole number for a chair, when in reality he was entitled to a third only.

While matters were thus settling between the old folks, the young lady agreed to admit Mr Wild's visits, and by degrees began to entertain him with all the show of affection which the great natural reserve of her temper, and the greater artificial reserve of her education, would permit.

At length, everything being agreed between their parents, settlements made, and the lady's fortune (to wit, seventeen pounds and nine shillings in money and goods) paid down, the day for their nuptials was fixed, and they were celebrated accordingly.

Most private histories, as well as comedies, end at this period – the historian and the poet both concluding they have done enough for their hero when they have married him – or intimating rather that the rest of his life must be a dull calm of happiness, very delightful indeed to pass through, but somewhat insipid to relate; and matrimony in general must, I believe, without any dispute, be allowed to be this state of tranquil felicity, including so little variety that like Salisbury Plain it affords only one prospect – a very pleasant one it must be confessed – but the same.

Now there was all the probability imaginable that this contract would have proved of such happy note – both from the great accomplishments of the young lady, who was thought to be possessed of every qualification necessary to make the marriage state happy, and from the truly ardent passion of Mr Wild – but whether it was that nature and fortune had great designs for him to execute, and would not suffer his vast abilities to be lost and sunk in the arms of a wife, or whether neither nature nor fortune had any hand in the matter, is a point I will not determine. Certain it is that this match did not produce that serene state we have mentioned above, but resembled the most turbulent and ruffled, rather than the most calm sea.

I cannot here omit a conjecture, ingenious enough, of a friend of mine, who had a long intimacy in the Wild family. He has often told me he fancied one reason of the dissatisfactions which afterwards fell out between Wild and his lady arose from the number of gallants to whom she had, before marriage, granted favours. For says he, and indeed very probable it is too, the lady might expect from her husband what she had before received from several, and being angry not to find one man as good as ten, she had, from that indignation, taken those steps which we cannot perfectly justify.

From this person I received the following dialogue, which he assured me he had overheard and taken down verbatim. It passed on the day fortnight after they were married.

CHAPTER VIII

A dialogue matrimonial, which passed between
Jonathan Wild, Esq., and Laetitia his wife,
on the morning of the day fortnight on which his
nuptials were celebrated; which concluded more
amicably than those debates generally do

Jonathan

My dear, I wish you would lie a little longer in bed this morning.

Laetitia

Indeed I cannot; I am engaged to breakfast with Jack Strongbow.

Jonathan

I don't know what Jack Strongbow does so often at my house. I assure you I am uneasy at it; for though I have no suspicion of your virtue, yet it may injure your reputation in the opinion of my neighbours.

Laetitia

I don't trouble my head about my neighbours; and they shall no more tell me what company I am to keep than my husband shall.

Jonathan

A good wife would keep no company which made her husband uneasy.

Laetitia

You might have found one of those good wives, sir, if you had pleased; I had no objection to it.

Jonathan

I thought I had found one in you.

Laetitia

You did! I am very much obliged to you for thinking me so poor-spirited a creature; but I hope to convince you to the contrary. What,

I suppose you took me for a raw senseless girl, who knew nothing what other married women do!

Jonathan
No matter what I took you for: I have taken you for better and worse.

Laetitia
And at your own desire too; for I am sure you never had mine. I should not have broken my heart if Mr Wild had thought proper to bestow himself on any other more happy woman. Ha, ha!

Jonathan
I hope, madam, you don't imagine that was not in my power, or that I married you out of any kind of necessity.

Laetitia
O no, sir; I am convinced there are silly women enough. And far be it from me to accuse you of any necessity for a wife. I believe you could have been very well contented with the state of a bachelor. I have no reason to complain of your necessities; but that, you know, a woman cannot tell beforehand.

Jonathan
I can't guess what you would insinuate, for I believe no woman had ever less reason to complain of her husband's want of fondness.

Laetitia
Then some, I am certain, have great reason to complain of the price they give for them. But I know better things. (These words were spoken with a very great air, and toss of the head.)

Jonathan
Well, my sweeting, I will make it impossible for you to wish me more fond.

Laetitia

Pray, Mr Wild, none of this nauseous behaviour, nor those odious words. I wish you were fond! I assure you, I don't know what you would pretend to insinuate of me. I have no wishes which misbecome a virtuous woman. No, nor should not, if I had married for love. And especially now, when nobody, I am sure, can suspect me of any such thing.

Jonathan

If you did not marry for love why did you marry?

Laetitia

Because it was convenient, and my parents forced me.

Jonathan

I hope, madam, at least, you will not tell me to my face you have made your convenience of me.

Laetitia

I have made nothing of you; nor do I desire the honour of making anything of you.

Jonathan

Yes, you have made a husband of me.

Laetitia

No, you made yourself so; for I repeat once more it was not my desire, but your own.

Jonathan

You should think yourself obliged to me for that desire.

Laetitia

La, sir! you was not so singular in it. I was not in despair. I have had other offers, and better too.

Jonathan

I wish you had accepted them with all my heart.

Laetitia

I must tell you, Mr Wild, this is a very brutish manner in treating a woman to whom you have such obligations; but I know how to despise it, and to despise you too for showing it me. Indeed I am well enough paid for the foolish preference I gave to you. I flattered myself that I should at least have been used with good manners. I thought I had married a gentleman; but I find you every way contemptible and below my concern.

Jonathan

Damn you, madam, have I not more reason to complain when you tell me you married for your convenience only?

Laetitia

Very fine truly. Is it behaviour worthy a man to swear at a woman? Yet why should I mention what comes from a wretch whom I despise.

Jonathan

Don't repeat that word so often. I despise you as heartily as you can me. And, to tell you a truth, I married you for my convenience likewise, to satisfy a passion which I have now satisfied, and you may be damned for anything I care.

Laetitia

The world shall know how barbarously I am treated by such a villain.

Jonathan

I need take very little pains to acquaint the world what a bitch you are, your actions will demonstrate it.

Laetitia

Monster! I would advise you not to depend too much on my sex, and provoke me too far – for I can do you a mischief, and will, if you dare use me so, you villain!

Jonathan

Begin whenever you please, madam; but assure yourself, the moment you lay aside the woman, I will treat you as such no longer; and if the first blow is yours, I promise you the last shall be mine.

Laetitia

Use me as you will; but damn me if ever you shall use me as a woman again; for may I be cursed if ever I enter into your bed more.

Jonathan

May I be cursed if that abstinence be not the greatest obligation you can lay upon me; for I assure you faithfully your person was all I had ever any regard for; and that I now loathe and detest as much as ever I liked it.

Laetitia

It is impossible for two people to agree better; for I always detested your person; and as for any other regard, you must be convinced I never could have any for you.

Jonathan

Why, then, since we are come to a right understanding, as we are to live together, suppose we agreed, instead of quarrelling and abusing, to be civil to each other.

Laetitia

With all my heart.

Jonathan

Let us shake hands then, and henceforwards never live like man and wife – that is, never be loving nor ever quarrel.

Laetitia

Agreed. But pray, Mr Wild, why bitch? Why did you suffer such a word to escape you?

Jonathan
It is not worth your remembrance.

Laetitia
You agree I shall converse with whomsoever I please?

Jonathan
Without control. And I have the same liberty?

Laetitia
When I interfere may every curse you can wish attend me!

Jonathan
Let us now take a farewell kiss, and may I be hanged if it is not the sweetest you ever gave me.

Laetitia
But why bitch? Methinks I should be glad to know why bitch?

At which words he sprang from the bed, damning her temper heartily. She returned it again with equal abuse, which was continued on both sides while he was dressing. However, they agreed to continue steadfast in this new resolution; and the joy arising on that occasion at length dismissed them pretty cheerfully from each other, though Laetitia could not help concluding with the words, 'why bitch?'

CHAPTER IX

Observations on the foregoing dialogue, together with a base design on our hero, which must be detested by every lover of greatness

Thus did this dialogue (which, though we have termed it matrimonial, had indeed very little savour of the sweets of matrimony in it) produce at last a resolution more wise than strictly pious, and which, if they could have rigidly adhered to it, might have prevented some unpleasant moments as well to our hero as to his serene consort; but their hatred was so very great and unaccountable that they never could bear to see the least composure in one another's countenance without attempting to ruffle it. This set them on so many contrivances to plague and vex one another that as their proximity afforded them such frequent opportunities of executing their malicious purposes, they seldom passed one easy or quiet day together.

And this, Reader, and no other, is the cause of those many inquietudes which you must have observed to disturb the repose of some married couples who mistake implacable hatred for indifference; for why should Corvinus – who lives in a round of intrigue, and seldom does, and never willingly would, dally with his wife – endeavour to prevent her from the satisfaction of an intrigue in her turn? Why does Camilla refuse a more agreeable invitation abroad, only to expose her husband at his own table at home? In short, to mention no more instances, whence can all the quarrels, and jealousies, and jars proceed in people who have no love for each other, unless from that noble passion above mentioned – that desire, according to my lady Betty Modish, of curing each other of a smile.[37]

We thought proper to give our reader a short taste of the domestic state of our hero, the rather to show him that great men are subject to the same frailties and inconveniences in ordinary life with little men, and that heroes are really of the same species with other human creatures, notwithstanding all the pains they themselves or their flatterers take to assert the contrary; and that they differ chiefly in the immensity of their greatness, or as the vulgar erroneously call it, villainy. Now, therefore – that we may not dwell too long on low scenes in a history of the sublime kind – we shall return to actions of a higher note and more suitable to our purpose.

When the boy Hymen had, with his lighted torch, driven the boy Cupid out of doors – that is to say, in common phrase, when the violence of Mr Wild's passion (or rather appetite) for the chaste Laetitia began to abate – he returned to visit his friend Heartfree, who was now in the liberties of the Fleet, and appeared to the commission of bankruptcy against him. Here he met with a more cold reception than he himself had apprehended. Heartfree had long entertained suspicions of Wild, but these suspicions had from time to time been confounded with circumstances, and principally smothered with that amazing confidence which was indeed the most striking virtue in our hero. Heartfree was unwilling to condemn his friend without certain evidence, and laid hold on every probable semblance to acquit him; but the proposal made at his last visit had so totally blackened his character in this poor man's opinion that it entirely fixed the wavering scale, and he no longer doubted but that our hero was one of the greatest villains in the world.

Circumstances of great improbability often escape men who devour a story with greedy ears; the reader, therefore, cannot wonder that Heartfree, whose passions were so variously concerned – first for the fidelity, and secondly for the safety of his wife, and lastly, who was so distracted with doubt concerning the conduct of his friend – should at this relation pass unobserved the incident of his being committed to the boat by the captain of the privateer, which he had at the time of his telling so lamely accounted for; but now when Heartfree came to reflect on the whole – and with a high prepossession against Wild – the absurdity of this fact glared in his eyes and struck him in the most sensible manner. At length a thought of great horror suggested itself to his imagination, and this was whether the whole was not a fiction, and Wild – who was, as he had learned from his own mouth, equal to any undertaking howsoever black – had not spirited away, robbed, and murdered his wife.

Intolerable as this apprehension was, he not only turned it round and examined it carefully in his own mind, but acquainted young Friendly with it at their next interview. Friendly, who detested Wild (from that envy probably with which these great characters naturally inspire low fellows), encouraged these suspicions so much that Heartfree resolved to attach our hero and carry him before a magistrate.

This resolution had been some time taken, and Friendly, with a warrant and a constable, had with the utmost diligence searched several days for our hero; but whether it was that in compliance with modern custom he had retired to spend the honeymoon with his bride, the only moon indeed in which it is fashionable or customary for the married parties to have any correspondence with each other – or perhaps his habitation might for particular reasons be usually kept a secret, like those of some few great men whom unfortunately the law has left out of that reasonable as well as honourable provision which it has made for the security of the persons of other great men.

But Wild resolved to perform works of supererogation in the way of honour, and though no hero is obliged to answer the challenge of my lord chief justice, or indeed of any other magistrate, but may with unblemished reputation slide away from it, yet such was the bravery, such the greatness, the magnanimity of Wild, that he appeared in person to it.

Indeed Envy may say one thing, which may lessen the glory of this action, namely that the said Mr Wild knew nothing of the said warrant or challenge; and as you may be assured, Reader, that the malicious fury will omit nothing which can anyways sully so great a character, so she has endeavoured to account for this second visit of our hero to his friend Heartfree from a very different motive than that of asserting his own innocence.

CHAPTER X

*Mr Wild with unprecedented generosity visits his friend Heartfree,
and the ungrateful reception he met with*

It has been said then that Mr Wild, not being able on the strictest examination to find in a certain spot of human nature called his own heart the least grain of that pitiful low quality called honesty, had resolved, perhaps a little too generally, that there was no such thing. He therefore imputed the resolution with which Mr Heartfree had so positively refused to concern himself in murder either to a fear of bloodying his hands or the apprehension of a ghost, or lest he should make an additional example in that excellent book called *God's Revenge against Murder*[38]; and doubted not but he would (at least in his present necessity) agree without scruple to a simple robbery, especially where any considerable booty should be proposed, and the safety of the attack plausibly made appear; which if he could prevail on him to undertake, he would immediately afterwards get him impeached, convicted, and hanged. He no sooner therefore had discharged his duties to Hymen, and heard that Heartfree had procured himself the liberties of the Fleet, than he resolved to visit him, and to propose a robbery with all the allurements of profit, ease, and safety.

This proposal was no sooner made than it was answered by Heartfree in the following manner:

'I might have hoped the answer which I gave to your former advice would have prevented me from the danger of receiving a second affront of this kind. An affront I call it, and surely, if it be so to call a man a villain, it can be no less to show him you suppose him one. Indeed, it may be wondered how any man can arrive at the boldness, I may say impudence, of first making such an overture to another; surely it is seldom done, unless to those who have previously betrayed some symptoms of their own baseness. If I have therefore shown you any such, these insults are more pardonable; but I assure you, if such appear, they discharge all their malignance outwardly, and reflect not even a shadow within. For to me baseness seems inconsistent with this rule – of doing no other person an injury from any motive or on any consideration whatever. This, sir, is the rule by which I am determined to walk, nor can that man justify disbelieving me who will not own he walks not by it himself. But, whether it be allowed to me or no, or whether I feel the good effects of its being practised by others, I am resolved to maintain it; for surely no man can reap a benefit from my pursuing it equal to the comfort I myself enjoy. For what a ravishing thought, how replete with ecstasy, must the consideration be that Almighty Goodness is by its own nature engaged to reward me! How indifferent must such a persuasion make a man to all the occurrences of this life! What trifles must he represent to himself both the enjoyments and the afflictions of this world! How easily must he acquiesce under missing the former, and how patiently will he submit to the latter, who is convinced that his failing of a transitory imperfect reward here is a most certain argument of his obtaining one permanent and complete hereafter! Do you think then – you little, paltry, mean animal (with such language did he treat our truly great man) – that I will forego such comfortable expectations for any pitiful reward which you can suggest or promise to me – for that sordid lucre for which all pains and labour are undertaken by the industrious, and all barbarities and iniquities committed by the vile – for a worthless acquisition, which such as you are can possess, can give, or can take away?' The former part of this speech occasioned much yawning in our hero, but the latter roused his anger; and he was collecting his rage to answer, when Friendly and the constable, who had been summoned by Heartfree on Wild's first appearance, entered the room, and seized the great man just as his wrath was bursting from his lips.

The dialogue which now ensued is not worth relating. Wild was soon acquainted with the reason of this rough treatment, and presently conveyed before a magistrate.

Notwithstanding the doubts raised by Mr Wild's lawyer on his examination – he insisting that the proceeding was improper, for that a *writ de homine replegiando* should issue, and on the return of that a *capias in withernam* – the justice inclined to commitment, so that Wild was driven to other methods for his defence. He therefore acquainted the justice that there was a young man likewise with him in the boat, and begged that he might be sent for – which request was accordingly granted, and the faithful Achates (Mr Fireblood) was soon produced to bear testimony for his friend; which he did with so much becoming zeal, and went through his examination with such coherence (though he was forced to collect his evidence from the hints given him by Wild in the presence of the justice and the accusers), that as here was direct evidence against mere presumption, our hero was most honourably acquitted, and poor Heartfree was charged by the justice, the audience, and all others who afterwards heard the story, with the blackest ingratitude, in attempting to take away the life of a man to whom he had such eminent obligations.

Lest so vast an effort of friendship as this of Fireblood's should too violently surprise the reader in this degenerate age, it may be proper to inform him that, beside the ties of engagement in the same employ, another nearer and stronger alliance subsisted between our hero and this youth, which latter was just departed from the arms of the lovely Laetitia when he received her husband's message. An instance which may also serve to justify those strict intercourses of love and acquaintance which so commonly subsist in modern history between the husband and gallant, displaying the vast force of friendship contracted by this more honourable than legal alliance, which is thought to be at present one of the strongest bonds of amity between great men, and the most reputable as well as easy way to their favour.

Four months had now passed since Heartfree's first confinement, and his affairs had begun to wear a more benign aspect; but they were a good deal injured by this attempt on Wild (so dangerous is any attack on a great man), several of his neighbours, and particularly one or two of his own trade, industriously endeavouring, from their bitter animosity against such kind of iniquity, to spread and exaggerate his ingratitude as much as possible; not in the least scrupling, in the violent ardour of their indignation, to add some small circumstances of their own knowledge of the many obligations conferred on Heartfree by Wild. To all these scandals he quietly submitted, comforting himself in the consciousness of his own innocence, and confiding in time the sure friend of justice to acquit him.

CHAPTER XI

A scheme so deeply laid that it shames all the politics of this our age; with digression and subdigression

Wild having now, to the hatred he bore Heartfree on account of those injuries he had done him, an additional spur from this injury received (for so it appeared to him, who no more than the most ignorant, considered how truly he deserved it), applied his utmost industry to accomplish the ruin of one whose very name sounded odious in his ears; when luckily a scheme arose in his imagination which not only promised to effect it securely, but (which pleased him most) by means of the mischief he had already done him; and which would at once load him with the imputation of having committed what he himself had done to him, and would bring on him the severest punishment for a fact of which he was not only innocent, but had already so greatly suffered by. And this was no other than to charge him with having conveyed away his wife, with his most valuable effects, in order to defraud his creditors.

He no sooner started this thought than he immediately resolved on putting it in execution. What remained to consider was only the *quomodo*, and the person or tool to be employed; for the stage of the world differs from that in Drury Lane principally in this – that whereas, on the latter, the hero or chief figure is almost continually before your eyes, whilst the under-actors are not seen above once in an evening – now, on the former, the hero or great man is always behind the curtain, and seldom or never appears or does anything in his own person. He does indeed, in this grand drama, rather perform the part of the prompter, and does instruct the well-dressed figures, who are strutting in public on the stage, what to say and do. To say the truth, a puppet show will illustrate our meaning better, where it is the master of the show (the great man) who dances and moves everything, whether it be the king of Muscovy or whatever other potentate, alias puppet which we behold on the stage; but he himself keeps wisely out of sight. For, should he once appear, the whole motion would be at an end. Not that anyone is ignorant of his being there, or supposes that the puppets are not mere sticks of wood, and he himself the sole mover; but as this (though every one knows it) does not appear visibly, i.e., to their eyes, no one is ashamed of consenting to be imposed upon – of helping on the drama, by calling the several sticks or puppets by the names which the master has allotted to them, and by assigning to each the character which the great man is pleased they shall move in, or rather in which he himself is pleased to move them.

It would be to suppose thee, gentle Reader, one of very little knowledge in this world, to imagine you have never seen some of these puppet shows which are so frequently acted on the great stage; but though you should have resided all your days in those remote parts of this island which great men seldom visit, yet, if you had any penetration, you must have had some occasions to admire both the solemnity of countenance in the actor and the gravity in the spectator, while some of those farces are carried on which are acted almost daily in every village in the kingdom. He must have a very despicable opinion of mankind indeed who can conceive them to be imposed on as often as they appear to be so. The truth is, they are in the same situation with the readers of romances who though they know the whole to be one entire fiction, nevertheless agree to be deceived. And as these find amusement, so do the others find ease and convenience in this concurrence. But, this being a subdigression, I return to my digression.

A great man ought to do his business by others – to employ hands, as we have before said, to his purposes, and keep himself as much behind the curtain as possible. And though it must be acknowledged that two very great men, whose names will be both recorded in history, did in these latter times come forth themselves on the stage, and did hack and hew and lay each other most cruelly open to the diversion of the spectators, yet this must be mentioned rather as an example of avoidance than imitation, and is to be ascribed to the number of those instances which serve to evince the truth of these maxims – *Nemo mortalium omnibus horis sapit. Ira furor brevis est*, etc.[39]

CHAPTER XII

New instances of Friendly's folly, etc.

To return to my history, which having rested itself a little, is now ready to proceed on its journey, Fireblood was the person chosen by Wild for this service. He had, on a late occasion, experienced the talents of this youth for a good round perjury. He immediately, therefore, found him out, and proposed it to him; when, receiving his instant assent, they consulted together, and soon framed an evidence, which being communicated to one of the most bitter and severe creditors of Heartfree, by him laid before a magistrate, and attested by the oath of Fireblood, the justice granted his warrant, and Heartfree was accordingly apprehended and brought before him.

When the officers came for this poor wretch, they found him meanly diverting himself with his little children, the younger of whom sat on his knees, and the elder was playing at a little distance from him with Friendly. One of the officers, who was a very good sort of a man, but one very laudably severe in his office, after acquainting Heartfree with his errand, bad him come along and be damned, and leave those little bastards – for so, he said, he supposed they were – for a legacy to the parish. Heartfree was much surprised at hearing there was a warrant for felony against him; but he showed less concern than Friendly did in his countenance. The elder daughter, when she saw the officer lay hold on her father, immediately quitted her play, and running to him and bursting into tears, cried out, 'You shall not hurt poor papa.' One of the other ruffians offered to take the little one rudely from his knees, but Heartfree started up and, catching the fellow by the collar, dashed his head so violently against the wall that had he had any brains, he might possibly have lost them by the blow.

The officer, like most of those heroic spirits who insult men in adversity, had some prudence mixed with his zeal for justice. Seeing, therefore, this rough treatment of his companion, he began to pursue more gentle methods, and very civilly desired Mr Heartfree to go with him, seeing he was an officer, and obliged to execute his warrant; that he was sorry for his misfortune, and hoped he would be acquitted. The other answered he should patiently submit to the laws of his country, and would attend him whither he was ordered to conduct him, then – taking leave of his children with a tender kiss, he recommended them to the care of Friendly, who promised to see them safe home, and then to attend him at the justice's, whose name and abode he had learned of the constable.

Friendly arrived at the magistrate's house just as that gentleman had signed the *mittimus* against his friend; for the evidence of Fireblood was so clear and strong, and the justice was so incensed against Heartfree, and so convinced of his guilt, that he would hardly hear him speak in his own defence, which the reader perhaps, when he hears the evidence against him, will be less inclined to censure. For this witness deposed that he had been, by Heartfree himself, employed to carry the orders of embezzling to Wild, in order to be delivered to his wife; that he had been afterwards present with Wild and her at the inn when they took coach for Harwich, where she showed him the casket of jewels, and desired him to tell her husband that she had fully executed his command – and this he swore to have been done after Heartfree had notice of the commission; and in order to bring it within that time, Fireblood, as well as Wild, swore that Mrs Heartfree lay several days concealed at Wild's house before her departure for Holland.

When Friendly found the justice obdurate, and that all he could say had no effect, nor was it any way possible for Heartfree to escape being committed to Newgate, he resolved to accompany him thither – where when they arrived, the turnkey would have confined Heartfree (he having no money) amongst the common felons – but Friendly would not permit it, and advanced every shilling he had in his pocket to procure a room in the press-yard for his friend – which indeed, through the humanity of the keeper, he did at a cheap rate.

They spent that day together, and in the evening the prisoner dismissed his friend, desiring him, after many thanks for his fidelity, to be comforted on his account. 'I know not,' says he, 'how far the malice of my enemy may prevail; but whatever my sufferings are, I am convinced my innocence will somewhere be rewarded. If, therefore, any fatal accident should happen to me (for he who is in the hands of perjury may apprehend the worst), my dear Friendly, be a father to my poor children' – at which words the tears gushed from his eyes. The other begged him not to admit any such apprehensions, for that he would employ his utmost diligence in his service, and doubted not but to subvert any villainous design laid for his destruction, and to make his innocence appear to the world as white as it was in his own opinion.

We cannot help mentioning a circumstance here, though we doubt it will appear very unnatural and incredible to our reader – which is, that notwithstanding the former character and behaviour of Heartfree, this story of his embezzling was so far from surprising his neighbours that many of them declared they expected no better from him. Some were assured he could pay forty shillings in the pound if he would. Others had overheard hints formerly pass between him and Mrs Heartfree which had given them suspicions. And what is most astonishing of all is that many of those who had before censured him for an extravagant heedless fool, now no less confidently abused him for a cunning, tricking, avaricious knave.

CHAPTER XIII

*Something concerning Fireblood which will surprise; and somewhat
touching one of the Miss Snaps, which will greatly concern the reader*

However, notwithstanding all these censures abroad, and in spite of all
his misfortunes at home, Heartfree in Newgate enjoyed a quiet,
undisturbed repose – while our hero, nobly disdaining rest, lay
sleepless all night, partly from the apprehensions of Mrs Heartfree's
return before he had executed his scheme, and partly from a suspicion
lest Fireblood should betray him – of whose infidelity he had nevertheless no other cause to maintain any fear, but from his knowing him to be
an accomplished rascal, as the vulgar term it, a complete great man in
our language. And indeed, to confess the truth, these doubts were not
without some foundation; for the very same thought unluckily entered
the head of that noble youth, who considered whether he might not
possibly sell himself for some advantage to the other side, as he had
yet no promise from Wild. But this was, by the sagacity of the latter,
prevented in the morning with a profusion of promises which showed
him to be of the most generous temper in the world, with which
Fireblood was extremely well satisfied, and made use of so many
protestations of his faithfulness that he convinced Wild of the justice of
his suspicions.

At this time an accident happened, which, though it did not
immediately affect our hero, we cannot avoid relating, as it occasioned
great confusion in his family, as well as in the family of Snap. It is indeed
a calamity highly to be lamented, when it stains untainted blood, and
happens to an honourable house – an injury never to be repaired – a
blot never to be wiped out – a sore never to be healed. To detain my
reader no longer, Miss Theodosia Snap was now safely delivered of a
male infant, the product of an amour which that beautiful (O that I
could say virtuous!) creature had with the Count.

Mr Wild and his lady were at breakfast when Mr Snap, with all the
agonies of despair both in his voice and countenance, brought them
this melancholy news. Our hero, who had (as we have said) wonderful
good nature when his greatness or interest was not concerned, instead

of reviling his sister-in-law, asked with a smile who was the father. But the chaste Laetitia – we repeat the chaste, for well did she now deserve that epithet – received it in another manner. She fell into the utmost fury at the relation, reviled her sister in the bitterest terms, and vowed she would never see nor speak to her more; then burst into tears and lamented over her father that such dishonour should ever happen to him and herself. At length she fell severely on her husband for the light treatment which he gave this fatal accident. She told him he was unworthy of the honour he enjoyed of marrying into a chaste family – that she looked on it as an affront to her virtue – that if he had married one of the naughty hussies of the town he could have behaved to her in no other manner. She concluded with desiring her father to make an example of the slut, and to turn her out of doors; for that she would not otherwise enter his house, being resolved never to set her foot within the same threshold with the trollop, whom she detested so much the more because (which was perhaps true) she was her own sister.

So violent, and indeed so outrageous, was this chaste lady's love of virtue that she could not forgive a single slip (indeed the only one Theodosia had ever made) in her own sister, in a sister who loved her, and to whom she owed a thousand obligations.

Perhaps the severity of Mr Snap, who greatly felt the injury done to the honour of his family, would have relented, had not the parish-officers been extremely pressing on this occasion, and for want of security conveyed the unhappy young lady to a place – the name of which, for the honour of the Snaps (to whom our hero was so nearly allied) we bury in eternal oblivion – where she suffered so much correction for her crime that the good-natured reader of the male kind may be inclined to compassionate her, at least to imagine she was sufficiently punished for a fault which, with submission to the chaste Laetitia and all other strictly virtuous ladies, it should be either less criminal in a woman to commit, or more so in a man to solicit her to it.

But to return to our hero, who was a living and strong instance that human greatness and happiness are not always inseparable – he was under a continual alarm of frights, and fears, and jealousies. He thought every man he beheld wore a knife for his throat, and a pair of scissors for his purse. As for his own gang particularly, he was thoroughly convinced there was not a single man amongst them who would not, for the value of five shillings, bring him to the gallows. These apprehensions so constantly broke his rest, and kept him so assiduously on his guard to frustrate and circumvent any designs which might be formed against him, that his condition, to any other than the glorious eye of ambition, might seem rather deplorable than the object of envy or desire.

CHAPTER XIV

In which our hero makes a speech well worthy to be celebrated; and the behaviour of one of the gang, perhaps more unnatural than any other part of this history

There was in the gang a man named Blueskin, one of those merchants who trade in dead oxen, sheep, etc. – in short, what the vulgar call a butcher. This gentleman had two qualities of a great man, viz. undaunted courage, and an absolute contempt of those ridiculous distinctions of *meum* and *tuum*[40], which would cause endless disputes did not the law happily decide them by converting both into *suum*[41]. The common form of exchanging property by trade seemed to him too tedious; he therefore resolved to quit the mercantile profession, and falling acquainted with some of Mr Wild's people, he provided himself with arms, and enlisted of the gang, in which he behaved for some time with great decency and order, and submitted to accept such share of the booty with the rest as our hero allotted him.

But this subserviency agreed ill with his temper; for we should have before remembered a third heroic quality – namely ambition – which was no inconsiderable part of his composition. One day, therefore, having robbed a gentleman at Windsor of a gold watch – which on its being advertised in the newspapers, with a considerable reward, was demanded of him by Wild – he peremptorily refused to deliver it.

'How, Mr Blueskin!' says Wild, 'you will not deliver the watch?' 'No, Mr Wild,' answered he, 'I have taken it, and will keep it; or if I dispose of it, I will dispose of it myself, and keep the money for which I sell it.' 'Sure,' replied Wild, 'you have not the assurance to pretend you have any property or right in this watch?' 'I am certain,' returned Blueskin, 'whether I have any right in it or no, you can prove none.' 'I will undertake,' cries the other, 'to show I have an absolute right to it, and that by the laws of our gang, of which I am providentially at the head.' 'I know not who put you at the head of it,' cries Blueskin, 'but those who did certainly did it for their own good, that you might conduct them the better in their robberies, inform them of the richest booties, prevent surprises, pack juries, bribe evidence, and so contribute to their benefit and safety; and not to convert all their labour and hazard to your own benefit and advantage.' 'You are greatly mistaken, sir,' answered Wild, 'you are talking of a legal society, where the chief magistrate is always chosen for the public good – which, as we see in all the legal societies of the world, he constantly consults, daily contributing, by his superior skill, to their prosperity, and not sacrificing their good to his own wealth, or pleasure, or humour – but in an illegal society or gang, as this of ours, it is otherwise, for who would be at the head of a gang, unless for his own interest? And without a head, you know, you cannot subsist. Nothing but a head, and obedience to that head, can preserve a gang a moment from destruction. It is absolutely better for you to content yourselves with a moderate reward, and enjoy that in safety at the disposal of your chief, than to engross the whole with the hazard to which you will be liable without his protection. And surely there is none in the whole gang who has less reason to complain than you. You have tasted of my favours: witness that piece of ribbon you wear in your hat, with which I dubbed you Captain. Therefore pray, Captain, deliver the watch.' 'Damn your cajoling,' says Blueskin, 'do you think I value myself on this bit of ribbon, which I could have bought myself for sixpence, and have worn without your leave? Do you imagine I think myself a Captain because you, whom I know not empowered to make one, call me so? The name of Captain is but a shadow. The men and the salary are the substance; and I am not to be bubbled with a shadow. I will be called Captain no longer, and he who flatters me by that name I shall think affronts me, and I will knock him down, I assure you.' 'Did ever man talk so unreasonably?' cries Wild. 'Are you not respected as a captain by the whole gang since my dubbing you so? But it is the shadow only, it seems; and you will knock a man down for affronting you who calls you Captain! Might not a man as reasonably tell a minister of state, sir, you have given me the shadow only? The ribbon or the bauble that you gave me implies that I have either signalised myself, by some great action, for the benefit and glory of my country, or at least that I am descended from those who have done so. I know myself to be a scoundrel, and so have been those few ancestors I can remember, or have ever heard of. Therefore, I am resolved to knock the first man down who calls me sir or right honourable. But all great and wise men think themselves sufficiently repaid by what procures them honour and precedence in the gang, without enquiring into substance; nay, if a title or a feather be equal to this purpose, they are substance – and not mere shadows. But I have not time to argue with you at present, so give me the watch without any more deliberation.' 'I am no more a friend to deliberation than yourself,' answered Blueskin, 'and so I tell you, once for all, by God – I never will give you the watch, no, nor will I ever hereafter surrender any part of my booty. I won it, and I will wear it. Take your pistols yourself, and go out on the highway, and don't lazily think to fatten yourself with the dangers and pains of other people.' At which words he departed in a fierce mood, and repaired to the tavern used by the gang, where he had appointed to meet some of his acquaintance, whom he informed of what had passed between him and Wild, and advised them all to follow his example; which they all readily agreed to, and Mr Wild's damnation was the universal toast. In drinking bumpers to which, they had finished a large bowl of punch, when a constable, with a numerous attendance, and Wild at their head, entered the room and seized on Blueskin, whom his companions, when they saw our hero, did not dare attempt to rescue. The watch was found upon him, which, together with Wild's information, was more than sufficient to commit him to Newgate.

In the evening Wild and the rest of those who had been drinking with Blueskin met at the tavern, where nothing was to be seen but the profoundest submission to their leader. They vilified and abused Blueskin, as much as they had before abused our hero, and now repeated the same toast, only changing the name of Wild into that of

Blueskin – all agreeing with Wild that the watch found in his pocket, and which must be a fatal evidence against him, was a just judgement on his disobedience and revolt.

Thus did this great man by a resolute and timely example (for he went directly to the justice when Blueskin left him) quell one of the most dangerous conspiracies which could possibly arise in a gang, and which, had it been permitted one day's growth, would inevitably have ended in his destruction – so much does it behove all great men to be eternally on their guard, and expeditious in the execution of their purposes – while none but the weak and honest can indulge themselves in remissness or repose.

The Achates, Fireblood, had been present at both these meetings; but though he had a little too hastily concurred in cursing his friend, and in vowing his perdition, yet now he saw all that scheme dissolved he returned to his integrity – of which he gave an incontestable proof, by informing Wild of the measures which had been concerted against him, in which he said he had pretended to acquiesce in order the better to betray them. But this, as he afterwards confessed on his deathbed at Tyburn, was only a copy of his countenance; for that he was, at that time, as sincere and hearty in his opposition to Wild as any of his companions.

Our hero received Fireblood's information with a very placid countenance. He said, as the gang had seen their errors, and repented, nothing was more noble than forgiveness. But, though he was pleased modestly to ascribe this to his lenity, it really arose from much more noble and political principles. He considered that it would be dangerous to attempt the punishment of so many; besides, he flattered himself that fear would keep them in order, and indeed Fireblood had told him nothing more than he knew before, viz. that they were all complete prigs, whom he was to govern by their fears, and in whom he was to place no more confidence than was necessary, and to watch them with the utmost caution and circumspection. For a rogue – he wisely said – like gunpowder, must be used with caution; since both are altogether as liable to blow up the party himself who uses them as to execute his mischievous purpose against some other person or animal.

We will now repair to Newgate, it being the place where most of the great men of this history are hastening as fast as possible; and to confess the truth, it is a castle very far from being an improper or misbecoming habitation for any great man whatever. And as this scene will continue during the residue of our history, we shall open it with a new book, and shall therefore take this opportunity of closing our third.

BOOK IV

CHAPTER I

*Sentiment of the ordinary's, worthy to be written in letters of gold;
a very extraordinary instance of folly in Friendly, and a dreadful
accident which befell our hero*

Heartfree had not been long in Newgate before his frequent conversation with his children, and other instances of a good heart, which betrayed themselves in his actions and conversation, created an opinion in all about him that he was one of the silliest fellows in the universe. The ordinary himself, a very sagacious as well as very worthy person, declared that he was a cursed rogue, but no conjuror.

What indeed might induce the former, i.e. the roguish part of this opinion in the ordinary, was a wicked sentiment which Heartfree one day disclosed in conversation – and which we, who are truly orthodox, will not pretend to justify – that he believed a sincere Turk would be saved. To this the good man, with becoming zeal and indignation, answered, 'I know not what may become of a sincere Turk – but if this be your persuasion, I pronounce it impossible you should be saved. No, sir; so far from a sincere Turk's being within the pale of salvation, neither will any sincere Presbyterian, Anabaptist, nor Quaker whatever, be saved.'

But neither did the one nor the other part of this character prevail on Friendly to abandon his old master. He spent his whole time with him, except only those hours when he was absent for his sake, in procuring evidence for him against his trial, which was now shortly to come on. Indeed this young man was the only comfort, besides a clear conscience and the hopes beyond the grave, which this poor wretch had; for the sight of his children was like one of those alluring pleasures which men in some diseases indulge themselves often fatally in, which at once flatter and heighten their malady.

Friendly being one day present while Heartfree was, with tears in his eyes, embracing his eldest daughter, and lamenting the hard fate to which he feared he should be obliged to leave her, spoke to him thus:

'I have long observed with admiration the magnanimity with which you go through your own misfortunes, and the steady countenance with which you look on death. I have observed that all your agonies arise from the thoughts of parting with your children, and of leaving them in a distressed condition; now, though I hope all your fears will prove ill grounded, yet, that I may relieve you as much as possible from them, be assured that as nothing can give me more real misery than to observe so tender and loving a concern in a master – to whose goodness I owe so many obligations, and whom I so sincerely love – so nothing can afford me equal pleasure with my contributing to lessen or to remove it. Be convinced, therefore, if you can place any confidence in my promise, that I will employ my little fortune, which you know to be not entirely inconsiderable, in the support of this your little family. Should any misfortune, which I pray Heaven avert, happen to you before you have better provided for these little ones, I will be myself their father, nor shall either of them ever know distress if it be any way in my power to prevent it. Your younger daughter I will provide for, and as for my little prattler, your elder, as I never yet thought of any woman for a wife, I will receive her as such at your hands – nor will I ever relinquish her for another.'

Heartfree flew to his friend, and embraced him with raptures of acknowledgment. He vowed to him that he had eased every anxious thought of his mind but one – and that he must carry with him out of the world.

'O Friendly!' cried he, 'it is my concern for that best of women, whom I hate myself for having ever censured in my opinion. O Friendly! You did know her goodness; yet sure, her perfect character none but myself was ever acquainted with. She had every perfection, both of mind and body, which Heaven has indulged to her whole sex, and possessed all in a higher excellence than nature ever indulged to another in any single virtue. Can I bear the loss of such a woman? Can I bear the apprehensions of what mischiefs that villain may have done to her, of which death is perhaps the lightest?'

Friendly gently interrupted him as soon as he saw any opportunity, endeavouring to comfort him on this head likewise, by magnifying every circumstance which could possibly afford any hopes of his seeing her again.

By this kind of behaviour, in which the young man exemplified so uncommon a height of friendship, he had soon obtained in the castle the character of as odd and silly a fellow as his master. Indeed they were both the byword, laughing-stock and contempt of the whole place.

The sessions now came on at the Old Bailey. The grand jury at Hick's Hall[42] had found the bill of indictment against Heartfree, and on the second day of the session he was brought to his trial where notwithstanding the utmost efforts of Friendly and the honest old female servant – the circumstances of the fact corroborating the evidence of Fireblood, as well as that of Wild, who counterfeited the most artful reluctance at appearing against his old friend Heartfree – the jury found the prisoner guilty.

Wild had now accomplished his scheme; for as to what remained, it was certainly unavoidable, seeing Heartfree was entirely void of interest with the great and was besides convicted on a statute the infringers of which could hope no pardon.

The catastrophe to which our hero had reduced this wretch was so wonderful an effort of greatness that it probably made Fortune envious of her own darling; but whether it was from this envy, or only from that known inconstancy and weakness so often and judiciously remarked in that lady's temper – who frequently lifts men to the summit of human greatness, only

ut lapsu graviore ruant[43] –

certain it is she now began to meditate mischief against Wild, who seems to have come to that period at which all heroes have arrived, and which she was resolved they never should transcend. In short, there seems to be a certain measure of mischief and iniquity which every great man is to fill up, and then Fortune looks on him of no more use than a silkworm whose bottom is spun, and deserts him. Mr Blueskin was convicted the same day of robbery, by our hero, an unkindness which, though he had drawn on himself, and necessitated him to, he took greatly amiss. As Wild, therefore, was standing near him, with that disregard and indifference which great men are too carelessly inclined to have for those whom they have ruined, Blueskin, privily drawing a knife, thrust the same into the body of our hero with such violence that all who saw it concluded he had done his business. And, indeed, had not Fortune, not so much out of love to our hero as from a fixed resolution to accomplish a certain purpose – of which we have formerly given a hint – carefully placed his guts out of the way, he must have fallen a sacrifice to the wrath of his enemy – which, as he afterwards said, he did not deserve. For, had he been contented to have robbed and only submitted to give him the booty, he might have still continued safe and unimpeached in the gang; but so it was that the knife, missing noble parts (the noblest of many), the guts, perforated only the hollow of his belly, and caused no other harm than an immoderate effusion of blood – of which, though it at present weakened him, he soon after recovered.

This accident, however, was in the end attended with worse consequences, for as very few people (those greatest of all men, absolute princes excepted) attempt to cut the thread of human life, like the fatal sisters, merely out of wantonness and for their diversion, but rather by so doing propose to themselves the acquisition of some future good, or the avenging some past evil; and as the former of these motives did not appear probable, it put inquisitive persons on examining into the latter. Now, as the vast schemes of Wild, when they were discovered, however great in their nature, seemed to some persons, like the projects of most other such persons, rather to be calculated for the glory of the great man himself than to redound to the general good of society, designs began to be laid by several of those who thought it principally their duty to put a stop to the future progress of our hero; and a learned judge particularly, a great enemy to this kind of greatness, procured a clause in an Act of Parliament as a trap for Wild, which he soon after fell into. By this law it was made capital in a prig to steal with the hands of other people. A law so plainly calculated for the destruction of all priggish greatness that it was indeed impossible for our hero to avoid it.

CHAPTER II

A short hint concerning popular ingratitude. Mr Wild's arrival
in the castle, with other occurrences to be found in no other history

If we had any leisure we would here digress a little on that ingratitude which so many writers have observed to spring up in the people in all free governments towards their great men – who while they have been consulting the good of the public, by raising their own greatness, in which the whole body (as the kingdom of France thinks itself in the glory of their grand monarch) was so deeply concerned, have been sometimes sacrificed by those very people for whose glory the said great men were so industriously at work. And this from a foolish zeal for a certain ridiculous imaginary thing called liberty, to which great men are observed to have a great animosity.

This law had been promulgated a very little time when Mr Wild, having received from some dutiful members of the gang a valuable piece of goods, did, for a consideration somewhat short of its original price, reconvey it to the right owner; for which fact, being ungratefully informed against by the said owner, he was surprised in his own house, and being overpowered by numbers, was hurried before a magistrate, and by him committed to that castle, which, suitable as it is to greatness, we do not choose to name too often in our history, and where many great men at this time happened to be assembled.

The governor, or as the law more honourably calls him, keeper of this castle, was Mr Wild's old friend and acquaintance. This made the latter greatly satisfied with the place of his confinement, as he promised himself not only a kind reception and handsome accommodation there, but even to obtain his liberty from him if he thought it necessary to desire it – but, alas! he was deceived; his old friend knew him no longer, and refused to see him, and the lieutenant-governor insisted on as high garnish for fetters, and as exorbitant a price for lodging, as if he had had a fine gentleman in custody for murder, or any other genteel crime.

To confess a melancholy truth, it is a circumstance much to be lamented that there is no absolute dependence on the friendship of great men – an observation which has been frequently made by those who have lived in courts, or in Newgate, or in any other place set apart for the habitation of such persons.

The second day of his confinement he was greatly surprised at receiving a visit from his wife – and more so when, instead of a countenance ready to insult him, the only motive to which he could ascribe her presence, he saw the tears trickling down her lovely cheeks. He embraced her with the utmost marks of affection, and declared he could hardly regret his confinement, since it had produced such an instance of the happiness he enjoyed in her, whose fidelity to him on this occasion would, he believed, make him the envy of most husbands, even in Newgate. He then begged her to dry her eyes, and be comforted; for that matters might go better with him than she expected. 'No, no,' says she, 'I am certain you would be found guilty. Death. I knew what it would always come to. I told you it was impossible to carry on such a trade long; but you would not be advised, and now you see the consequence, now you repent when it is too late. All the comfort I shall have when you are nubbed[a] is that I gave you a good advice. If you had always gone out by yourself, as I would have had you, you might have robbed on to the end of the chapter; but you was wiser than all the world, or rather lazier, and see what your laziness is come to – to the cheat[b], for thither you will go now, that's infallible. And a just judgement on you for following your headstrong will; I am the only person to be pitied. Poor I, who shall be scandalised for your fault. "There goes she whose husband was hanged," methinks I hear them crying so already.' At which words she burst into tears. He could not then forbear chiding her for this unnecessary concern on his account, and begged her not to trouble him any more. She answered with some spirit, 'On your account, and be damned to you! No, if the old cull of a justice had not sent me hither, I believe it would have been long enough before I should have come hither to see after you; damn me, I am committed for the filinglay[c], man, and we shall be both nubbed together. I' faith, my dear, it almost makes me amends for being nubbed myself, to have the pleasure of seeing thee nubbed too.' 'Indeed, my

a. The cant word for hanging.
b. The gallows.
c. Picking pockets.

dear,' answered Wild, 'it is what I have long wished for thee; but I do not desire to bear thee company, and I have still hopes to have the pleasure of seeing you go without me; at least I will have the pleasure to be rid of you now.' And so saying, he seized her by the waist, and with strong arm flung her out of the room; but not before she had with her nails left a bloody memorial on his cheek. And thus this fond couple parted.

Wild had scarce recovered himself from the uneasiness into which this unwelcome visit, proceeding from the disagreeable fondness of his wife, had thrown him, than the faithful Achates appeared. The presence of this youth was indeed a cordial to his spirits. He received him with open arms, and expressed the utmost satisfaction in the fidelity of his friendship, which so far exceeded the fashion of the times, and said many things which we have forgotten on the occasion; but we remember they all tended to the praise of Fireblood, whose modesty, at length, put a stop to the torrent of compliments, by asserting he had done no more than his duty, and that he should have detested himself could he have forsaken his friend in his adversity. And after many protestations that he came the moment he heard of his misfortune, he asked him if he could be of any service. Wild answered – since he had so kindly proposed that question – he must say he should be obliged to him if he could lend him a few guineas – for that he was very seedy. Fireblood replied that he was greatly unhappy in not having it then in his power, adding many hearty oaths that he had not a farthing of money in his pocket – which was indeed strictly true; for he had only a banknote, which he had that evening purloined from a gentleman in the playhouse passage. He then asked for his wife, to whom, to speak truly, the visit was intended, her confinement being the misfortune of which he had just heard; for as for that of Mr Wild himself, he had known it from the first minute, without ever intending to trouble him with his company. Being informed therefore of the visit which had lately happened, he reproved Wild for his cruel treatment of that good creature; then taking as sudden a leave as he civilly could of the gentleman, he hastened to comfort his lady, who received him with great kindness.

CHAPTER III

Curious anecdotes relating to the history of Newgate

There resided in the castle at the same time with Mr Wild one Roger Johnson, a very great man, who had long been at the head of all the prigs in Newgate, and had raised contributions on them. He examined into the nature of their defence, procured and instructed their evidence, and made himself, at least in their opinion, so necessary to them that the whole fate of Newgate seemed entirely to depend upon him.

Wild had not been long in confinement before he began to oppose this man. He represented him to the prigs as a fellow who under the plausible pretence of assisting their causes was in reality undermining the liberties of Newgate. He at first threw out certain sly hints and insinuations, but having by degrees formed a party against Roger, he one day assembled them together, and spoke to them in the following florid manner:

'Friends and fellow-citizens,

'The cause which I am to mention to you this day is of such mighty importance that when I consider my own small abilities, I tremble with an apprehension lest your safety may be rendered precarious by the weakness of him who has undertaken to represent to you your danger. Gentlemen, the liberty of Newgate is at stake; your privileges have been long undermined, and are now openly violated by one man; by one who has engrossed to himself the whole conduct of your trials, under colour of which he exacts what contributions on you he pleases; but are those sums appropriated to the uses for which they are raised? Your frequent convictions at the Old Bailey, those depredations of justice, must too sensibly and sorely demonstrate the contrary. What evidence does he ever produce for the prisoner, which the prisoner himself could not have provided, and often better instructed? How many noble youths have there been lost when a single alibi would have saved them! Should I be silent – nay, could your own injuries want a tongue to remonstrate, the very breath, which by his neglect has been stopped at the cheat, would cry out loudly against him. Nor is the exorbitancy of his plunders visible only in the dreadful consequences it has produced to the prigs, nor glares it only in the miseries brought on them. It blazes forth in the more desirable effects it has wrought for himself, in the rich perquisites acquired by it. Witness that silk nightgown, that robe of shame, which to his eternal dishonour, he publicly wears – that gown which I will not scruple to call the winding-sheet of the liberties of Newgate. Is there a prig who has the interest and honour of Newgate so little at heart that he can refrain from blushing when he beholds that trophy, purchased with the breath of so many prigs? Nor is this all. His waistcoat embroidered with silk, and his velvet cap, bought with the same price, are ensigns of the same disgrace. Some would think the rags which covered his nakedness when first he was committed hither well exchanged for these gaudy trappings; but in my eye no exchange can be profitable when dishonour is the condition. If, therefore, Newgate –'

Here the only copy which we could procure of this speech breaks off abruptly; however we can assure the reader, from very authentic information, that he concluded with advising the prigs to put their affairs into other hands. After which, one of his party, as had been before concerted, in a very long speech recommended him (Wild himself) to their choice.

Newgate was divided into parties on this occasion, the prigs on each side representing their chief or great man to be the only person by whom the affairs of Newgate could be managed with safety and advantage. The prigs had indeed very incompatible interests; for whereas the supporters of Johnson, who was in possession of the plunder of Newgate, were admitted to some share under their leader, so the abettors of Wild had, on his promotion, the same views of dividing some part of the spoil among themselves. It is no wonder, therefore, they were both so warm on each side. What may seem more remarkable was that the debtors, who were entirely unconcerned in the dispute, and who were the destined plunder of both parties, should interest themselves with the utmost violence, some on behalf of Wild, and others in favour of Johnson. So that all Newgate resounded with 'Wild for ever', 'Johnson for ever'. And the poor debtors re-echoed the liberties of Newgate, which, in the cant language, signifies plunder, as loudly as the thieves themselves. In short, such quarrels and animosities happened between them that they seemed rather the people of two countries long at war with each other than the inhabitants of the same castle.

Wild's party at length prevailed, and he succeeded to the place and power of Johnson, whom he presently stripped of all his finery; but when it was proposed that he should sell it and divide the money for the good of the whole, he waved that motion, saying it was not yet time – that he should find a better opportunity – that the clothes wanted cleaning – with many other pretences; and within two days, to the surprise of many, he appeared in them himself. For which he vouchsafed no other apology than that they fitted him much better than they did Johnson, and that they became him in a much more elegant manner.

This behaviour of Wild greatly incensed the debtors, particularly those by whose means he had been promoted. They grumbled extremely, and vented great indignation against Wild; when one day a very grave man, and one of much authority among them, bespake them as follows:

'Nothing sure can be more justly ridiculous than the conduct of those who should lay the lamb in the wolf's way, and then should lament his being devoured. What a wolf is in a sheep-fold, a great man is in society. Now, when one wolf is in possession of a sheep-fold, how little would it avail the simple flock to expel him and place another in his stead! Of the same benefit to us is the overthrowing one prig in favour of another. And for what other advantage was your struggle? Did you not all know that Wild and his followers were prigs, as well as Johnson and his? What then could the contention be among such but that which you have now discovered it to have been? Perhaps some would say, "Is it then our duty tamely to submit to the rapine of the prig who now plunders us for fear of an exchange?" Surely no, but I answer, "It is better to shake the plunder off than to exchange the plunderer." And by what means can we effect this but by a total change in our manners? Every prig is a slave. His own priggish desires, which enslave him, themselves betray him to the tyranny of others. To preserve, therefore, the liberty of Newgate is to change the manners of Newgate. Let us, therefore, who are confined here for debt only, separate ourselves entirely from the prigs; neither drink with them nor converse with them. Let us at the same time separate ourselves further from

138

priggism itself. Instead of being ready, on every opportunity, to pillage each other, let us be content with our honest share of the common bounty, and with the acquisition of our own industry. When we separate from the prigs, let us enter into a closer alliance with one another. Let us consider ourselves all as members of one community, to the public good of which we are to sacrifice our private views; not to give up the interest of the whole for every little pleasure or profit which shall accrue to ourselves. Liberty is consistent with no degree of honesty inferior to this, and the community where this abounds no prig will have the impudence or audaciousness to endeavour to enslave; or if he should, his own destruction would be the only consequence of his attempt. But while one man pursues his ambition, another his interest, another his safety – while one has a roguery (a priggism they here call it) to commit, and another a roguery to defend – they must naturally fly to the favour and protection of those who have power to give them what they desire, and to defend them from what they fear – nay, in this view it becomes their interest to promote this power in their patrons. Now, gentlemen, when we are no longer prigs, we shall no longer have these fears or these desires. What remains, therefore, for us but to resolve bravely to lay aside our priggism – our roguery– in plainer words, and preserve our liberty, or to give up the latter in the preservation and preference of the former?'

This speech was received with much applause; however, Wild continued as before to levy contributions among the prisoners, to apply the garnish to his own use, and to strut openly in the ornaments which he had stripped from Johnson. To speak sincerely, there was more bravado than real use or advantage in these trappings. As for the nightgown, its outside indeed made a glittering tinsel appearance, but it kept him not warm, nor could the finery of it do him much honour, since every one knew it did not properly belong to him; as to the waistcoat, it fitted him very ill, being infinitely too big for him; and the cap was so heavy that it made his head ache. Thus these clothes, which perhaps (as they presented the idea of their misery more sensibly to the people's eyes) brought him more envy, hatred, and detraction, than all his deeper impositions and more real advantages, afforded very little use or honour to the wearer – nay, could scarce serve to amuse his own vanity when this was cool enough to reflect with the least seriousness. And, should I speak in the language of a man who estimated human happiness without regard to that greatness, which we have so laboriously endeavoured to paint in this history, it is probable he never took (i.e. robbed the prisoners of) a shilling, which he himself did not pay too dear for.

CHAPTER IV

The dead-warrant arrives for Heartfree; on which occasion Wild betrays some human weakness

The dead-warrant, as it is called, now came down to Newgate for the execution of Heartfree among the rest of the prisoners. And here the reader must excuse us – who profess to draw natural, not perfect characters, and to record the truths of history, not the extravagances of romance – while we relate a weakness in Wild of which we are ourselves ashamed, and which we would willingly have concealed, could we have preserved at the same time that strict attachment to truth and impartiality, which we have professed in recording the annals of this great man. Know then, Reader, that this dead-warrant did not affect Heartfree, who was to suffer a shameful death by it, with half the concern it gave Wild, who had been the occasion of it. He had been a little struck the day before on seeing the children carried away in tears from their father. This sight brought the remembrance of some slight injuries he had done the father to his mind, which he endeavoured as much as possible to obliterate; but when one of the keepers (I should say lieutenants of the castle) repeated Heartfree's name among those of the malefactors who were to suffer within a few days, the blood forsook his countenance, and in a cold still stream moved heavily to his heart, which had scarce strength enough left to return it through his veins. In short, his body so visibly demonstrated the pangs of his mind, that to escape observation he retired to his room, where he sullenly gave vent to such bitter agonies that even the injured Heartfree, had not the apprehension of what his wife had suffered shut every avenue of compassion, would have pitied him.

When his mind was thoroughly fatigued, and worn out with the horrors which the approaching fate of the poor wretch, who lay under a sentence which he had iniquitously brought upon him had suggested, sleep promised him relief; but this promise was, alas! delusive. This certain friend to the tired body is often the severest enemy to the oppressed mind. So at least it proved to Wild, adding visionary to real horrors, and tormenting his imagination with phantoms too dreadful to be described. At length, starting from these visions, he no sooner recovered his waking senses than he cried out, 'I may yet prevent this catastrophe. It is not too late to discover the whole.' He then paused a moment; but greatness, instantly returning to his assistance, checked the base thought, as it first offered itself to his mind. He then reasoned thus coolly with himself, 'Shall I, like a child, or a woman, or one of those mean wretches whom I have always despised, be frightened by dreams and visionary phantoms to sully that honour which I have so difficultly acquired and so gloriously maintained? Shall I, to redeem the worthless life of this silly fellow, suffer my reputation to contract a stain which the blood of millions cannot wipe away? Was it only that the few, the simple part of mankind, should call me a rogue – perhaps I could submit; but to be for ever contemptible to the prigs, as a wretch who wanted spirit to execute my undertaking, can never be digested. What is the life of a single man? Have not whole armies and nations been sacrificed to the honour of one great man? Nay, to omit that first class of greatness, the conquerors of mankind, how often have numbers fallen by a fictitious plot only to satisfy the spleen, or perhaps exercise the ingenuity, of a member of that second order of greatness – the ministerial! What have I done then? Why, I have ruined a family, and brought an innocent man to the gallows. I ought rather to weep with Alexander that I have ruined no more, than to regret the little I have done.' He at length, therefore, bravely resolved to consign over Heartfree to his fate, though it cost him more struggling than may easily be believed utterly to conquer his reluctance and to banish away every degree of humanity from his mind, these little sparks of which composed one of those weaknesses which we lamented in the opening of our history.

But, in vindication of our hero, we must beg leave to observe that Nature is seldom so kind as those writers who draw characters absolutely perfect. She seldom creates any man so completely great, or completely low, but that some sparks of humanity will glimmer in the former, and some sparks of what the vulgar call evil will dart forth in the latter. Utterly to extinguish which will give some pain, and uneasiness to both; for I apprehend no mind was ever yet formed entirely free from blemish, unless peradventure that of a sanctified hypocrite, whose praises some well-fed flatterer has gratefully thought proper to sing forth.

CHAPTER V

Containing various matters

The day was now come when poor Heartfree was to suffer an ignominious death. Friendly had in the strongest manner confirmed his assurance of fulfilling his promise of becoming a father to one of his children and a husband to the other. This gave him inexpressible comfort, and he had the evening before taken his last leave of the little wretches with a tenderness which drew a tear from one of the keepers, joined to a magnanimity which would have pleased a stoic. When he was informed that the coach which Friendly had provided for him was ready, and that the rest of the prisoners were gone, he embraced that faithful friend with great passion, and begged that he would leave him here; but the other desired leave to accompany him to his end, which at last he was forced to comply with. And now he was proceeding towards the coach when he found his difficulties were not yet over; for now a friend arrived of whom he was to take a harder and more tender leave than he had yet gone through. This friend, Reader, was no other than Mrs Heartfree herself, who ran to him with a look all wild, staring, and frantic, and having reached his arms, fainted away in them without uttering a single syllable. Heartfree was, with great difficulty, able to preserve his own senses in such a surprise at such a season. And indeed our good-natured reader will be rather inclined to wish this miserable couple had, by dying in each other's arms, put a final period to their woes, than have survived to taste those bitter moments which were to be their portion, and which the unhappy wife, soon recovering from the short 'intermission of being', now began to suffer. When she became first mistress of her voice she burst forth into the following accents: 'O my husband! Is this the condition in which I find you after our cruel separation? Who has done this? Cruel Heaven! What is the occasion? I know you can deserve no ill. Tell me, somebody who can speak, while I have my senses left to understand, what is the matter?' At which words several laughed, and one answered, 'The matter! Why, no great matter. The gentleman is not the first, nor won't be the last. The worst of the matter is that if we are to stay all the morning here I shall lose my dinner.' Heartfree, pausing a moment and recollecting himself, cried out, 'I will bear all with patience.' And then, addressing himself to the commanding officer, begged he might only have a few minutes by himself with his wife, whom he had not seen before since his misfortunes. The great man answered he had compassion on him, and would do more than he could answer; but he supposed he was too much a gentleman not to know that something was due for such civility. On this hint, Friendly, who was himself half dead, pulled five guineas out of his pocket, which the great man took, and said he would be so generous to give him ten minutes; on which one observed that many a gentleman had bought ten minutes with a woman dearer, and many other facetious remarks were made, unnecessary to be here related. Heartfree was now suffered to retire into a room with his wife, the commander informing him at his entrance that he must be expeditious, for that the rest of the good company would be at the tree before him, and he supposed he was a gentleman of too much breeding to make them wait.

This tender wretched couple were now retired for these few minutes, which the commander without carefully measured with his watch, and Heartfree was mustering all his resolution to part with what his soul so ardently doted on, and to conjure her to support his loss for the sake of her poor infants, and to comfort her with the promise of Friendly on their account; but all his design was frustrated. Mrs Heartfree could not support the shock, but again fainted away, and so entirely lost every symptom of life that Heartfree called vehemently for assistance. Friendly rushed first into the room, and was soon followed by many others – and, what was remarkable, one who had unmoved beheld the tender scene between these parting lovers was touched to the quick by the pale looks of the woman, and ran up and down for water, drops, etc., with the utmost hurry and confusion. The ten minutes were expired, which the commander now hinted; and seeing nothing offered for the renewal of the term (for indeed Friendly had unhappily emptied his pockets), he began to grow very importunate, and at last told Heartfree he should be ashamed not to act more like a man. Heartfree begged his pardon, and said he would make him wait no longer. Then, with the deepest sigh, cried, 'Oh, my angel!' and, embracing his wife with the utmost eagerness, kissed her pale lips with more fervency than ever bridegroom did the blushing cheeks of his bride. He then cried, 'The Almighty bless thee! And, if it be his pleasure, restore thee to life; if not, I beseech him we may presently meet again in a better world than this.' He was breaking from her when, perceiving her sense returning, he could not forbear renewing his embrace, and again pressing her lips, which now recovered life and warmth so fast that he begged one ten minutes more to tell her what her swooning had prevented her hearing. The worthy commander, being perhaps a little touched at this tender scene, took Friendly aside, and asked him what he would give if he would suffer his friend to remain half-an-hour? Friendly answered, anything – that he had no more money in his pocket, but he would certainly pay him that afternoon. 'Well, then, I'll be moderate,' said he; 'twenty guineas.' Friendly answered, 'It is a bargain.' The commander, having exacted a firm promise, cried, 'Then I don't care if they stay a whole hour together; for what signifies hiding good news? The gentleman is reprieved,' of which he had just before received notice in a whisper. It would be very impertinent to offer at a description of the joy this occasioned to the two friends, or to Mrs Heartfree, who was now again recovered. A surgeon, who was happily present, was employed to bleed them all. After which the commander, who had his promise of the money again confirmed to him, wished Heartfree joy, and shaking him very friendly by the hands, cleared the room of all the company, and left the three friends together.

CHAPTER VI

In which the foregoing happy incident is accounted for

But here, though I am convinced my good-natured reader may almost want the surgeon's assistance also, and that there is no passage in this whole story which can afford him equal delight, yet, lest our reprieve should seem to resemble that in *The Beggar's Opera*[44], I shall endeavour to show him that this incident, which is undoubtedly true, is at least as natural as delightful; for we assure him we would rather have suffered half mankind to be hanged than have saved one contrary to the strictest rules of writing and probability.

Be it known, then (a circumstance which I think highly credible), that the great Fireblood had been, a few days before, taken in the fact of a robbery, and carried before the same justice of peace who had, on his evidence, committed Heartfree to prison. This magistrate, who did indeed no small honour to the commission he bore, duly considered the weighty charge committed to him, by which he was entrusted with decisions affecting the lives, liberties, and properties of his countrymen. He therefore examined always with the utmost diligence and caution into every minute circumstance. And, as he had a good deal balanced, even when he committed Heartfree, on the excellent character given him by Friendly and the maid; and as he was much staggered on finding that, of the two persons on whose evidence alone Heartfree had been committed, and had been since convicted, one was in Newgate for a felony, and the other was now brought before him for a robbery, he thought proper to put the matter very home to Fireblood at this time. The young Achates was taken, as we have said, in the fact – so that denial he saw was in vain. He therefore honestly confessed what he knew must be proved – and desired, on the merit of the discoveries he made, to be admitted as an evidence against his accomplices. This afforded the happiest opportunity to the justice to satisfy his conscience in relation to Heartfree. He told Fireblood that, if he expected the favour he solicited, it must be on condition that he revealed the whole truth to him concerning the evidence which he had lately given against a bankrupt, and which some circumstances had induced a suspicion of; that he might depend on it the truth would be discovered by other means, and gave some oblique hints (a deceit entirely justifiable) that Wild himself had offered such a discovery. The very mention of Wild's name immediately alarmed Fireblood, who did not in the least doubt the readiness of that great man to hang any of the gang when his own interest seemed to require it. He therefore hesitated not a moment; but having obtained a promise from the justice that he should be accepted as an evidence, he discovered the whole falsehood, and declared that he had been seduced by Wild to depose as he had done.

The justice, having thus luckily and timely discovered this scene of villainy, alias greatness, lost not a moment in using his utmost endeavours to get the case of the unhappy convict represented to the sovereign, who immediately granted him that gracious reprieve which caused such happiness to the persons concerned, and which we hope we have now accounted for to the satisfaction of the reader.

The good magistrate, having obtained this reprieve for Heartfree, thought it incumbent on him to visit him in the prison, and to sound, if possible, the depth of this affair, that if he should appear as innocent as he now began to conceive him, he might use all imaginable methods to obtain his pardon and enlargement.

The next day therefore after that when the miserable scene above described had passed, he went to Newgate, where he found those three persons – namely Heartfree, his wife, and Friendly – sitting together. The justice informed the prisoner of the confession of Fireblood, with the steps which he had taken upon it. The reader will easily conceive the many outward thanks, as well as inward gratitude, which he received from all three; but those were of very little consequence to him compared with the secret satisfaction he felt in his mind from reflecting on the preservation of innocence, as he soon after very clearly perceived was the case.

When he entered the room, Mrs Heartfree was speaking with some earnestness. As he perceived, therefore, he had interrupted her, he begged she would continue her discourse, which if he prevented by his presence, he desired to depart; but Heartfree would not suffer it. He said she had been relating some adventures which perhaps might entertain him to hear, and which she the rather desired he would hear, as they might serve to illustrate the foundation on which this falsehood had been built, which had brought on her husband all his misfortunes.

The justice very gladly consented, and Mrs Heartfree, at her husband's desire, began the relation from the first renewal of Wild's acquaintance with him; but though this recapitulation was necessary for the information of our good magistrate, as it would be useless, and perhaps tedious, to the reader, we shall only repeat that part of her story to which he is only a stranger, beginning with what happened to her after Wild had been turned adrift in the boat by the captain of the French privateer.

CHAPTER VII

Mrs Heartfree relates her adventures

Mrs Heartfree proceeded thus: 'The vengeance which the French captain exacted on that villain (our hero) persuaded me that I was fallen into the hands of a man of honour and justice – nor indeed was it possible for any person to be treated with more respect and civility than I now was. But if this could not mitigate my sorrows when I reflected on the condition in which I had been betrayed to leave all that was dear to me, much less could it produce such an effect when I discovered, as I soon did, that I owed it chiefly to a passion which threatened me with great uneasiness, as it quickly appeared to be very violent – and as I was absolutely in the power of the person who possessed it, or was rather possessed by it. I must however do him the justice to say my fears carried my suspicions further than I afterwards found I had any reason to carry them. He did indeed very soon acquaint me with his passion, and used all those gentle methods which frequently succeed with our sex to prevail with me to gratify it, but never once threatened, nor had the least recourse to force. He did not even once insinuate to me that I was totally in his power, which I myself sufficiently saw, and whence I drew the most dreadful apprehensions – well knowing that, as there are some dispositions so brutal that cruelty adds a zest and savour to their pleasures, so there are others whose gentler inclinations are better gratified when they win us by softer methods to comply with their desires. Yet that even these may be often compelled by an unruly passion to have recourse at last to the means of violence, when they despair of success from persuasion, but I was happily the captive of a better man. My conqueror was one of those over whom vice has a limited jurisdiction; and though he was too easily prevailed on to sin, he was proof against any temptation to villainy.

'We had been two days almost totally becalmed, when a brisk gale rising as we were in sight in Dunkirk, we saw a vessel making full sail towards us. The captain of the privateer was so strong that he apprehended no danger but from a man-of-war, which the sailors discerned this not to be. He therefore struck his colours, and furled his sails as much as possible, in order to lie by and expect her, hoping she might be a prize.' (Here Heartfree smiling, his wife stopped and enquired the cause. He told her it was from her using the sea terms so aptly. She laughed, and answered he would wonder less at this when he heard the long time she had been on board; and then proceeded.) 'This vessel now came alongside of us, and hailed us, having perceived that on which we were aboard to be of her own country; they begged us not to put into Dunkirk, but to accompany them in their pursuit of a large English merchantman, whom we should easily overtake, and both together as easily conquer. Our captain immediately consented to this proposition, and ordered all his sail to be crowded. This was most unwelcome news to me; however, he comforted me all he could by assuring me I had nothing to fear, that he would be so far from offering the least rudeness to me himself; that he would, at the hazard of his life, protect me from it. This assurance gave me all the consolation which my present circumstances and the dreadful apprehensions I had on your dear account would admit.' (At which words the tenderest glances passed on both sides between the husband and wife.)

'We sailed near twelve hours, when we came in sight of the ship we were in pursuit of, and which we should probably have soon come up with had not a very thick mist ravished her from our eyes. This mist continued several hours, and when it cleared up we discovered our companion at a great distance from us; but what gave us (I mean the captain and his crew) the greatest uneasiness was the sight of a very large ship within a mile of us, which presently saluted us with a gun, and now appeared to be a third-rate English man-of-war. Our captain declared the impossibility of either fighting or escaping, and accordingly struck without waiting for the broadside which was preparing for us, and which perhaps would have prevented me from the happiness I now enjoy.' This occasioned Heartfree to change colour; his wife therefore passed hastily to circumstances of a more smiling complexion.

'I greatly rejoiced at this event, as I thought it would not only restore me to the safe possession of my jewels, but to what I value beyond all the treasure in the universe. My expectation, however, of both these was somewhat crossed for the present. As to the former, I was told they should be carefully preserved; but that I must prove my right to them before I could expect their restoration – which, if I mistake not, the captain did not very eagerly desire I should be able to accomplish. And as to the latter, I was acquainted that I should be put on board the first ship which they met on her way to England, but that they were proceeding to the West Indies.

'I had not been long on board the man-of-war before I discovered just reason rather to lament than rejoice at the exchange of my captivity – for such I concluded my present situation to be. I had now another lover in the captain of this Englishman, and much rougher and less gallant than the Frenchman had been. He used me with scarce common civility, as indeed he showed very little to any other person, treating his officers little better than a man of no great good-breeding would exert to his meanest servant – and that too on some very irritating provocation. As for me, he addressed me with the insolence of a basha to a Circassian slave[45]; he talked to me with the loose licence in which the most profligate libertines converse with harlots, and which women abandoned only in a moderate degree detest and abhor. He often kissed me with very rude familiarity, and one day attempted further brutality; when a gentleman on board – and who was in my situation, that is had been taken by a privateer and was retaken – rescued me from his hands, for which the captain confined him (though he was not under his command) two days in irons. When he was released (for I was not suffered to visit him in his confinement) I went to him and thanked him with the utmost acknowledgment for what he had done and suffered on my account. The gentleman behaved to me in the handsomest manner on this occasion; told me he was ashamed of the high sense I seemed to entertain of so small an obligation of an action to which his duty as a Christian and his honour as a man obliged him. From this time I lived in great familiarity with this man, whom I regarded as my protector, which he professed himself ready to be on all occasions, expressing the utmost abhorrence of the captain's brutality, especially that shown towards me, and the tenderness of a parent for the preservation of my virtue, for which I was not myself more solicitous than he appeared. He was, indeed, the only man I had hitherto met since my unhappy departure who did not endeavour by all his looks, words, and actions, to assure me he had a liking to my unfortunate person – the rest seeming desirous of sacrificing the little beauty they complimented to their desires, without the least consideration of the ruin which I earnestly represented to them they were attempting to bring on me and on my future repose.

'I now passed several days pretty free from the captain's molestation, until one fatal night.' Here, perceiving Heartfree grew pale, she comforted him by an assurance that Heaven had preserved her chastity, and again had restored her unsullied to his arms. She continued thus: 'Perhaps I give it a wrong epithet in the word fatal – but a wretched night I am sure I may call it, for no woman who came off victorious was, I believe, ever in greater danger. One night I say, having drunk his spirits high with punch, in company with the purser, who was the only man in the ship he admitted to his table, the captain sent for me into his cabin; whither, though unwilling, I was obliged to go. We were no sooner alone together than he seized me by the hand, and after affronting my ears with discourse which I am unable to repeat, he swore a great oath that his passion was to be dallied with no longer; that I must not expect to treat him in the manner to which a set of blockhead land-men submitted. "None of your coquette airs, therefore, with me, madam," said he, "for I am resolved to have you this night. No struggling nor squalling, for both will be impertinent. The first man who offers to come in here, I will have his skin flea'd off at the gangway." He then attempted to pull me violently towards his bed. I threw myself on my knees, and with tears and entreaties besought his compassion;

but this was, I found, to no purpose. I then had recourse to threats, and endeavoured to frighten him with the consequence; but neither had this, though it seemed to stagger him more than the other method, sufficient force to deliver me. At last a stratagem came into my head, of which my perceiving him reel gave me the first hint. I entreated a moment's reprieve only – when, collecting all the spirits I could muster, I put on a constrained air of gaiety, and told him, with an affected laugh, he was the roughest lover I had ever met with, and that I believed I was the first woman he had ever paid his addresses to. 'Addresses,' said he; 'damn your dresses! I want to undress you.' I then begged him to let us drink some punch together; for that I loved a can as well as himself, and never would grant the favour to any man until I had drunk a hearty glass with him. 'O!' said he, 'if that be all, you shall have punch enough to drown yourself in'. At which words he rung the bell, and ordered in a gallon of that liquor. I was in the meantime obliged to suffer his nauseous kisses, and some rudenesses which I had great difficulty to restrain within moderate bounds. When the punch came in, he took up the bowl and drank my health ostentatiously, in such a quantity that it considerably advanced my scheme. I followed him with bumpers as fast as possible, and was myself obliged to drink so much that at another time it would have staggered my own reason, but at present it did not affect me. At length, perceiving him very far gone, I watched an opportunity, and ran out of the cabin, resolving to seek protection of the sea if I could find no other; but Heaven was now graciously pleased to relieve me – for in his attempt to pursue me he reeled backwards, and falling down the cabin stairs, he dislocated his shoulder and so bruised himself that I was not only preserved that night from any danger of my intended ravisher, but the accident threw him into a fever which endangered his life, and whether he ever recovered or no I am not certain; for during his delirious fits the eldest lieutenant commanded the ship. This was a virtuous and a brave fellow, who had been twenty-five years in that post without being able to obtain a ship, and had seen several boys, the bastards of noblemen, put over his head. One day while the ship remained under his command an English vessel bound to Cork passed by; myself and my friend, who had formerly lain two days in irons on my account, went on board this ship with the leave of the good lieutenant, who made us such presents as he was able of provisions, and congratulating me on my delivery from a danger to which none of the ship's crew had been strangers, he kindly wished us both a safe voyage.'

CHAPTER VIII

In which Mrs Heartfree continues the relation of her adventures

The first evening after we were aboard this vessel, which was a brigantine, we being then at no very great distance from the Madeiras, the most violent storm arose from the north-west, in which we presently lost both our masts; and indeed death now presented itself as inevitable to us. I need not tell my Tommy what were then my thoughts. Our danger was so great that the captain of the ship, a professed atheist, betook himself to prayers, and the whole crew, abandoning themselves for lost, fell with the utmost eagerness to the emptying a cask of brandy, not one drop of which they swore should be polluted with salt water. I observed here my old friend displayed less courage than I expected from him. He seemed entirely swallowed up in despair. But Heaven be praised! We were all at last preserved. The storm, after above eleven hours' continuance, began to abate and by degrees entirely ceased, but left us still rolling at the mercy of the waves, which carried us at their own pleasure to the south-east a vast number of leagues. Our crew were all dead drunk with the brandy which they had taken such care to preserve from the sea; but indeed, had they been awake, their labour would have been of very little service, as we had lost all our rigging, our brigantine being reduced to a naked hulk only. In this condition we floated above thirty hours, until in the midst of a very dark night we spied a light, which seeming to approach us, grew so large that our sailors concluded it to be the lantern of a man-of-war; but when we were cheering ourselves with the hopes of our deliverance from this wretched situation, on a sudden, to our great concern, the light entirely disappeared, and left us in despair, increased by the remembrance of those pleasing imaginations with which we had entertained our minds during its appearance. The rest of the night we passed in melancholy conjectures on the light which had deserted us, which the major part of the sailors concluded to be a meteor. In this distress we had one comfort, which was a plentiful store of provisions; this so supported the spirits of the sailors that they declared had they but a sufficient quantity of brandy they cared not whether they saw land for a month to come; but indeed we were much nearer it than we imagined, as we perceived at break of day. One of the most knowing of the crew declared we were near the continent of Africa; but when we were within three leagues of it a second violent storm arose from the north, so that we again gave over all hopes of safety. This storm was not quite so outrageous as the former, but of much longer continuance, for it lasted near three days, and drove us an immense number of leagues to the south. We were within a league of the shore, expecting every moment our ship to be dashed in pieces, when the tempest ceased all on a sudden. But the waves still continued to roll like mountains, and before the sea recovered its calm motion, our ship was thrown so near the land that the captain ordered out his boat, declaring he had scarce any hopes of saving her; and indeed we had not quitted her many minutes before we saw the justice of his apprehensions, for she struck against a rock and immediately sunk. The behaviour of the sailors on this occasion very much affected me; they beheld their ship perish with the tenderness of a lover or a parent; they spoke of her as the fondest husband would of his wife; and many of them, who seemed to have no tears in their composition, shed them plentifully at her sinking. The captain himself cried out, "Go thy way, charming Molly, the sea never devoured a lovelier morsel. If I have fifty vessels I shall never love another like thee. Poor slut! I shall remember thee to my dying day." Well, the boat now conveyed us all safe to shore, where we landed with very little difficulty. It was now about noon, and the rays of the sun, which descended almost perpendicular on our heads, were extremely hot and troublesome. However, we travelled through this extreme heat about five miles over a plain. This brought us to a vast wood, which extended itself as far as we could see, both to the right and left, and seemed to me to put an entire end to our progress. Here we decreed to rest and dine on the provision which we had brought from the ship, of which we had sufficient for very few meals – our boat being so overloaded with people that we had very little room for luggage of any kind. Our repast was salt pork broiled, which the keenness of hunger made so delicious to my companions that they fed very heartily upon it. As for myself, the fatigue of my body and the vexation of my mind had so thoroughly weakened me that I was almost entirely deprived of appetite; and the utmost dexterity of the most accomplished French cook would have been ineffectual had he endeavoured to tempt me with delicacies. I thought myself very little a gainer by my late escape from the tempest, by which I seemed only to have exchanged the element in which I was presently to die. When our company had sufficiently, and indeed very plentifully feasted themselves, they resolved to enter the wood and endeavour to pass it, in expectation of finding some inhabitants, or at least some provision. We proceeded therefore in the following order: one man in the front with a hatchet, to clear our way, and two others followed him with guns, to protect the rest from wild beasts; then walked the rest of our company, and last of all the captain himself, being armed likewise with a gun, to defend us from any attack behind – in the rear, I think you call it. And thus our whole company, being fourteen in number, travelled on until night overtook us, without seeing anything unless a few birds and some very insignificant animals. We rested all night under the covert of some trees, and indeed we very little wanted shelter at that season, the heat in the day being the only inclemency we had to combat with in this climate. I cannot help telling you my old friend lay still nearest me on the ground, and declared he would be my protector should any of the sailors offer rudeness. But I can acquit them of any such attempt; nor was I ever affronted by anyone more than with a coarse expression, proceeding rather from the roughness and ignorance of their education than from any abandoned principle, or want of humanity.

'We had now proceeded very little way on our next day's march when one of the sailors, having skipped nimbly up a hill, with the assistance of a speaking trumpet informed us that he saw a town a very little way off. This news so comforted me, and gave me such strength, as well as spirits, that with the help of my old friend and another, who suffered me to lean on them, I with much difficulty attained the summit.

But was so absolutely overcome in climbing it that I had no longer sufficient strength to support my tottering limbs, and was obliged to lay myself again on the ground. Nor could they prevail on me to undertake descending through a very thick wood into a plain, at the end of which indeed appeared some houses, or rather huts, but at a much greater distance than the sailor assured us; the little way, as he had called it, seeming to me full twenty miles, nor was it, I believe, much less.'

CHAPTER IX

Containing incidents very surprising

'The captain declared he would, without delay, proceed to the town before him; in which resolution he was seconded by all the crew. But when I could not be persuaded, nor was I able to travel any further before I had rested myself, my old friend protested he would not leave me, but would stay behind as my guard; and when I had refreshed myself with a little repose, he would attend me to the town, which the captain promised he would not leave before he had seen us.

'They were no sooner departed than (having first thanked my protector for his care of me) I resigned myself to sleep, which immediately closed my eyelids, and would probably have detained me very long in his gentle dominions, had I not been awaked with a squeeze by the hand by my guard, which I at first thought intended to alarm me with the danger of some wild beast; but I soon perceived it arose from a softer motive, and that a gentle swain was the only wild beast I had to apprehend. He began now to disclose his passion in the strongest manner imaginable, indeed with a warmth rather beyond that of both my former lovers, but as yet without any attempt of absolute force. On my side remonstrances were made in more bitter exclamations and revilings than I had used to any, that villain Wild excepted. I told him he was the basest and most treacherous wretch alive; that his having cloaked his iniquitous designs under the appearance of virtue and friendship added an ineffable degree of horror to them; that I detested him of all mankind the most, and could I be brought to yield to prostitution, he should be the last to enjoy the ruins of my honour. He suffered himself not to be provoked by this language, but only changed his manner of solicitation from flattery to bribery. He unripped the lining of his waistcoat, and pulled forth several jewels – these, he said, he had preserved from infinite danger to the happiest purpose, if I could be won by them. I rejected them often with the utmost indignation, until at last – casting my eye, rather by accident than design, on a diamond necklace – a thought, like lightning, shot through my mind, and in an instant I remembered that this was the very necklace you had sold the cursed Count, the cause of all our misfortunes. The confusion of ideas into which this surprise hurried me prevented my reflecting on the villain who then stood before me; but the first recollection presently told me it could be no other than the Count himself, the wicked tool of Wild's barbarity. Good heavens! What was then my condition! How shall I describe the tumult of passions which then laboured in my breast? However, as I was happily unknown to him, the least suspicion on his side was altogether impossible. He imputed, therefore, the eagerness with which I gazed on the jewels to a very wrong cause, and endeavoured to put as much additional softness into his countenance as he was able. My fears were a little quieted, and I was resolved to be very liberal of promises, and hoped so thoroughly to persuade him of my venality that he might, without any doubt, be drawn in to wait the captain and crew's return, who would, I was very certain, not only preserve me from his violence, but secure the restoration of what you had been so cruelly robbed of. But, alas! I was mistaken.' Mrs Heartfree, again perceiving symptoms of the utmost disquietude in her husband's countenance, cried out, 'My dear, don't you apprehend any harm. But, to deliver you as soon as possible from your anxiety – when he perceived I declined the warmth of his addresses, he begged me to consider – he changed at once his voice and features, and in a very different tone from what he had hitherto affected, he swore I should not deceive him as I had the captain; that fortune had kindly thrown an opportunity in his way which he was resolved not foolishly to lose; and concluded with a violent oath that he was determined to enjoy me that moment, and therefore I knew the consequence of resistance. He then caught me in his arms, and began such rude attempts that I screamed out with all the force I could, though I had so little hopes of being rescued; when there suddenly rushed forth from a thicket a creature which at his first appearance, and in the hurry of spirits I then was, I did not take for a man – but indeed, had he been the fiercest of wild beasts, I should have rejoiced at his devouring us both. I scarce perceived he had a musket in his hand before he struck my ravisher such a blow with it that he felled him at my feet. He then advanced with a gentle air towards me, and told me in French he was extremely glad he had been luckily present to my assistance. He was naked, except his middle and his feet, if I can call a body so which was covered with hair almost equal to any beast whatever. Indeed, his appearance was so horrid in my eyes that the friendship he had shown me, as well as his courteous behaviour, could not entirely remove the dread I had conceived from his figure. I believe he saw this very visibly – for he begged me not to be frightened, since whatever accident had brought me thither, I should have reason to thank heaven for meeting him, at whose hands I might assure myself of the utmost civility and protection. In the midst of all this consternation, I had spirits enough to take up the casket of jewels, which the villain, in falling, had dropped out of his hands, and conveyed it into my pocket. My deliverer, telling me that I seemed extremely weak and faint, desired me to refresh myself at his little hut – which, he said, was hard by. If his demeanour had been less kind and obliging, my desperate situation must have lent me confidence; for sure the alternative could not be doubtful, whether I should rather trust this man – who, notwithstanding his savage outside, expressed so much devotion to serve me, which at least I was not certain of the falsehood of – or should abide with one whom I so perfectly well knew to be an accomplished villain. I therefore committed myself to his guidance, though with tears in my eyes, and begged him to have compassion on my innocence, which was absolutely in his power. He said, the treatment he had been witness of, which he supposed was from one who had broken his trust towards me, sufficiently justified my suspicion; but begged me to dry my eyes, and he would soon convince me that I was with a man of different sentiments. The kind accents, which accompanied these words, gave me some comfort, which was assisted by the repossession of our jewels by an accident so strongly savouring of the disposition of Providence in my favour.

'We left the villain weltering in his blood, though beginning to recover a little motion, and walked together to his hut, or rather cave, for it was underground, on the side of a hill. The situation was very pleasant, and from its mouth we overlooked a large plain and the town I had before seen. As soon as I entered it, he desired me to sit down on a bench of earth, which served him for chairs, and then laid before me some fruits, the wild product of that country, one or two of which had an excellent flavour. He likewise produced some baked flesh, a little resembling that of venison. He then brought forth a bottle of brandy, which he said had remained with him ever since his settling there, now above thirty years, during all which time he had never opened it, his only liquor being water. That he had reserved this bottle as a cordial in sickness – but, he thanked heaven, he had never yet had occasion for it. He then acquainted me that he was a hermit, that he had been formerly cast away on that coast, with his wife, whom he dearly loved, but could not preserve from perishing; on which account he had resolved never to return to France, which was his native country, but to devote himself to prayer and a holy life, placing all his hopes in the blessed expectation of meeting that dear woman again in heaven, where he was convinced she was now a saint and an interceder for him. He said he had exchanged a watch with the king of that country – whom he described to be a very just and good man – for a gun, some powder, shot, and ball, with which he sometimes provided himself food, but more generally used it in defending himself against wild beasts; so that his diet was chiefly of the vegetable kind. He told me many more circumstances, which I may relate to you hereafter. But, to be as concise as possible at present, he at length greatly comforted me by promising to conduct me to a seaport, where I might have an opportunity to meet with some vessels trafficking for slaves, and whence I might once more commit myself to that element which, though I had already suffered so much on it, I must again trust to put me in possession of all I loved.

'The character he gave me of the inhabitants of the town we saw below us, and of their king, made me desirous of being conducted thither; especially as I very much wished to see the captain and sailors, who had behaved very kindly to me, and with whom, notwithstanding all the civil behaviour of the hermit, I was rather easier in my mind than alone with this single man; but he dissuaded me greatly from attempting such a walk until I had recruited my spirits with rest, desiring me to repose myself on his couch or bank, saying that he himself would retire without the cave, where he would remain as my guard. I accepted this kind proposal, but it was long before I could procure any slumber. However, at length, weariness prevailed over my fears, and I enjoyed several hours' sleep. When I awaked I found my faithful sentinel on his post and ready at my summons. This behaviour infused some confidence into me, and I now repeated my request that he would go with me to the town below; but he answered it would be better advised to take some repast before I undertook the journey, which I should find much longer than it appeared. I consented, and he set forth a greater variety of fruits than before, of which I ate very plentifully. My collation being ended, I renewed the mention of my walk, but he still persisted in dissuading me, telling me that I was not yet strong enough; that I could repose myself nowhere with greater safety than in his cave; and that for his part he could have no greater happiness than that of attending me – adding, with a sigh, it was a happiness he should envy any other more than all the gifts of fortune. You may imagine I began now to entertain suspicions; but he presently removed all doubt by throwing himself at my feet and expressing the warmest passion for me. I should have now sunk with despair had he not accompanied these professions with the most vehement protestations that he would never offer me any other force but that of entreaty, and that he would rather die the most cruel death by my coldness than gain the highest bliss by becoming the occasion of a tear of sorrow to these bright eyes – which he said were stars, under whose benign influence alone he could enjoy, or indeed suffer life.' She was repeating many more compliments he made her, when a horrid uproar, which alarmed the whole gate, put a stop to her narration at present. It is impossible for me to give the reader a better idea of the noise which now arose than by desiring him to imagine I had the hundred tongues the poet once wished for, and was vociferating from them all at once, by hollowing, scolding, crying, swearing, bellowing – and, in short, by every different articulation which is within the scope of the human organ.

CHAPTER X

A horrible uproar in the gate

But however great an idea the reader may hence conceive of this uproar, he will think the occasion more than adequate to it when he is informed that our hero (I blush to name it) had discovered an injury done to his honour – and that in the tenderest point. In a word, Reader (for you must know it, though it give thee the greatest horror imaginable), he had caught Fireblood in the arms of his lovely Laetitia.

As the generous bull who, having long depastured among a number of cows, and thence contracted an opinion that these cows are all his own property, if he beholds another bull bestride a cow within his walks he roars aloud, and threatens instant vengeance with his horns until the whole parish are alarmed with his bellowing – not with less noise nor less dreadful menaces did the fury of Wild burst forth and terrify the whole gate. Long time did rage render his voice inarticulate to the hearer – as when, at a visiting day, fifteen or sixteen or perhaps twice as many females, of delicate but shrill pipes, ejaculate all at once on different subjects, all is sound only, the harmony entirely melodious indeed, but conveys no idea to our ears – but at length, when reason began to get the better of his passion, which latter, being deserted by his breath, began a little to retreat, the following accents leapt over the hedge of his teeth – or rather the ditch of his gums, whence those hedge-stakes had long since been displaced in battle with an Amazon of Drury.

'...[a]Man of honour! Does this become a friend? Could I have expected such a breach of all the laws of honour from thee, whom I had taught to walk in its paths? Had you chosen any other way to injure my confidence I could have forgiven it; but this is a stab in the tenderest part, a wound never to be healed, an injury never to be repaired; for it is not only the loss of an agreeable companion – of the affection of a wife dearer to my soul than life itself – it is not this loss alone I lament. This loss is accompanied with disgrace and with dishonour. The blood of the Wilds, which has run with such uninterrupted purity through

a. The beginning of this speech is lost.

so many generations, this blood is fouled, is contaminated; hence flow my tears, hence arises my grief. This is the injury never to be redressed, nor even to be with honour forgiven.' 'M–in a bandbox!' answered Fireblood, 'here is a noise about your honour! If the mischief done to your blood be all you complain of, I am sure you complain of nothing; for my blood is as good as yours.' 'You have no conception,' replied Wild, 'of the tenderness of honour – you know not how nice and delicate it is in both sexes – so delicate that the least breath of air which rudely blows on it destroys it.' 'I will prove from your own words,' says Fireblood, 'I have not wronged your honour. Have you not often told me that the honour of a man consisted in receiving no affront from his own sex, and that of woman in receiving no kindness from ours? Now, sir, if I have given you no affront, how have I injured your honour?' 'But does not everything,' cried Wild, 'of the wife belong to the husband? A married man, therefore, has his wife's honour as well as his own, and by injuring hers you injure his. How cruelly you have hurt me in this tender part I need not repeat; the whole gate knows it, and the world shall. I will apply to Doctors' Commons[46] for my redress against her; I will shake off as much of my dishonour as I can by parting with her; and as for you, expect to hear of me in Westminster Hall – the modern method of repairing these breaches and of resenting this affront.' 'Damn your eyes!' cries Fireblood; 'I fear you not, nor do I believe a word you say.' 'Nay, if you affront me personally,' says Wild, 'another sort of resentment is prescribed.' At which word, advancing to Fireblood, he presented him with a box on the ear, which the youth immediately returned; and now our hero and his friend fell to boxing, though with some difficulty, both being encumbered with the chains which they wore between their legs. A few blows passed on both sides before the gentlemen who stood by stepped in and parted the combatants; and now both parties, having whispered each other that if they outlived the ensuing sessions and escaped the tree one should give and the other should receive satisfaction in single combat, they separated and the gate soon recovered its former tranquillity.

Mrs Heartfree was then desired by the justice and her husband both to conclude her story, which she did in the words of the next chapter.

CHAPTER XI

The conclusion of Mrs Heartfree's adventures

'If I mistake not, I was interrupted just as I was beginning to repeat some of the compliments made me by the hermit.' 'Just as you had finished them, I believe, madam,' said the justice. 'Very well, sir,' said she, 'I am sure I have no pleasure in the repetition. He concluded then with telling me, though I was in his eyes the most charming woman in the world, and might tempt a saint to abandon the ways of holiness, yet my beauty inspired him with a much tenderer affection towards me than to purchase any satisfaction of his own desires with my misery. If therefore I could be so cruel to him to reject his honest and sincere address, nor could submit to a solitary life with one who would endeavour by all possible means to make me happy, I had no force to dread – for that I was as much at my liberty as if I was in France, or England, or any other free country. I repulsed him with the same civility with which he advanced, and told him that as he professed great regard to religion, I was convinced he would cease from all further solicitation when I informed him that, if I had no other objection, my own innocence would not admit of my hearing him on this subject, for that I was married. He started a little at that word, and was for some time silent; but at length, recovering himself, he began to urge the uncertainty of my husband's being alive, and the probability of the contrary. He then spoke of marriage as of a civil policy only, on which head he urged many arguments not worth repeating, and was growing so very eager and importunate that I know not whither his passion might have hurried him had not three of the sailors, well armed, appeared at that instant in sight of the cave. I no sooner saw them than, exulting with the utmost inward joy, I told him my companions were come for me, and that I must now take my leave of him; assuring him that I would always remember, with the most grateful acknowledgment, the favours I had received at his hands. He fetched a very heavy sigh, and squeezing me tenderly by the hand, he saluted my lips with a little more eagerness than the European salutations admit of, and told me he should likewise remember my arrival at his cave to the last day of his life, adding, – O, that he could there spend the whole in the company of one whose bright eyes had kindled – but I know you will think, sir, that we women love to repeat the compliments made us – I will therefore omit them. In a word, the sailors being now arrived, I quitted him with some compassion for the reluctance with which he parted from me, and went forward with my companions.

'We had proceeded but a very few paces before one of the sailors said to his comrades, "Damn me, Jack, who knows whether yon fellow has not some good flip in his cave?" I innocently answered, "The poor wretch has only one bottle of brandy." "Has he so?" cries the sailor. "Fore George[43], we will taste it;" and so saying they immediately returned back, and myself with them. We found the poor man prostrate on the ground, expressing all the symptoms of misery and lamentation. I told him in French (for the sailors could not speak that language) what they wanted. He pointed to the place where the bottle was deposited, saying they were welcome to that and whatever else he had, and added he cared not if they took his life also. The sailors searched the whole cave, where finding nothing more which they deemed worth their taking, they walked off with the bottle, and immediately emptying it without offering me a drop, they proceeded with me towards the town.

'In our way I observed one whisper another, while he kept his eye steadfastly fixed on me. This gave me some uneasiness; but the other answered, "No, damn me, the captain will never forgive us. Besides, we have enough of it among the black women, and in my mind, one colour is as good as another." This was enough to give me violent apprehensions; but I heard no more of that kind until we came to the town, where, in about six hours, I arrived in safety.

'As soon as I came to the captain, he enquired what was become of my friend, meaning the villainous Count. When he was informed by me of what had happened, he wished me heartily joy of my delivery, and expressing the utmost abhorrence of such baseness, swore if ever he met him he would cut his throat – but, indeed, we both concluded that he had died of the blow which the hermit had given him.

'I was now introduced to the chief magistrate of this country, who was desirous of seeing me. I will give you a short description of him. He was chosen (as is the custom there) for his superior bravery and wisdom. His power is entirely absolute during his continuance; but on the first deviation from equity and justice, he is liable to be deposed and punished by the people, the elders of whom once a year assemble to examine into his conduct. Besides the danger which these examinations, which are very strict, expose him to, his office is of such care and trouble that nothing but that restless love of power so predominant in the mind of man could make it the object of desire, for he is indeed the only slave of all the natives of this country. He is obliged, in time of peace, to hear the complaint of every person in his dominions and to render him justice; for which purpose every one may demand an audience of him, unless during the hour which he is allowed for dinner, when he sits alone at the table, and is attended in the most public manner with more than European ceremony. This is done to create an awe and respect towards him in the eye of the vulgar – but lest it should elevate him too much in his own opinion, in order to his humiliation, he receives every evening in private, from a kind of beadle, a gentle kick on his posteriors. Besides which he wears a ring in his nose, somewhat resembling that we ring our pigs with, and a chain round his neck not unlike that worn by our aldermen – both which I suppose to be emblematical, but heard not the reasons of either assigned. There are many more particularities among these people, which when I have an opportunity, I may relate to you. The second day after my return from court one of his officers, whom they call "Schach Pimpach"[47], waited upon me, and, by a French interpreter who lives here, informed me that the chief magistrate liked my person, and offered me an immense present if I would suffer him to enjoy it (this is, it seems, their common form of making love). I rejected the present, and never heard any further solicitations; for as it is no shame for women here to consent at the first proposal, so they never receive a second.

'I had resided in this town a week when the captain informed me that a number of slaves, who had been taken captives in war, were to be guarded to the seaside, where they were to be sold to the merchants who traded in them to America; that if I would embrace this opportunity I might assure myself of finding a passage to America, and thence to England; acquainting me at the same time that he himself intended to go with them. I readily agreed to accompany him. The chief, being advertised of our designs, sent for us both to court, and without mentioning a word of love to me, having presented me with a very rich jewel – of less value, he said, than my chastity – took a very civil leave, recommending me to the care of Heaven, and ordering us a large supply of provisions for our journey.

'We were provided with mules for ourselves and what we carried with us, and in nine days reached the seashore, where we found an English vessel ready to receive both us and the slaves. We went aboard it, and sailed the next day with a fair wind for New England, where I hoped to get an immediate passage to the Old; but Providence was kinder than my expectation, for the third day after we were at sea we met an English man-of-war homeward bound; the captain of it was a very good-natured man, and agreed to take me on board. I accordingly took my leave of my old friend, the master of the shipwrecked vessel, who went on to New England, whence he intended to pass to Jamaica, where his owners lived. I was now treated with great civility, had a little cabin assigned me, and dined every day at the captain's table, who was indeed a very gallant man – and, at first, made me a tender of his affections; but when he found me resolutely bent to preserve myself pure and entire for the best of husbands, he grew cooler in his addresses, and soon behaved in a manner very pleasing to me, regarding my sex only so far as to pay me a deference, which is very agreeable to us all.

'To conclude my story; I met with no adventure in this passage at all worth relating, until my landing at Gravesend, whence the captain brought me in his own boat to the Tower. In a short hour after my arrival we had that meeting which, however dreadful at first, will, I now hope, by the good offices of the best of men – whom Heaven for ever bless – end in our perfect happiness, and be a strong instance of what I am persuaded is the surest truth: that Providence will sooner or later procure the felicity of the virtuous and innocent.'

Mrs Heartfree thus ended her speech, having before delivered to her husband the jewels which the Count had robbed him of, and that presented her by the African chief, which last was of immense value. The good magistrate was sensibly touched at her narrative, as well on the consideration of the sufferings she had herself undergone as for those of her husband, which he had himself been innocently the instrument of bringing upon him. That worthy man, however, much rejoiced in what he had already done for his preservation, and promised to labour with his utmost interest and industry to procure the absolute pardon, rather of his sentence than of his guilt, which he now plainly discovered was a barbarous and false imputation.

CHAPTER XII

The history returns to the contemplation of greatness

But we have already perhaps detained our reader too long in this relation from the consideration of our hero, who daily gave the most exalted proofs of greatness in cajoling the prigs, and in exactions on the debtors; which latter now grew so great, i.e. corrupted in their morals, that they spoke with the utmost contempt of what the vulgar call honesty. The greatest character among them was that of a pickpocket, or in truer language, a file; and the only censure was want of dexterity. As to virtue, goodness, and such like, they were the objects of mirth and derision, and all Newgate was a complete collection of prigs, every man being desirous to pick his neighbour's pocket, and every one was as sensible that his neighbour was as ready to pick his; so that (which is almost incredible) as great roguery was daily committed within the walls of Newgate as without. The glory resulting from these actions of Wild probably animated the envy of his enemies against him. The day of his trial now approached – for which, as Socrates did, he prepared himself – but not weakly and foolishly, like that philosopher, with patience and resignation, but with a good number of false witnesses. However, as success is not always proportioned to the wisdom of him who endeavours to attain it, so are we more sorry than ashamed to relate that our hero was, notwithstanding his utmost caution and prudence, convicted and sentenced to a death which, when we consider not only the great men who have suffered it, but the much larger number of those whose highest honour it has been to merit it, we cannot call otherwise than honourable. Indeed, those who have unluckily missed it seem all their days to have laboured in vain to attain an end, which Fortune, for reasons only known to herself, has thought proper to deny them. Without any further preface then, our hero was sentenced to be hanged by the neck. But, whatever was to be now his fate, he might console himself that he had perpetrated what

> *Nec Judicis ira, nec ignis*
> *Nec poterit ferrum, nec edax abolere vetustas.*[48]

For my own part, I confess, I look on this death of hanging to be as proper for a hero as any other, and I solemnly declare that had Alexander the Great been hanged it would not in the least have diminished my respect to his memory. Provided a hero in his life does but execute a sufficient quantity of mischief – provided he be but well and heartily cursed by the widow, the orphan, the poor, and the oppressed (the sole rewards, as many authors have bitterly lamented both in prose and verse, of greatness, i. e. priggism), I think it avails little of what nature his death be, whether it be by the axe, the halter, or the sword. Such names will be always sure of living to posterity, and of enjoying that fame which they so gloriously and eagerly coveted; for according to a great dramatic poet,

> *Fame*
> *Not more survives from good than evil deeds.*
> *The aspiring youth that fired the Ephesian dome*
> *Outlives in fame the pious fool that raised it.* [49]

Our hero now suspected that the malice of his enemies would overpower him. He therefore betook himself to that true support of greatness in affliction – a bottle – by means of which he was enabled to curse, swear, and bully and brave his fate. Other comfort indeed he had not much, for not a single friend ever came near him. His wife, whose trial was deferred to the next sessions, visited him but once, when she plagued, tormented, and upbraided him so cruelly that he forbade the keeper ever to admit her again. The ordinary of Newgate had frequent conferences with him, and greatly would it embellish our history could we record all which that good man delivered on these occasions; but unhappily we could procure only the substance of a single conference, which was taken down in shorthand by one who overheard it. We shall transcribe it therefore exactly in the same form and words we received it; nor can we help regarding it as one of the most curious pieces which either ancient or modern history has recorded.

CHAPTER XIII

A dialogue between the ordinary of Newgate and Mr Jonathan Wild the Great; in which the subjects of death, immortality, and other grave matters, are very learnedly handled by the former

Ordinary
Good morrow to you, sir; I hope you rested well last night.

Jonathan
Damned ill, sir. I dreamt so confoundedly of hanging, that it disturbed my sleep.

Ordinary
Fie upon it! You should be more resigned. I wish you would make a little better use of those instructions which I have endeavoured to inculcate into you, and particularly last Sunday – and from these words: 'Those who do evil shall go into everlasting fire, prepared for the devil and his angels', I undertook to show you, first, what is meant by everlasting fire; and, secondly, who were the devil and his angels. I then proceeded to draw some inferences from the whole[a]; in which I am mightily deceived if I did not convince you that you yourself was one of those angels, and, consequently, must expect everlasting fire to be your portion in the other world.

Jonathan
Faith, doctor, I remember very little of your inferences; for I fell asleep

a. He pronounced this word 'hull', and perhaps would have spelt it so.

soon after your naming your text. But did you preach this doctrine then, or do you repeat it now in order to comfort me?

Ordinary

I do it in order to bring you to a true sense of your manifold sins, and by that means, to induce you to repentance. Indeed, had I the eloquence of Cicero, or of Tully, it would not be sufficient to describe the pains of hell or the joys of heaven. The utmost that we are taught is that ear has not heard, nor can heart conceive. Who then would, for the pitiful consideration of the riches and pleasures of this world, forfeit such inestimable happiness! Such joys! Such pleasures! Such delights? Or who would run the venture of such misery – which, but to think on, shocks the human understanding? Who, in his senses, then, would prefer the latter to the former?

Jonathan

Ay, who indeed? I assure you, doctor, I had much rather be happy than miserable. But[a] *****************

Ordinary

Nothing can be plainer. St.**********************************

Jonathan

******If once convinced***** no man ** lives of***** whereas sure the clergy***opportunity*** better informed ***** all manner of vice

Ordinary

*are**atheist***deist****ari****cinian****hanged***burnt* oiled* oasted***** dev ****his an***** ell fire****** ternal da**** tion.

Jonathan

You***to frighten me out of my wits. But the good**** is, I doubt not, more merciful than his ****If I should believe all you say, I am sure I should die in inexpressible horror.

---

a. This part was so blotted that it was illegible.

Ordinary

Despair is sinful. You should place your hopes in repentance and grace; and though it is most true that you are in danger of the judgement, yet there is still room for mercy; and no man, unless excommunicated, is absolutely without hopes of a reprieve.

Jonathan

I am not without hopes of a reprieve from the cheat yet. I have pretty good interest; but if I cannot obtain it, you shall not frighten me out of my courage. I will not die like a pimp. Damn me, what is death? It is nothing but to be with Platos and with Caesars, as the poet says, and all the other great heroes of antiquity*****************

Ordinary

Ay, all this is very true, but life is sweet for all that – and I had rather live to eternity than go into the company of any such heathens, who are, I doubt not, in hell with the devil and his angels; and, as little as you seem to apprehend it, you may find yourself there before you expect it. Where, then, will be your tauntings and your vauntings, your boastings and your braggings? You will then be ready to give more for a drop of water than you ever gave for a bottle of wine.

Jonathan

Faith, doctor! well minded. What say you to a bottle of wine?

Ordinary

I will drink no wine with an atheist. I should expect the devil to make a third in such company, for, since he knows you are his, he may be impatient to have his due.

Jonathan

It is your business to drink with the wicked, in order to amend them.

Ordinary

I despair of it; and so I consign you over to the devil, who is ready to receive you.

Jonathan

You are more unmerciful to me than the judge, doctor. He recommended my soul to Heaven; and it is your office to show me the way thither.

Ordinary

No: the gates are barred against all revilers of the clergy.

Jonathan

I revile only the wicked ones – if any such are, which cannot affect you – who, if men were preferred in the church by merit only, would have long since been a bishop. Indeed, it might raise any good man's indignation to observe one of your vast learning and abilities obliged to exert them in so low a sphere, when so many of your inferiors wallow in wealth and preferment.

Ordinary

Why, it must be confessed that there are bad men in all orders; but you should not censure too generally. I must own I might have expected higher promotion, but I have learnt patience and resignation; and I would advise you to the same temper of mind – which, if you can attain, I know you will find mercy. Nay, I do now promise you will. It is true you are a sinner; but your crimes are not of the blackest dye: you are no murderer, nor guilty of sacrilege. And, if you are guilty of theft, you make some atonement by suffering for it, which many others do not. Happy is it indeed for those few who are detected in their sins, and brought to exemplary punishment for them in this world. So far, therefore, from repining at your fate when you come to the tree, you should exult and rejoice in it; and, to say the truth, I question whether, to a wise man, the catastrophe of many of those who die by a halter is not more to be envied than pitied. Nothing is so sinful as sin, and murder is the greatest of all sins. It follows that whoever commits murder is happy in suffering for it. If, therefore, a man who commits murder is so happy in dying for it, how much better must it be for you, who have committed a less crime!

Jonathan

All this is very true; but let us take a bottle of wine to cheer our spirits.

Ordinary

Why wine? Let me tell you, Mr Wild, there is nothing so deceitful as the spirits given us by wine. If you must drink, let us have a bowl of punch –a liquor I the rather prefer, as it is nowhere spoken against in Scripture, and as it is more wholesome for the gravel, a distemper with which I am grievously afflicted.

Jonathan (having called for a bowl)

I ask your pardon, doctor; I should have remembered that punch was your favourite liquor. I think you never taste wine while there is any punch remaining on the table.

Ordinary

I confess I look on punch to be the more eligible liquor, as well for the reasons I before mentioned as likewise for one other cause, viz. it is the properest for a draught. I own I took it a little unkind of you to mention wine, thinking you knew my palate.

Jonathan

You are in the right; and I will take a swinging cup to your being made a bishop.

Ordinary

And I will wish you a reprieve in as large a draught. Come, don't despair; it is yet time enough to think of dying; you have good friends, who very probably may prevail for you. I have known many a man reprieved who had less reason to expect it.

Jonathan

But if I should flatter myself with such hopes, and be deceived – what then would become of my soul?

Ordinary

Pugh! Never mind your soul – leave that to me; I will render a good account of it, I warrant you. I have a sermon in my pocket which may be of some use to you to hear. I do not value myself on the talent of preaching, since no man ought to value himself for any gift in this world. But perhaps there are not many such sermons. But to proceed, since we have nothing else to do until the punch comes. My text is the latter part of a verse only.

... To the Greeks foolishness.[50]

The occasion of these words was principally that philosophy of the Greeks which at that time had overrun great part of the heathen world, had poisoned and, as it were, puffed up their minds with pride, so that they disregarded all kinds of doctrine in comparison of their own; and however safe and however sound the learning of the others might be, yet if it anywise contradicted their own laws, customs, and received opinions, away with it – it is not for us. It was to the Greeks foolishness.

In the former part, therefore, of my discourse on these words, I shall principally confine myself to the laying open and demonstrating the great emptiness and vanity of this philosophy, with which these idle and absurd sophists were so proudly blown up and elevated.

And here I shall do two things. First, I shall expose the matter; and secondly, the manner of this absurd philosophy.

And first, for the first of these, namely the matter. Now, here we may retort the unmannerly word which our adversaries have audaciously thrown in our faces; for what was all this mighty matter of philosophy, this heap of knowledge, which was to bring such large harvests of honour to those who sowed it, and so greatly and nobly to enrich the ground on which it fell – what was it but foolishness? An inconsistent heap of nonsense, of absurdities and contradictions, bringing no ornament to the mind in its theory, nor exhibiting any usefulness to the body in its practice. What were all the sermons and the savings, the fables and the morals of all these wise men but, to use the word mentioned in my text once more, foolishness? What was their great master Plato, or their other great light Aristotle? Both fools, mere quibblers and sophists, idly and vainly attached to certain ridiculous notions of their own, founded neither on truth nor on reason. Their whole works are a strange medley of the greatest falsehoods, scarce covered over with the colour of truth. Their precepts are neither borrowed from nature nor guided by reason; mere fictions serving only to evince the dreadful height of human pride – in one word, foolishness. It may be perhaps expected of me that I should give some instances from their works to prove this charge; but as to transcribe every passage to my purpose would be to transcribe their whole works, and as in such a plentiful crop it is difficult to choose. Instead of trespassing on your patience, I shall conclude this first head with asserting what I have so fully proved, and what may indeed be inferred from the text – that the philosophy of the Greeks was foolishness.

Proceed we now, in the second place, to consider the manner in which this inane and simple doctrine was propagated. And here – but here the punch by entering waked Mr Wild, who was fast asleep, and put an end to the sermon; nor could we obtain any further account of the conversation which passed at this interview.

CHAPTER XIV

Wild proceeds to the highest consummation of human greatness

The day now drew nigh when our great man was to exemplify the last and noblest act of greatness by which any hero can signalise himself. This was the day of execution, or consummation, or apotheosis (for it is called by different names), which was to give our hero an opportunity of facing death and damnation without any fear in his heart, or, at least, without betraying any symptoms of it in his countenance. A completion of greatness which is heartily to be wished to every great man; nothing being more worthy of lamentation than when Fortune, like a lazy poet, winds up her catastrophe awkwardly, and bestowing too little care on her fifth act, dismisses the hero with a sneaking and private exit, who had in the former part of the drama performed such notable exploits as must promise to every good judge among the spectators a noble, public and exalted end.

But she was resolved to commit no such error in this instance. Our hero was too much and too deservedly her favourite to be neglected by her in his last moments; accordingly all efforts for a reprieve were vain, and the name of Wild stood at the head of those who were ordered for execution.

From the time he gave over all hopes of life, his conduct was truly great and admirable. Instead of showing any marks of dejection or contrition, he rather infused more confidence and assurance into his looks. He spent most of his hours in drinking with his friends and with the good man above commemorated. In one of these compotations, being asked whether he was afraid to die, he answered, 'Damn me, it is only a dance without music.' Another time, when one expressed some sorrow for his misfortune, as he termed it, he said with great fierceness, 'A man can die but once.' Again, when one of his intimate acquaintance hinted his hopes that he would die like a man, he cocked his hat in defiance, and cried out greatly – 'Zounds! Who's afraid?'

Happy would it have been for posterity, could we have retrieved any entire conversation which passed at this season, especially between our hero and his learned comforter, but we have searched many pasteboard records in vain.

On the eve of his apotheosis, Wild's lady desired to see him, to which he consented. This meeting was at first very tender on both sides; but it could not continue so, for, unluckily, some hints of former miscarriages intervening – as particularly when she asked him how he could have used her so barbarously once as calling her bitch, and whether such language became a man, much less a gentleman – Wild flew into a violent passion, and swore she was the vilest of bitches to upbraid him at such a season with an unguarded word spoke long ago. She replied, with many tears, she was well enough served for her folly in visiting such a brute – but she had one comfort however, that it would be the last time he could ever treat her so; that indeed she had some obligation to him, for that his cruelty to her would reconcile her to the fate he was tomorrow to suffer; and indeed, nothing but such brutality could have made the consideration of his shameful death (so this weak woman called hanging), which was now inevitable, to be borne even without madness. She then proceeded to a recapitulation of his faults in an exacter order, and with more perfect memory, than one would have imagined her capable of; and it is probable would have rehearsed a complete catalogue had not our hero's patience failed him, so that with the utmost fury and violence he caught her by the hair and kicked her, as heartily as his chains would suffer him, out of the room.

At length the morning came which Fortune at his birth had resolutely ordained for the consummation of our hero's greatness. He had himself indeed modestly declined the public honour she intended him, and had taken a quantity of laudanum, in order to retire quietly off the stage; but we have already observed in the course of our wonderful history that to struggle against this lady's decrees is vain and impotent; and whether she has determined you shall be hanged or be a prime minister, it is in either case lost labour to resist. Laudanum, therefore, being unable to stop the breath of our hero – which the fruit of hemp-seed, and not the spirit of poppy-seed, was to overcome – he was at the usual hour attended by the proper gentleman appointed for that purpose, and acquainted that the cart was ready. On this occasion he exerted that greatness of courage which has been so much celebrated in other heroes; and knowing it was impossible to resist, he gravely declared he would attend them. He then descended to that room where the fetters of great men are knocked off in a most solemn and ceremonious manner. Then, shaking hands with his friends (to wit, those who were conducting him to the tree), and drinking their healths in a bumper of brandy, he ascended the cart, where he was no sooner seated than he received the acclamations of the multitude, who were highly ravished with his greatness.

The cart now moved slowly on, being preceded by a troop of horse-guards bearing javelins in their hands, through streets lined with crowds all admiring the great behaviour of our hero, who rode on, sometimes sighing, sometimes swearing, sometimes singing or whistling, as his humour varied.

When he came to the tree of glory, he was welcomed with a universal shout of the people, who were there assembled in prodigious numbers to behold a sight much more rare in populous cities than one would reasonably imagine it should be, viz. the proper catastrophe of a great man.

But though envy was, through fear, obliged to join the general voice in applause on this occasion, there were not wanting some who maligned this completion of glory, which was now about to be fulfilled to our hero, and endeavoured to prevent it by knocking him on the head as he stood under the tree, while the ordinary was performing his last office. They therefore began to batter the cart with stones, brickbats, dirt, and all manner of mischievous weapons, some of which, erroneously playing on the robes of the ecclesiastic, made him so expeditious in his repetition, that with wonderful alacrity he had ended almost in an instant, and conveyed himself into a place of safety in a hackney-coach, where he waited the compulsion with a temper of mind described in these verses:

Suave mari magno, turbantibus aequora ventis,
E terra magnum alterius spectare laborem. [51]

We must not, however, omit one circumstance, as it serves to show the most admirable conservation of character in our hero to his last moment, which was that whilst the ordinary was busy in his ejaculations, Wild, in the midst of the shower of stones, etc., which played upon him, applied his hands to the parson's pocket and emptied it of his bottle-screw, which he carried out of the world in his hand.

The ordinary being now descended from the cart, Wild had just opportunity to cast his eyes around the crowd, and to give them a hearty curse, when immediately the horses moved on, and with universal applause our hero swung out of this world.

Thus fell Jonathan Wild the Great, by a death as glorious as his life had been, and which was so truly agreeable to it, that the latter must have been deplorably maimed and imperfect without the former – a death which has been alone wanting to complete the characters of several ancient and modern heroes, whose histories would then have been read with much greater pleasure by the wisest in all ages. Indeed we could almost wish that whenever Fortune seems wantonly to deviate from her purpose, and leaves her work imperfect in this particular, the historian would indulge himself in the license of poetry and romance, and even do a violence to truth, to oblige his reader with a page which must be the most delightful in all his history, and which could never fail of producing an instructive moral.

Narrow minds may possibly have some reason to be ashamed of going this way out of the world, if their consciences can fly in their faces and assure them they have not merited such an honour; but he must be a fool who is ashamed of being hanged – who is not weak enough to be ashamed of having deserved it.

CHAPTER XV

The character of our hero, and the conclusion of this history

We will now endeavour to draw the character of this great man; and by bringing together those several features as it were of his mind which lie scattered up and down in this history, to present our readers with a perfect picture of greatness.

Jonathan Wild had every qualification necessary to form a great man. As his most powerful and predominant passion was ambition, so nature had, with consummate propriety, adapted all his faculties to the attaining those glorious ends to which this passion directed him. He was extremely ingenious in inventing designs, artful in contriving the means to accomplish his purposes, and resolute in executing them. For as the most exquisite cunning and most undaunted boldness qualified him for any undertaking, so was he not restrained by any of those weaknesses which disappoint the views of mean and vulgar souls, and which are comprehended in one general term of honesty, which is a corruption of 'honosty', a word derived from what the Greeks call an ass. He was entirely free from those low vices of modesty and good nature, which, as he said, implied a total negation of human greatness, and were the only qualities which absolutely rendered a man incapable of making a considerable figure in the world. His lust was inferior only to his ambition; but as for what simple people call love, he knew not what it was. His avarice was immense, but it was of the rapacious, not of the tenacious kind. His rapaciousness was indeed so violent that nothing ever contented him but the whole; for however considerable the share was which his coadjutors allowed him of a booty, he was restless in inventing means to make himself master of the smallest pittance reserved by them. He said laws were made for the use of prigs only, and to secure their property. They were never therefore more perverted than when their edge was turned against these; but that this generally happened through their want of sufficient dexterity.

The character which he most valued himself upon, and which he principally honoured in others, was that of hypocrisy. His opinion was that no one could carry priggism very far without it; for which reason, he said, there was little greatness to be expected in a man who acknowledged his vices, but always much to be hoped from him who professed great virtues. Wherefore, though he would always shun the person whom he discovered guilty of a good action, yet he was never deterred by a good character, which was more commonly the effect of profession than of action. For which reason, he himself was always very liberal of honest professions, and had as much virtue and goodness in his mouth as a saint – never in the least scrupling to swear by his honour, even to those who knew him the best – nay, though he held good-nature and modesty in the highest contempt, he constantly practised the affectation of both, and recommended this to others, whose welfare, on his own account, he wished well to. He laid down several maxims as the certain methods of attaining greatness, to which, in his own pursuit of it, he constantly adhered, as:

1. Never to do more mischief to another than was necessary to the effecting his purpose; for that mischief was too precious a thing to be thrown away.
2. To know no distinction of men from affection; but to sacrifice all with equal readiness to his interest.
3. Never to communicate more of an affair than was necessary to the person who was to execute it.
4. Not to trust him who has deceived you, nor who knows he has been deceived by you.

5. To forgive no enemy; but to be cautious and often dilatory in revenge.

6. To shun poverty and distress, and to ally himself as close as possible to power and riches.

7. To maintain a constant gravity in his countenance and behaviour, and to affect wisdom on all occasions.

8. To foment eternal jealousies in his gang, one of another.

9. Never to reward anyone equal to his merit; but always to insinuate that the reward was above it.

10. That all men were knaves or fools, and much the greater number a composition of both.

11. That a good name, like money, must be parted with, or at least greatly risked, in order to bring the owner any advantage.

12. That virtues, like precious stones, were easily counterfeited; that the counterfeits in both cases adorned the wearer equally, and that very few had knowledge or discernment sufficient to distinguish the counterfeit jewel from the real.

13. That many men were undone by not going deep enough in roguery; as in gaming any man may be a loser who does not play the whole game.

14. That men proclaim their own virtues, as shopkeepers expose their goods, in order to profit by them.

15. That the heart was the proper seat of hatred, and the countenance of affection and friendship.

He had many more of the same kind, all equally good with these and which were after his decease found in his study, as the twelve excellent and celebrated rules were in that of King Charles I; for he never promulgated them in his lifetime, not having them constantly in his mouth, as some grave persons have the rules of virtue and morality, without paying the least regard to them in their actions. Whereas our hero, by a constant and steady adherence to his rules in conforming everything he did to them, acquired at length a settled habit of walking by them, until at last he was in no danger of inadvertently going out of the way; and by these means he arrived at that degree of greatness, which few have equalled – none, we may say, have exceeded. For though it must be allowed that there have been some few heroes who have done greater mischiefs to mankind – such as those who have betrayed the liberty of their country to others, or have undermined and overpowered it themselves; or conquerors who have impoverished, pillaged, sacked, burnt, and destroyed the countries and cities of their fellow-creatures, from no other provocation than that of glory, i. e., as the tragic poet calls it,

> *A privilege to kill,*
> *A strong temptation to do bravely ill –* [52]

Yet, if we consider it in the light wherein actions are placed in this line,

> *Laetius est, quoties magno tibi constat honestum –* [53]

when we see our hero, without the least assistance or pretence, setting himself at the head of a gang, which he had not any shadow of right to govern – if we view him maintaining absolute power, and exercising tyranny over a lawless crew, contrary to all law but that of his own will – we consider him setting up an open trade publicly, in defiance not only of the laws of his country but of the common sense of his countrymen – if we see him first contriving the robbery of others, and again the defrauding the very robbers of that booty, which they had ventured their necks to acquire, and which without any hazard, they might have retained – here sure he must appear admirable, and we may challenge not only the truth of history, but almost the latitude of fiction, to equal his glory.

Nor had he any of those flaws in his character which, though they have been commended by weak writers, have (as I hinted in the beginning of this history) by the judicious reader been censured and despised. Such was the clemency of Alexander and Caesar, which nature had so grossly erred in giving them, as a painter would who should dress a peasant in robes of state or give the nose or any other feature of a Venus to a satyr. What had the destroyers of mankind, that glorious pair – one of whom came into the world to usurp the dominion and abolish the constitution of his own country, the other to conquer, enslave and rule over the whole world, at least as much as was well known to him, and the shortness of his life would give him leave to visit – what had, I say, such as these to do with clemency? Who cannot see the absurdity and contradiction of mixing such an ingredient with those noble and great qualities I have before mentioned? Now, in Wild everything was truly great, almost without alloy, as his imperfections (for surely some small ones he had) were only such as served to denominate him a human creature, of which kind none ever arrived at consummate excellence. But surely his whole behaviour to his friend Heartfree is a convincing proof that the true iron or steel greatness of his heart was not debased by any softer metal. Indeed, while greatness consists in power, pride, insolence, and doing mischief to mankind – to speak out – while a great man and a great rogue are synonymous terms, so long shall Wild stand unrivalled on the pinnacle of greatness. Nor must we omit here, as the finishing of his character, what indeed ought to be remembered on his tomb or his statue: the conformity above mentioned of his death to his life – and that Jonathan Wild the Great, after all his mighty exploits, was what so few great men can accomplish – hanged by the neck until he was dead.

Having thus brought our hero to his conclusion, it may be satisfactory to some readers (for many, I doubt not, carry their concern no further than his fate) to know what became of Heartfree. We shall acquaint them, therefore, that his sufferings were now at an end; that the good magistrate easily prevailed for his pardon, nor was contented until he had made him all the reparation he could for his troubles, though the share he had in bringing these upon him was not only innocent but from its motive laudable. He procured the restoration of the jewels from the man-of-war at her return to England, and above all, omitted no labour to restore Heartfree to his reputation, and to persuade his neighbours, acquaintance and customers, of his innocence. When the commission of bankruptcy was satisfied, Heartfree had a considerable sum remaining, for the diamond presented to his wife was of prodigious value, and infinitely recompensed the loss of those jewels which Miss Straddle had disposed of. He now set up again in his trade; compassion for his unmerited misfortunes brought him many customers among those who had any regard to humanity, and he has by industry joined with parsimony amassed a considerable fortune. His wife and he are now grown old in the purest love and friendship, but never had another child. Friendly married his elder daughter at the age of nineteen, and became his partner in trade. As to the younger, she never would listen to the addresses of any lover, not even of a young nobleman, who offered to take her with two thousand pounds, which her father would have willingly produced, and indeed did his utmost to persuade her to the match; but she refused absolutely, nor would give any other reason, when Heartfree pressed her, than that she had dedicated her days to his service, and was resolved no other duty should interfere with that which she owed the best of fathers, nor prevent her from being the nurse of his old age.

Thus Heartfree, his wife, his two daughters, his son-in-law, and his grandchildren, of which he has several, live all together in one house; and that with such amity and affection towards each other that they are in the neighbourhood called the family of love.

As to all the other persons mentioned in this history in the light of greatness, they had all the fate adapted to it, being every one hanged by the neck, save two, viz. Miss Theodosia Snap, who was transported to America, where she was pretty well married, reformed, and made a good wife; and the Count, who recovered of the wound he had received from the hermit and made his escape into France, where he committed a robbery, was taken, and broke on the wheel.

Indeed, whoever considers the common fate of great men must allow they well deserve and hardly earn that applause which is given them by the world; for when we reflect on the labours and pains, the cares, disquietudes and dangers which attend their road to greatness, we may say with the divine that a man may go to heaven with half the pains which it costs him to purchase hell. To say the truth, the world have this reason at least to honour such characters as that of Wild: that while it is in the power of every man to be perfectly honest, not one in a thousand is capable of being a complete rogue; and few indeed there are who, if they were inspired with the vanity of imitating our hero, would not after much fruitless pains be obliged to own themselves inferior to Mr Jonathan Wild the Great.

NOTES

1. Plutarch (*c*.46–*c*.120), Cornelius Nepos (*c*.110–*c*.24 BC), and Suetonius (*c*.70–*c*.130) were all writers of famous works of biography in classical times.

2. Here Fielding provides us with both a negative and a positive example of a Greek and Roman leader respectively. Aristides (*c*.530–468 BC) was an Athenian statesman, praised by Plutarch and Cornelius Nepos; Marcus Junius Brutus (*c*.85–42 BC), was cited by Plutarch as an example of a virtuous Roman senator; the Greek leader Lysander (d. 395 BC) was heavily criticised by both Plutarch and Cornelius Nepos; and Nero (37–68) was reputed to be notoriously cruel.

3. Alexander the Great (356–323 BC), and Julius Caesar (*c*.101–44 BC) respectively.

4. According to *A Complete History of England* (1706), Hengist the Saxon invaded Britain after 458, invited the Britons to a feast, and with the words, '*Nemet eour Saxes*', slaughtered 300 of them.

5. The chief law court in England until the late nineteenth century.

6. 'Bounteous mother'. (Latin)

7. 'Try to cure the malady straight away'. From Persius' *Satires* (III.64).

8. The dream is described in Herodotus' *The Histories*. Herodotus tells how Astyages tries to have his young grandson killed, but fails, and the prophecy comes true.

9. This dream by Hecuba, Queen of Troy, is described by Cicero in *De divinatione*. Urged to have her baby, Paris, killed, Hecuba instead abandoned him on nearby Mount Ida. Years later, Paris was to elope with Helen, wife of Menelaus, King of Sparta, leading to the Trojan War.

10. The Bubonic Plague, otherwise known as the Black Death spread rapidly through London in early 1665; this devastating outbreak became known as the Great Plague.

11. Titus Oates (1649–1705) was a perjurer who fabricated a fradulent Catholic plot to kill King Charles II.

12. A popular Latin dictionary used in schools in the seventeenth and eighteenth centuries. Parnassus was a mountain in Greece, revered by Apollo; its name became synonymous with achievement in literature, especially poetry.

13. Homer tells how Achilles once caught Isus and Antiphus as they looked after their sheep on Mount Ida, and tied them up, but afterwards released them after accepting a ransom.

14. As the Greek army faces disaster, Nestor contrasts his present decline with a long-ago successful raid against the Eleans, during which he and his men rounded up a substantial 'booty'.

15. In Virgil's *Aeneid*, King Evander tells of the 'half-human' Cacus, offspring of Vulcan, who stole four bulls and four heifers. When Hercules discovers this theft, he kills Cacus.

16. Alexander the Great was widely regarded as a criminal conqueror. Charles XII of Sweden (1682–1718) was an expansionist ruler who was eventually killed in battle. A controversial figure of the time, he was praised by the Tories, and condemned by the Whigs, including Henry Fielding.

17. A possible reference to the retreat of Peter the Great after Charles XII's victory at Narva (1700) in the Great Northern War (1700–21).

18. Mateo Alemán's novel, *The Life of Guzmán de Alfarache, or, The Spanish Rogue*, became popular in England after its first English translation in 1622. Thomas Otway's (1652–85) farce, *The Cheats of Scapin*, was adapted from Molière's play, *Les Fourberies de Scapin* (1671).

19. A popular form of the card-game 'whist'.

20. Aristocrats who were found guilty of major crimes were usually beheaded on the block at Tower Hill. Common criminals were hanged from the gallows at Tyburn, near Marble Arch.

21. Hazard was a game of chance played with dice.

22. 'He who was once white, is now the opposite of white'. From Ovid's *Metamorphoses* (II, 541).

23. *Pius* (good, dutiful) and *pater* (father) were epithets regularly used by Virgil to describe Aeneas, the hero of the *Aeneid*. Occasionally Virgil omitted these labels in episodes where the hero fell short of the high standards required by the description.

24. 'Thus, thus, it pleases me'; part of Queen Dido's lament in the *Aeneid*, as she kills herself. (*Aeneid* 4. 660)

25. In Homer's *Odyssey*, Penelope is left alone for years, while her husband, Odysseus (Ulysses), is away. Encouraged to marry again, she stalls by stating that first she must weave a sheet for her father-in-law, Laertes. Each night, in secret, she unpicks the work she has done by day.

26. Bartholomew Fair, which took place at Smithfield each year, offered a variety of entertainments, including farces and burlesques played by live actors and puppets.

27. A reference to William Deards (d. 1761), a toy- and trinket-seller whom Fielding sued in 1739.

28. Drawcansir is a character in the farce, *The Rehearsal* (1672), by George Villiers, 2nd Duke of Buckingham (1628–87).

29. From Horace's *Ars Poetica* (lines 191–2).

30. 'You may drive out Nature with a pitchfork, yet she will ever hurry back.' Horace, *Epistles* (1. 10. 24).

31. The story as told here does not actually appear in Herodotus.

32. From Edward Young's poem, *The Complaint, or, Night Thoughts on Life, Death and Immortality*, first published in 1742.

33. When Socrates' friend Crito tells him that a ship which will signal his execution is expected that day, he replies, 'If this be the will of the gods, so be it'. (Plato, *Crito*, 43c–44a)

34. Achates was the faithful servant of Aeneas in Virgil's *Aeneid*, and Hephaestion the close friend of Alexander the Great.

35. This is most likely another reference to William Deards (see note 27). A 'bubble' is a term for a cheat or fraud.

36. In Jonathan Swift's Lilliput of *Gulliver's Travels*, a 'Hurgo' was a 'great Lord'. In 1738, Parliament banned accounts of its debates being reproduced in newspapers, and to get

round this, the *Gentleman's Magazine* started to print its accounts of the goings-on in parliament as 'Debates in the Senate of Lilliput'.

37. A reference to Colley Cibber's (1671–1757) play, *The Careless Husband* (1705).

38. The phrase is taken from John Reynolds' *The Triumphs of Gods Revenge against the Crying and Execrable Sin of (Wilful and Premeditated) Murder*, originally published between 1621 and 1635.

39. 'None among mortals is right all the time'. From Pliny, *Natural History* (VII. xl. 131). 'Anger is short-lived madness'. From Horace, *Epistles* (I. ii. 62).

40. 'Mine and yours'. (Latin)

41. 'His'. (Latin)

42. Hick's Hall in Clerkenwell was where the justices of Middlesex held their sessions from 1612 until 1778. Anyone convicted here would then be sent to the Old Bailey for trial.

43. 'That he may be hurled down in more headlong ruin.' From Claudian's *Against Rufinus* (I. 21–3).

44. At the end of the play *The Beggar's Opera* (1728), by John Gay (1685–1732), the condemned highwayman, Macheath, is reprieved because 'an opera must end happily… to comply with the taste of the town'.

45. A 'basha' was a Turkish governor. Such men were renowned for keeping slaves in a harem.

46. The name formerly applied to a society of ecclesiastical lawyers in London.

46. 'St George' was the battle cry of English soldiers.

47. 'King Pimp'.

48. Taken from the last paragraph of Ovid's *Metamorphoses*. The original quotation, in which Ovid refers to his literary immortality, translates as 'which neither the wrath of Jove, nor fire, nor sword, nor the gnawing tooth of time shall ever be able to undo'. Here, Fielding changes *Iovis*, 'of Jove', to *Judicis*, 'of the judge'.

49. A reference to Colley Cibbers' version of Shakespeare's *Richard III*. (Act III)

50. I Corinthians (1: 22–3).

51. 'Pleasant it is, when over a great sea the winds trouble the waters, to gaze from shore upon another's great tribulation.' Lucretius, *De Rerum Natura* (II. 1–2).

52. From the opening scene of *Sophonisba* (1676) by Nathaniel Lee (*c.*1649–92).

53. From Lucan's *Civil War* (IX. 404), in which Cato praises his soldiers for their courage in the face of hardship.

Henry Fielding was born in Somerset on 22nd April 1707, the son of a lieutenant. Following his mother's death when he was eleven, Fielding was educated at Eton, where he made the acquaintance of George Lyttelton (1709–73) and Pitt the elder (1708–78). After a failed attempt to elope with a beautiful heiress, he moved to London in the late 1720s, and began a career writing comedies, burlesques and satires for the stage. His first play, *Love in Several Masques*, was performed in 1728, and between 1729 and 1737 he wrote over twenty-five dramas. His most successful was *Tom Thumb*, an extravagant burlesque which was performed in 1730. The Licensing Act of 1737 effectively brought an end to Fielding's career as a dramatist, and he turned briefly to law, before turning his attention to political journalism, writing most often for *The Champion*, a satirical, anti-Jacobite journal. After this, he concentrated largely on prose. His novels include *Shamela* (1741), *Joseph Andrews* (1742), *Jonathan Wild the Great* (1743), *Tom Jones* (1749), and *Amelia* (1751). It is thought that his first wife, Charlotte Cradock, whom he married in 1734, was the inspiration behind at least two of his famous heroines. Some years after her death in 1744, he caused a scandal by marrying Charlotte's maid, Mary Daniel.

In 1748, Fielding was appointed Justice of the Peace for Westminster – a role which, along with his half-brother and fellow-magistrate, Sir John Fielding, saw him working tirelessly for legal reforms, and introducing the first organised police force in London.

Fielding died in Lisbon on 8th October 1754, at the age of forty-seven, having suffered from gout and asthma, amongst other afflictions.

SELECTED TITLES FROM HESPERUS PRESS

Author	Title	Foreword writer
Jane Austen	*Love and Friendship*	Fay Weldon
Aphra Behn	*The Lover's Watch*	
Charlotte Brontë	*The Green Dwarf*	Libby Purves
Anton Chekhov	*Three Years*	William Fiennes
Wilkie Collins	*Who Killed Zebedee?*	Martin Jarvis
William Congreve	*Incognita*	Peter Ackroyd
Joseph Conrad	*The Return*	Colm Tóibín
Daniel Defoe	*The King of Pirates*	Peter Ackroyd
Charles Dickens	*The Haunted House*	Peter Ackroyd
Fyodor Dostoevsky	*The Double*	Jeremy Dyson
George Eliot	*Amos Barton*	Matthew Sweet
F. Scott Fitzgerald	*The Rich Boy*	John Updike
Gustave Flaubert	*Memoirs of a Madman*	Germaine Greer
E.M. Forster	*Arctic Summer*	Anita Desai
Elizabeth Gaskell	*Lois the Witch*	Jenny Uglow
Thomas Hardy	*Fellow-Townsmen*	Emma Tennant
L.P. Hartley	*Simonetta Perkins*	Margaret Drabble
Nathaniel Hawthorne	*Rappaccini's Daughter*	Simon Schama
D.H. Lawrence	*Daughters of the Vicar*	Anita Desai
Katherine Mansfield	*In a German Pension*	Linda Grant
Prosper Mérimée	*Carmen*	Philip Pullman
Alexander Pope	*Scriblerus*	Peter Ackroyd
Marcel Proust	*Pleasures and Days*	A.N. Wilson
Robert Louis Stevenson	*Dr Jekyll and Mr Hyde*	Helen Dunmore
Jonathan Swift	*Directions to Servants*	Colm Tóibín
Leo Tolstoy	*Hadji Murat*	Colm Tóibín
Mark Twain	*Tom Sawyer, Detective*	
Oscar Wilde	*The Portrait of Mr W.H.*	Peter Ackroyd
Virginia Woolf	*Carlyle's House and Other Sketches*	Doris Lessing